fitting ends and other stories

fitting ends

ends

and Other Stories by

DAN CHAON

TRIQUARTERLY BOOKS
NORTHWESTERN UNIVERSITY PRESS

evanston, illinois

TriQuarterly Books
Northwestern University Press
Evanston, Illinois 60208-4210

ISBN 0-8101-5021-2 (cloth)
ISBN 0-8101-5022-0 (paper)

Library of Congress Cataloging-in-Publication Data

Chaon, Dan.
     Fitting ends and other stories / by Dan Chaon.
        p. cm.
     ISBN 0-8101-5021-2 (cloth : alk. paper).–
ISBN 0-8101-5022-0 (pbk. : alk. paper)
     1. United States–Social life and customs–20th
century–Fiction. 2. Young adults–United States–
Fiction. I. Title.
PS3553.H277F58 1995
813'.54–dc20   95-23447
                                     CIP

Cover: *Grey and Gold* (detail). Oil on canvas, 1942, 90.8 x 125.7 cm. John
Rogers Cox, American, 1915-1990. © The Cleveland Museum of Art, 1995,
Mr. and Mrs. William H. Marlatt Fund, 43.60

For my parents, and

with love and respect, for Sheila

"Before I draw nearer to that stone to which you point," said Scrooge, "answer me one question. Are these the shadows of things that Will be, or are they the shadows of things that May be, only?"

Charles Dickens, *A Christmas Carol*

contents

acknowledgments

The author is grateful for permission to reprint stories that appeared, sometimes in slightly different form, in the following publications: "Fitting Ends," "Rapid Transit," "Going Out," and "Sure I Will" in *TriQuarterly;* "Fraternity" in *Ploughshares;* "Spirit Voices" in *American Short Fiction;* "Dread" in *Indiana Review;* "Accidents" in *MSS;* "Transformations" in *Story* and also in the collection *Conversations,* ed. John Seltzer (New York: Macmillan, 1993).

Excerpt in "Spirit Voices" is from Liz Rosenberg, *Adelaide and the Night Train* (New York: HarperCollins, 1989); excerpt in "My Sister's Honeymoon: A Videotape" is from the song "Top of the World" by Richard Carpenter and John Bettis (Alamo Music Corp./Hammer and Nails Music [ASCAP]).

The author would like to thank the Ragdale Foundation and the Illinois Arts Council for their assistance in writing this book.

spirit voices

I turned twenty-seven on a quiet Saturday in April, shortly after the birth of our second child. The day was dull and ominous: it had been raining off and on since I woke, and I spent most of the morning working on our taxes. My birthday gifts had been practical– socks, underwear, shirts in a style that made me feel that I wasn't really young anymore. When I went out for a drive in the late after- noon, the light drizzle began to turn to sleet, and the houses, the telephone poles, the street signs, became sharp-edged and spectral against the gray sky. Dark birds lifted out of the bare trees as I passed.

I had only meant to go to the drugstore, but as I turned onto the quiet main street, I thought I saw my brother-in-law's wife, Rhonda, the one my wife's family hated, driving alone in a long white car. Though I knew it was foolish, I couldn't help but follow.

We'd known for a week or so that she was back, but I hadn't seen her. In that dark weath- er, I couldn't even be certain it *was* her–I only caught a glimpse of the face, the pale skin and short black hair. I drifted behind the car as it headed out toward the edge of town.

The town we live in is small by most stan- dards, little more than a cluster of trees and buildings in the middle of the Nebraska prairie –a main street the teenagers drive up and down at night, with a few storefronts in the center, the town wisping away at both ends into gas stations, motels, then open road. The car was going under the viaduct, to the west side, where I knew Rhonda was staying.

Rhonda lived in a low-income tract called Sioux Villa, and most of the residents there were pretty bad off–destitute elderly, single mothers, Indians, alcoholics. If there was a murder in St. Bonaventure, it usually happened in Sioux Villa. The apartments were in rows of six, so that the place looked like the old one-story stucco motel my family had owned until I was seven, when my father bought the more elegant Bonaventure Motor Lodge.

I didn't know which apartment was Rhonda's, so I cruised in and out of the rows until I saw that white car parked in front of one of the unnumbered doorways.

I stopped the car. That was all–I didn't have any plan in mind. I idled the car outside, listening to the rain, to the rhythmic wing-beating of the windshield wipers. The defroster was on high, and the car smelled heavy with it.

Then I pulled the hood up on my jacket and opened the car door, but I left the engine running. I thought, why not be a good person? I thought, why not go ring her bell, and tell her welcome back. I imagined myself saying: "If there's anything you need, give us a call," though I knew Susan, my wife, wouldn't want anything to do with her. Susan would probably hang up on her if she called.

I hesitated there on her stoop, thinking of this. I remembered Susan telling me: "If I see her, I have half a mind to kick her ass. Seriously." The rain trickled from my hood, and I wiped the droplets from my glasses, leaving a blurry film before my eyes. Maybe this wasn't even her place.

I opened the screen door and pressed my face close to the little diamond-shaped window in the inside door. I cupped my hand over my eyes and peered in. The window was fogged over: droplets of condensation ran down the steamy glass, leaving little bars through which I could spot an old Naugahyde couch, a crumpled bag of potato chips lying on it. Then, just at the edge of my vision, I spotted an arm. I leaned closer, and the rest of her tilted into view: she was standing at the mouth of a dark hallway, with her back to me. I saw that she was shirtless, and as I watched, she pushed her jeans down to her ankles and stepped out of them. She was a small woman, yet her body was hard-looking, almost muscular; different from the shapes of women I was used to seeing around St. B. She stood there in her underwear and stocking feet for a moment, looking down at something I couldn't see. Then her shoulders tightened, and her arms contorted behind her back as she unhooked her bra. My own breath was fogging up the outside glass, and I passed my hand through it as she turned, startled. She crossed her arms over her bare breasts: she'd seen my face at the window, I thought, and my heart leapt. What was I doing? Peeping in—a person could get arrested for that. I let the screen door slam and backed away quickly, hurrying toward my idling car: how could I explain myself to Rhonda now, or worse, what would Susan say if she found out? My body felt luminous, visible.

I put the car in reverse, and my wheels spun in the wet gravel. I sped out of the row of houses, and as I turned the corner, I caught a glimpse of her as she stumbled to the door. I stepped on the gas, and as I roared away, I could see her standing on the doorstep in only a towel, her hands tented over her head to shield herself from the rain. I imagined I heard her shouting something after me.

Afterwards, when I thought of what I'd done, I felt actually trembly with embarrassment and confusion. What if she'd recognized the car? What if she'd seen me? I'd never really known Rhonda that well, not enough to think of her as a friend, anyway. I'd talked to her a few times at family gatherings, and we'd seemed to hit it off. There was a kind of cynical edge in what she said, and I secretly relished her dry comments about our in-laws, the loose, almost bored posture as she sat, listening to them talk. I remembered the Thanksgiving afternoon when she sipped casually from a pint bottle of peach schnapps after dinner, reclining in the living room, watching sports while the rest of the women washed dishes. I was the one that sat next to her. But the vague camaraderie between us was not enough to justify my behavior. It might even give Rhonda the idea that I was after her, a married man eager to prey on a "fallen woman."

It had been six months since Rhonda left my wife's brother, Kent, and their two-year-old daughter. She'd run off with a Puerto Rican, so people said. Rhonda and Kent had been living in Virginia at the time. Kent had just been discharged from the Navy, where he'd learned a trade–some kind of mechanics, I gathered– and he was looking for a job when she went off. My mother-in-law claimed the Puerto Rican was both a pimp and a dope dealer, and had gotten Rhonda hooked on something. In any case, Kent came home to Nebraska with his little girl, and I gave him a job at the motel I run–the motel I inherited from my father. My mother-in-law cared for the child while he was at work.

Kent got a few letters from Rhonda, but he didn't let anyone know what they said. And then, after several months, Rhonda appeared in St. Bonaventure. My mother-in-law imagined that the man had beat her up and dumped her somewhere along their "journey of sin," a journey she'd followed through the postmarks on the letters–Atlantic City, Philadelphia, Baltimore. She talked of these cities as if they were distant constellations.

Ever since Rhonda returned, my mother-in-law had been imagining that she wanted Kent back. "He'd have to be out of his mind," she murmured when Kent was out of the room.

It wasn't that I approved of what Rhonda had done, of course. But I wasn't sure that I blamed her, either. I wanted to know her side of the story.

When I got home, my sister Joan was there. She had come to cook us dinner. We had planned to go out dancing for my birthday that night, but by the afternoon we decided to postpone until some other time. The baby was colicky, and our two-year-old, Joshua, hadn't taken well to his change in status. Recently, he'd begun to wake up in the middle of the night, too, calling for us jealously. So Joan said she was going to come over and fix us a steak.

My sister is six years older than me. My mother had had two miscarriages in between us, and perhaps that had hardened Joan to the idea of siblings. In any case, we'd never been close as children, not, in fact, until after our parents had passed away, and Joan had divorced. There wasn't any real reason for her to stay in St. Bonaventure besides me, I guess.

Joan looked at me shrewdly when I came in. She often seemed to loom over people, though she wasn't exactly tall—just, as she put it, big-boned. "Where were you?" she said. "I've been here for nearly an hour."

"I was driving," I told her, and she nodded. She was big on the notion of "private time." Everyone in our family had been, in individual ways, a bit of a loner. Still, I couldn't picture her following someone for no reason, or peeping into their home.

"Where's Susan?" I said, and she looked back to the green pepper she was dissecting.

"She's in the bedroom with the baby. The J-monster is in there, too." She had recently started to be a little antagonistic toward Joshua, our oldest. I could tell she thought he was spoiled, but it still surprised me. She'd always seemed so delighted by him before. Not too long ago, she'd told me that she was glad she never had any children of her own. I hoped she wouldn't keep calling Joshua the J-monster.

"Any major disasters while I was out?" I asked.

"Just the usual," she said. "Tell Susan dinner will be ready soon."

Susan was sitting on our bed, nursing Molly, and reading a book to Joshua. He huddled into the crook of her arm, listening grimly. I sat down beside her, with Joshua between us, and I slipped my arm around her waist, encompassing all of them.

"'They passed the restless ocean,'" Susan read, "'combing out her hair.'" She winked at me. "What took you so long?" she said.

"Oh, I got lost," I said. "It's the perfect day for the end of my youth." I put my hand to my brow melodramatically.

"Come on," she said. "You're not allowed to brood until you turn thirty."

"I'm advanced," I said, and Joshua pushed against us impatiently. "Read," he said. "Read." And so Susan continued, and I looked down at Molly. She was nursing intensely, her eyes closed, her brow furrowed. Susan hadn't breast-fed Joshua, and it was still strange to see her breasts, with their new roundness, almost opaque so I could just barely see her veins deep beneath her skin. She had always been hearty and athletic-looking, and the leftover softness of pregnancy made her seem almost exotic. We hadn't made love since the baby was born, and I hadn't pressed her, yet. But sometimes, when her nipple slipped out of the baby's mouth, erect and red, I would feel a twinge of urgency. And then, almost involuntarily, I thought of Rhonda, the flash of the brown aureoles of her breasts before her pale arms covered them. I cleared my throat.

"Joan says supper's almost ready," I said, and Susan nodded.

At supper, Joan insisted on a chorus of "Happy Birthday" and I sat there, listening to their low, female voices intertwining, echoing hollowly. Joshua watched with amazed horror. Afterwards, Joan went right into one of her heavy conversations. There were several recurring themes when Joan visited–her ex-husband, and what happened to her marriage; her dislike for St. Bonaventure; lack of suitable male companionship, etc. Tonight, she told us that her boss, a married man, wanted to have an affair with her.

"The worst part of it," she said, "is that we're friends, sort of. At least, I have to work closely with him every day. It's not like I can just say 'screw you' and forget about it. I can see what it is. His wife is this matronly, country-club type, and he's got what? Three or four kids. And I think it's something that all married people go through at some point. Especially men."

"Plus you're pretty," my wife said. "And vulnerable."

"What do you mean, 'especially men,'" I said.

"Oh shut up," Joan told me. "Not you." Joshua got up from the table, and I warned him that the baby was sleeping. He turned his back to me, bitterly, and sat down among his toys. "Anyway," Joan said. "The truth is, in a lot of ways, I'm really attracted to him, and I would do it, I would. But look at me. I've been divorced for almost as long as I was married now, and I've passed the point in my life when I could allow that sort of thing to happen to me. I mean, here I am in this tiny town, with his wife and children living not so far away, and him involved in all these domestic things. I wouldn't be able to call him if I wanted. We'd have to sneak around, quickies on abandoned roads, that sort of thing. I'm sure that's just the kind of adventure he'd love. But me? I'd end up like what's-her-name. Your brother's wife. Rhonda. Wandering around St. Bonaventure like a spook."

"Don't do it," my wife said. "You deserve better. You really do."

"Yeah," Joan said. "I know I do." She cut her steak carefully, glancing down to where Joshua was driving a toy truck against her foot. She made a face. "So what's with the whole Rhonda thing, anyway? Anything new?"

"Not that I know of," Susan said. She looked over at me, and it sent a sudden prickle across my neck. "It's still in progress, as far as I know," she said. She shot me another quick look, one that was meant to convey sympathy for Joan.

"Poor Joan," Susan would say later, when we were up with the baby in the middle of the night. "I wish there was something we could do for her." She went on to remark on how sweet and smart and good-looking Joan was. "Why doesn't someone wonderful come along for her," she asked, and I murmured, "I don't know." But the truth was, I thought, even if a wonderful man came along, he wouldn't be good enough. At least Rhonda had made a choice. Joan acted like she could go through life, making excuses but never doing anything, as if there were an infinity of possibilities to choose from. Sooner or later she was going to find those possibilities were disappearing, one by one. But I wouldn't tell Susan this, because generalities annoyed her. "What possibilities?" she'd ask. "Disappeared how?" and I wouldn't be able to explain.

Saturdays are my only day off, and in the morning I was back to work at the motel. I tried to put all the thoughts of the previous day–of Rhonda, and my sister, and disappearing possibilities–out of my mind. To a certain extent, I guess I was feeling a little guilty. I kept imagining that she had recognized me, and I pictured her, eventually getting back together with Kent, telling him. I tried to think of what I would say to Susan. I knew how she would interpret it: I secretly had the hots for Rhonda, she'd say. I was getting restless. That's what she would think, no matter how carefully I explained myself.

Susan honestly hated Rhonda. "She's beneath contempt," she'd always say. "How could a mother leave her child like that, for any reason?" In a way, I suppose, I was surprised at the hard edge in her voice, just as I was surprised at how easily she'd settled into being a mother. She had once been pretty wild herself, and I thought she'd have more sympathy.

When we first met, Susan had seemed so dangerous to me: she hung around with older men, who gave her rides on their motorcycles and jacked-up cars, and she was a drinker. I guess it was what I needed at the time. My mother had just died, and my father had just had the first in the series of strokes that would eventually kill him. He once told me that the best thing he'd ever done was to be there for his parents when they were old–his brothers were never around–and that stuck with me. I'd come home from college to help with the motel, and Susan would come over late and talk me into turning on the "No Vacancy" light before we'd filled. She'd get me to do things I never would have done without her. I still thought fondly of how we'd stayed up all night, how she and her tough girlfriends taught me how to bounce a quarter into a glass of beer, or the time she'd tricked me into trying marijuana by feeding it to me in a cake. We used to drive a hundred miles just to check into small town motels, pretending we were having an illicit affair. Once an old woman had refused to give us a room because we didn't have the same last names. "I don't believe in it," she told us darkly.

When I walked into the office of the motel, Kent was asleep, slumped in the swivel chair behind the desk. He worked the night shift, from ten until seven, and usually the motel was as full as it was going to get by the time he started. He didn't have to deal much with customers at all, and I figured he would be good at taking care of the type of problems that sometimes arise late at night. He was a big man, with thick dark eyebrows and a kind of steely, mean-looking face. He was a nice enough person, actually, though I remembered being afraid of him when we first met.

Of course, my father wouldn't have liked to see him there, unshaven, a full ashtray on the desk, his heavy head tucked against his shoulder. My parents had always run the place themselves. We'd lived in the little three-bedroom apartment connected to the office, and my mother or father had registered every guest. There was a buzzer at the front that brought them, no matter what the hour, out of bed.

I'd hired out. The little apartment behind the office had been converted into storage. Still, I was there six days a week, ten hours a day. I hadn't abandoned the place.

I rang the bell, and Kent stirred a little, his brow furrowing. "Fuck," he murmured. Then he opened his eyes, glowering up at whoever had disturbed him.

I frowned. "Rise and shine," I said. "Shift's over."

"Oh," he said, and his look softened. "Robert. Hey, happy birthday, man."

"Thanks," I said. "You know . . . you really have to be careful about your language around the guests."

"Yeah," he said, and looked down. "I know it. Sorry about that." He glanced around sheepishly, as if there might be someone else in the room, and his look reminded me that he'd had a rough time of it lately. I didn't want to be another problem in his life.

"It's no big deal," I said. "Any major disasters last night?"

"Nada," he said. "All quiet. Did you and Sue go out?"

I shrugged. "In a few weeks, maybe. Joan came over and fixed us a nice dinner. " I shrugged again, as if I had to make excuses, to apologize. "It was all right," I said.

Kent nodded, and his voice dropped a little, the way men's voices do when they exchange something that passes for personal. I'd never been exactly sure what it meant. "Yeah, well, I know how it is, man."

He smiled, pursing his lips. "I guess maybe I'm lucky to be a bachelor again."

"Yes, well," I said. I wished that I could ask him what was going on between him and Rhonda. He surely must have known she was in town. Had he seen her? Talked to her? "So how are things going with you?" I said. "You're getting along okay?"

"Oh, fine." Now it was Kent's turn to shrug. "Brittany's running Mom ragged. You know how Mom can get to complaining. But she loves it, you can tell." He sighed, and stood up. His hair was flattened on one side, stiff. I watched as he tried to neaten the clutter on the desk, piling the scattered papers together. "I guess you heard that Rhonda's back in town," he said at last.

"Yeah," I said.

"Yeah," he said. "Fucking everybody's heard." He stared into my eyes, and I tried to keep my face noncommittal, but I could feel my expression wavering, the muscles moving beneath the skin. Finally he looked away and picked up his ashtray, dumping it into the wastebasket. "I don't know, man," he said. "I just don't know."

The motel, the Bonaventure Motor Lodge, was not the most profitable business around. The town was in a valley and couldn't be seen by cars passing on the interstate. All they could see were the mesas and treeless hills, the empty pastureland that surrounded us, and despite the cheerful signs that promised food, gas, lodging, most of them just kept on going. Still there were always a few forced to straggle in come nightfall, enough to keep us in business.

I liked to watch them in the mornings, as they loaded up their vehicles and went on their various ways. This time of year, there weren't too many vacationers. They were mostly, I imagined, off on more desperate pursuits: nomadic men and women, fugitives, lovers, addled old folks, young families on their way to new jobs, working men fleeing their dying cities, or parts of families, single mothers and fathers, escaping some domestic situation. There was something heroic about these people, I thought. I would walk down the row, glancing at the license plates, peeking in the windows of the cars. You could tell a lot about people from what they left in the backseat of their cars: toys, books, empty beer cans, little barking dogs with their toenails painted bright red. Once I saw a semiautomatic, tossed casually on a blanket in the back; another time, a limbless mannequin gazed blankly at me when I peered into a hatchback. For a minute, I thought it was a body. Sometimes, when I was sure no one was looking, I would trace my name or my initials in the dusty film on the back of a car. Sometimes I would be out there when a guest came out the door, and I'd talk to them for a bit–ask them if they slept comfortably, inquire casually as to where they were headed. Mostly, people didn't have much to say. To them, I was just another provincial busybody, another obstacle in their path.

In the afternoon, after all the keys had been turned in, and while the maids were cleaning out the rooms, my sister stopped by for lunch. She was working at the courthouse, in the County Attorney's office, and she hadn't been getting along with her co-workers– she didn't want to spend her lunch period with them. They were all secretary types, dumb as dirt, she said. Besides, she suspected they had been gossiping about her and Mr. Trencher, her boss.

She'd brought a bucket of chicken from a local fast-food place, and we ate in the apartment in back of the office, in the old kitchen. The table we'd had when we were kids was still there, though the kitchen itself was cluttered with fresh towels and boxes of toilet paper and complimentary soap. "Don't you find it a little creepy, eating back here," Joan said as she spread out the plastic silverware and plates, and opened the Styrofoam containers of mashed potatoes and gravy. "I think of all the hours Mother spent in this kitchen, and now look at it. It would kill her to see."

"I think it's sort of comforting, actually," I said. "Nostalgic."

"You would," she said. She peeled the crisp skin off her chicken and set it on my plate. "Trencher's been moon-eyed all morning," she said. "It's really driving me crazy."

"Tell him to cut it out," I said. "Give him a karate chop."

She grimaced. "Well," she said. "It's not like he's chasing me around the desk or something. That's the trouble. It's this very subtle thing–little looks, and this weird tension in the air. So if I tell him to cut it out, he can act like I'm just paranoid. He'll say I'm reading things into it."

I nodded slowly, scoping my mind for good advice. I didn't know what she expected me to say. I didn't understand this Mr. Trencher any more than I understood Rhonda, or Joan herself, whose unfaithful ex-husband used to call late at night, used to drive hundreds of miles to camp out on her door. Why did she seem to draw this type of man? I had never been a person who could follow that kind of love, with its hidden agendas and uncertainty, its mazes of fear and desire. I hadn't been in love very many times. As far as I knew, my wife was the only woman who'd ever been in love with me. What did I know about any of it? "You could quit," I suggested hesitantly.

"Why should I have to quit," she said sharply. I shrugged. She was right–I hadn't been thinking. "I didn't do anything wrong. If anything, I should file harassment charges," she said.

I nodded. "You could." But then she just pursed her lips. It seemed a distant possibility; and as we looked at one another, I had the feeling that she wasn't completely unhappy with the situation. We ate for a moment in silence.

I was trying to think of some other subject to bring up when the front desk buzzer rang. I scooted my chair back, and Joan stood up as I did.

"I've got to get going anyway," Joan said. "I've got some errands to run."

But when we walked out to the office, both of us stopped cold. Rhonda was standing at the desk, and when she saw Joan, her eyes narrowed. She glanced from Joan to me, holding herself stiffly, formally, like a messenger. She was wearing one of those coats that looked like it was made out of red vinyl, the kind a rock singer might wear, with big shoulderpads. But her face looked tired and drawn. She stared at me, and I felt myself blushing, for a moment imagining she had come to accuse me of spying on her.

"I wanted to leave this for Kent," she said, and held out an envelope. She set it on the desk, on top of the guest register. "I heard he was working here."

"He's not here now," I said, and she brushed her eyes over me, a quick once-over. She kept her face expressionless.

"I know," she said. "Could you just see that Kent gets it?"

"Sure," I said, and she turned, without looking at me again, and went out the door. I was almost as surprised by the abruptness of her exit as I had been to see her standing there. I guess I had imagined some little conversation between us, some slight acknowledgment. I watched her car pull through the motel's cul-de-sac and back onto the street.

"Well, well," Joan said. She breathed, a sigh that seemed somewhere between puzzled and gratified. "This should be interesting. I can hardly wait for Susan to hear about this." She looked at me sidelong and I watched her gently lift the envelope. For a moment, I thought she was going to open it, and it sent an odd, possessive jolt through me. I wanted to snatch it from her. But she just examined it, front and back: blank. Then she put it down. "I'll drop by the house after work," she said.

Susan didn't say much at first. Miraculously, both babies were asleep, and she was stretched out on the couch, watching music videos. I sat down and she slid her feet onto my lap. "So you didn't open this letter, I suppose," she said at last.

"Of course not," I said.

"Hmmmm," she said. I ran my thumb along the sole of her bare foot, reproachfully, and she shifted, stretching her leg muscles. "I'd like to know what that bitch is telling him." She leaned her head back, looking at me thoughtfully.

"You could ask Kent," I said.

"Yeah, right," she said. "If my mom hasn't gotten it out of him, then no one will." She eyed me for a minute, and when my finger grazed the underside of her foot again, she moved her feet from my lap and tucked them beneath her. "He still loves her, I guess," she said. "Thinks he loves her."

"Could be," I agreed. But I wasn't sure what the difference was between loving someone and thinking you do. It made me uncomfortable, puzzling over it, because it suggested layers of reality—what you thought was solid suddenly gave way, like a secret panel in a haunted house. "Maybe she thinks she loves him, too," I said.

"Oh, I'm sure," Susan said. She squinted, as if trying to see something far in the distance. "I'm sure that's the line she's feeding him, among others. 'Kent, I made a little mistake,'" she mimicked, in a soft breathy voice—nothing like Rhonda's, I thought. Susan pouted her lips. "'I'm so-o sorry,'" she purred.

"Well . . . " I said hesitantly. "Maybe she did make a mistake." I shrugged, and she peered at me, the corners of her mouth moving, but not quite smiling.

"That's not a mistake," she said at last. "A mistake

is when your account is overdrawn a few bucks at the bank. It isn't a mistake when you leave your husband and baby daughter to run off with some pimp." Her expression shifted again, but I couldn't guess what she was thinking. "If I were to do something like that, is that what you'd call it? A mistake?"

"I'd take you back," I said.

"No you wouldn't," she said. "You may think you would, but I know you. You wouldn't." I couldn't help but flinch a little, pinned by that look. What did she see in me, or think she saw? She shook her head. "Besides," she said. "I wouldn't go back if you'd have me. I couldn't respect you." We stared at each other, and I couldn't think of what to say next. The baby monitor crackled in the silence, humming with transistor noise. We waited. I saw her straighten, tensing like an animal seen briefly in a clearing, before it bolts. "Oh, no," she whispered, and Molly's voice, that high, strange mechanical cry that infants have, began to unravel–soft at first, but gaining force.

When Joan showed up a while later, I was walking the baby, trying to quiet her. Susan and Joan sat down at the kitchen table, and I could hear Susan going on in the same vein. "I've told Kent what my opinion is," she was saying. I didn't concentrate on the rest. The baby kept wailing, her cries shuddering in my ears. The radio was turned up, playing static in hopes that the white noise might calm her as it sometimes did. But it was having the opposite effect on me: the radio and the crying baby and the bitter voices of the women in the next room layered over me, like heavy, stale air. I looked into the kitchen, I was surprised by the shudder of disgust that passed through me. I stared at them from the threshold, and I couldn't help but think how primitive they seemed, like pictures of Russian peasant women I'd seen in books, with their hard, judgmental mouths and their drab clothes. At that moment, they seemed to represent everything that was small and compromised and unlovely about my life. I thought about the time I'd gotten into Joan's car and found the radio tuned to a Muzak station; I thought about the scuffed terry-cloth houseslippers my wife had taken to wearing, even in the middle of the day. They should want to run off with dark-skinned lovers, I thought, they should want to do crazy drugs and wander through strange cities after midnight. I rocked Molly insistently, shushing her without much gentleness in my voice.

"Has your mother heard about it?" Joan was saying. Susan was at the refrigerator, and I watched as she took out a single beer and poured it into two glasses. I thought sadly of those nights before we were married, walking her home after we'd been out drinking, Susan leaning against me, her lips pressed close to my ear. All that stuff, I thought, was behind us; now she couldn't even manage to drink a whole beer by herself.

"I pray to God she doesn't," Susan said. She offered Joan the glass of beer, and I watched them both take little sips. "She's on twenty-four-hour watch as it is."

"I'm sure," Joan said. She smiled—grotesquely, enjoying herself. "But don't you think Rhonda's going to eventually want to see the baby?"

"Not if Mom can help it."

"That's ridiculous," I said, and they both looked up. Molly had quieted a bit, and maybe they hadn't noticed me listening. "They can't keep her from seeing her own child," I said, and the pulse of annoyance I felt toward them crept into my voice. "I mean, legally, doesn't she have visitation rights or something?"

They both eyed me. Susan made a wry face, and the way she tilted her head made me realize she needed a haircut. Her hair constantly looked like it needed to be combed, and the word "unbecoming" came suddenly into my mind. "She'd need a damn good lawyer," Susan said. "And if you think she's going to get past Mom without a fight, you don't know my mother." She let her gaze linger over me for a moment, and I frowned. "He's been Rhonda's biggest fan lately," she told Joan.

"Oh, I know," Joan said. "You should have seen them making goo-goo eyes at each other at the motel." It was supposed to be a joke, but I felt my face getting warm. I wasn't in the mood for Joan's humor. "Little do we know," Joan said. "He's actually Rhonda's secret sex slave."

"Shut up, Joan," I said. "That's all you think about, isn't it? Why don't you just sleep with Trencher and get it over with." I hesitated, a little taken aback by my own meanness, but before Joan could say anything, Molly started to shriek again, and the sound made my shoulders go rigid, made my whole body hum with irritation. "Jesus Christ!" I snapped at Susan. "Can you please take this *thing* off my hands—it wants to nurse." I thrust the baby toward her, and her cries stopped abruptly; her tiny eyes widened in terror or accusation. Then her mouth contorted and she screamed again.

"What's wrong with you? Are you crazy?" Glaring, she took the baby and cradled her gently, sheltering her from me.

"How do you expect me to get her to sleep with you two in here harping away like a couple of old biddies?" I said. Susan lifted her blouse roughly, and the baby affixed herself desperately to the breast, as if she'd been held against her will and starved by some torturer. "Oh, it makes me sick," I said. "My whole life is nothing but work and screaming kids and listening to you two gossip and complain. I'm so bored and tired of this same old thing that I could just jump out a window."

"Why don't you then," Susan said. "You're the one that complains all the time! All you do is sit around like a lump and brood. And now you can't even stand to take a few minutes to comfort your own sick baby.

If you're so bored, why don't you leave? Maybe you could hook up with your precious Rhonda. I'm sure she'd show you a great time."

"Maybe I will," I said.

"Good," Susan said. She narrowed her eyes at me, then lifted her glass and drained the beer defiantly. "There's the door."

I hesitated for a moment, opening my mouth with no words–no quick retorts or parting shots. I just stared at them, shaking my head. "I'm leaving," I said. Then I turned and walked out, slamming the door.

It was a cool night, full of those heavy, earthy-smelling spring shadows, and by the time I was in the car my heart was shriveling. It wasn't an anger I'd be able to hang onto very long, and I knew in a few hours I'd be turning various apologies over in my mind. At least, I thought, I'd go out to a bar; then I'd walk down to the motel and spend the night there.

I drove slowly down our street, through the tunnel of newly budding trees, the rows of my neighbor's houses with their basketball hoops above the garage doors or their toy-scattered lawns, curling down into the valley, toward Euclid. It was about nine o'clock; the movie had let out, and the high school kids were cruising, just as I had done at their age, idling rest-lessly at the three stoplights, roaring from one end of town to the other and back, honking as they passed their friends. I thought of the worn path a zoo animal makes around the circumference of its cage. They'd get out of St. Bonaventure soon, they'd graduate and never come back. That's what they were thinking.

I pulled onto Euclid, maybe the only grown-up on the street, merging with them, pacing the twelve blocks or so between eastern and western city limits. A car full of heavily made-up teenaged girls slowed, and they stretched to peer at me. I could see their mouths laughing and chattering as they passed. We had been trying to stop the kids from using the motel lot as a place to make a U-turn, but I watched them come to the end of the street and spin through the cul-de-sac at the motor lodge, riding the big speed bumps we'd put in as if they were some carnival ride. I could see from a distance the "No Vacancy" light was on. But when I drove through, making my own U-turn, I counted only six cars in the lot. The office was dark, and the thought of Kent in there, fast asleep, brought back a wave of that old irritation.

As I parked the car I clenched my fists, imagining Kent huddled up in the back, eyes closed tight, breathing through his nose. I thought of the money he'd lost me; not much, probably, but it added up, it meshed with all the other worries on my mind. I was never going to get anywhere, I thought.

It was silent when I opened the door. My keys chimed against one another, dangling in the lock. "Kent?" I said sternly. I flipped the lights on and the fluorescent bulbs slowly flickered to life. Kent's dirty ashtray was on the desk, and papers were scattered everywhere. I glanced outside, thinking maybe some emergency had taken him away, but my mother-in-law's pickup, the one she let Kent drive, was still out there in the space marked "manager."

"Kent," I called again, less certainly, and I stepped cautiously toward the dark, bare rooms. For a moment I thought I could hear music coming from back there–vague, distant sounds, like marimba tones, bamboo windchimes brushing one another. I used to check out this book at the library from time to time, *Omens and Superstitions of the World,* and I remembered reading that if you imagine you hear music, then you are in the presence of benevolent spirits. It's an American Indian belief. But the music didn't sound benevolent: it seemed sad; something has been lost, I thought, and it made me shiver. The sound seemed to drift off into the distance, just barely at the edge of my hearing. Then it was gone.

"Kent," I whispered. I stood there, not really wanting to move into the shadows, imagining terrible things: Kent lying on the floor back there, with a gun still gripped in his fist, or his body swinging slowly over a tipped chair. "Hello? Is someone there?" I called. And then I noticed, laying there on the desk, the cash box—just sitting out, for all to see. I picked it up quickly and opened it. Of course it was empty, except for a few credit card vouchers and a page of motel stationery, with Kent's handwriting on it.

"Dear Robert," I read, beneath the motel letterhead. "I know what I am doing is wrong. But part of it can count towards this week's wages I guess. I hope you will consider the rest a loan. I will pay you back as soon as I can. I am going to get back with Rhon. We will get Brittany after Mom is asleep. And go somewhere, I'm not sure. Please tell Mom that I will send for our stuff when we are settled. And tell her and Susan I am sorry and love to them. But this is the only way it seems because nothing can work under so much pressure and everyone's mind made up, etc. I swear I'll pay back every cent to you." It was signed "Kent Barnhart."

I didn't know how much they'd taken; there might have been almost five hundred dollars there. I'd planned to go to the bank and deposit it in the morning. But I knew this much: I couldn't really afford to lose it. I stood there at the window, the sound of my pulse beating in my ears. I stared out at the parking lot—six lousy cars. But someone would have to be there to check them out in the morning. Then, as I gazed out at the line of doorways, the familiar shape of the building and the walk, I recognized the car at the end of the row. It was Rhonda's old white Buick.

I knew they must have been in there at that very moment, in the room just in front of her car—B19, the one with the king-sized bed. My muscles tightened, and for a moment, I pressed my hands to the window, as if I were locked inside. I wasn't, of course; I could march down there myself and open the door with my master key, throw it open wide and demand my money back. That's what Susan would do, I thought. And if it was Joan, she'd have already been on the phone to the cops. But I was just sitting there, listening to the ticks and hums of the empty office, waiting. Coward, I thought.

I pulled my keys out of the lock and went out, moving like a burglar across my own property, hanging close to the wall. I tried to goad myself, picturing them making love on a nest of my money, picturing them mocking me. My insides felt wavery, like something seen through thick, imperfect glass, and I pinched the key tightly between my fingers. By the time I got to the door, that wavering feeling seemed to be spreading, extending beyond my body like an aura. I saw myself fit the key into the lock, sliding the metal teeth silently into the slot, and I felt my hand turning the knob. But I didn't push the door open. I hesitated there, the knob cool and smooth against my skin, and I drew my face closer to the door. I could hear voices. I inched the door open, just a crack. They were whispering, and though I held my breath, I couldn't make out the words–only gentle, sad voices, and when I pushed the door open a bit further I could see them, reflected in the dresser mirror, sitting there on the bed, their heads almost touching, holding hands. I don't know how long I stood there, staring at their reflection, but they didn't look up. I felt as if something large and dark was hovering over me, opening its wings. After a time I edged back. I let the door pull quietly closed. Then I went back to my car and drove away.

For a long time afterward, I felt ashamed of myself; there was something unmanly, there was some weakness, I guess, in letting someone rob you and just letting them go. I never told Susan about it. When my mother-in-law called early the next morning, I acted as shocked as the rest of them.

By the time I got back to the motel that night, they'd left. I'd driven out a little beyond the edge of town and parked there by the side of the road, like Susan and I used to do. Euclid turned into Highway 30 just outside of town, and Highway 30 fed into the interstate that stretched either way across the country, toward both coasts. Even as I drove past the city limits, the big chamber-of-commerce welcome sign and the glow of the all-night gas station, I knew that I was not the type of person who could ever run off, except to a life of loneliness and sorrow. My fate was already mapped out–smooth straight lines of married and familial love–and I could see everything clearly: in a few days or weeks Susan and I would make love again, the first time in a long while, and everything would fall back in place, all would be well. Joan and Mr. Trencher would continue that slow strange dance they'd been engaged in, and I'd keep going to work, and the children would grow, and in a hundred years there wouldn't be a trace of any of us. Maybe Rhonda and Kent would end up back in town, too, eventually, but I couldn't be certain about them. What did I know about that kind of love, that kind of life?

chinchilla

Arlinda had known for a long time that her mother was not like a real mother. She had seen mothers on TV, read about them in books. She had been at other children's houses and had viewed the mothers on display there–fat mothers who made pies and cookies and cakes; beautiful mothers who wore long coats and jewels, who went dancing with fathers and would not come home till late; cross mothers who spanked and whose children had many chores and rules. But Arlinda's mother was nothing like such women.

Years later, Arlinda would come to hate her mother. She would eagerly and deliberately seek out ways to hurt her, and there would be a time when she would slap her mother and watch those thick glasses fly to the floor and shatter. And it would be even more years before she would pause to find herself using her mother's phrases and gestures, words, movements that had lain hidden inside her.

But all this was still a long time away. Now Arlinda merely believed that her mother had a secret. Many secrets. This was how Arlinda came to become a spy and a thief.

It all started with her mother's illness. Her mother had been sick almost as long as Arlinda could remember, but Arlinda knew very little about the actual sickness, only the symptoms, which were always changing: there were dull, angry pains that seemed to travel around her mother's body, wherever Arlinda touched her– the legs, the back, the face. Her mother would wince when she was hugged. Her illness was as mysterious as the medicine that was meant to cure it–wrapped in Kleenex, hidden at the bottom of her mother's purse like little colored beads, or hoarded in unlabeled vials. Once Arlinda had found a nest of them secreted in the crack of the couch, like little orange and yellow eggs. She had heard her mother saying their names in a whisper over the phone–Thorazine, codeine. They sounded like the names of cowgirls, or princesses. She had scooped up some of them, held them tightly in her dry hand, sure that no one had seen. Then, late at night, she'd studied them, found that the orange half separated from the yellow, and that there was a fine, bitter powder inside, which blew away as she drew near and breathed.

Her mother had come into her room later, demanding: "Were you digging around in that couch? Did you take some medicine?"

Arlinda denied everything, and not knowing what better to say, told her mother: "I saw Daddy! He was looking there."

Her mother's eyes narrowed. "When?" her mother hissed. "When?"

"I don't know!" Arlinda had cried, and her mother asked her more and more questions, until Arlinda began to believe her own lie, to defend it with tears and outrage, until it was hard to remember that she had taken them and buried them deep in the dirt of the jade plant in the kitchen.

But none of this was really a secret. Her mother had taken the pills and hidden them for as long as Arlinda could remember, it was a game played routinely always, and the only secret was that she had stolen them that once. The real mysteries were shadowy, frightening–things she knew about her mother that could not be reconciled with what she saw.

When her mother was gone, in town shopping or visiting someone, Arlinda went exploring. She would creep around the house, sometimes crawling on all fours under beds, discovering hatboxes filled with unfinished embroidery napkins, stunning high heels of aquamarine and black lace, beautiful skirts patterned with scenes of forests and sunsets and palm trees. Hidden. These things were her mother's, but she could never have imagined her wearing them. Her mother wore jeans, turtlenecks, plain colors, flat shoes. It was nearly impossible to imagine her as a lovely woman, bright lips, long hair, in these shimmering clothes, laughing or dancing, gliding through crowded ballrooms.

She would go into her parents' bedroom and carefully open the dresser, gently lifting things out, one by one, discovering, underneath old clothes or check stubs, her mother's most secret things.

At first it was her mother's jewelry boxes that were fascinating. Arlinda would sort through necklaces and glittering earrings with just her finger and thumb. She knew when she touched something she would take it for her own; she crouched, still as a rabbit, listening for the sound of her mother's car approaching the driveway. And then she spirited the jewelry away.

She was not afraid of being discovered. Her mother never wore the jewelry, she would never miss it. What really frightened her was that her mother had some secret that should never be revealed, something as terrible as Bluebeard's locked room, waiting. She had no specific evil in mind, just a tingling aura of dread.

Perhaps this was why she hadn't taken anything since she'd found the photographs. She came across them in a white envelope nestled at the very back of a drawer, so tucked away she hadn't noticed it before.

There were five Polaroid pictures of her mother and father in their younger days. They were dirty pictures—in them, her mother and father were naked.

In one photo, her mother faced forward; there was a mirror behind her, and the light of a lamp was reflected in it, big and wavering, like the sun at dusk.

Her mother's hair was long, like wisps of dark smoke around her shoulders, and she had a vague, dreamy smile, her eyes half closed. Her mother was holding her breasts in her hands. In another photo, her father was stretched out on the bed with a knowing look on his face, the kind of look that Arlinda would get when he was teasing her.

Seeing them like this, she felt a warm, liquid rush of fear run through her. They looked like ghosts or mystics, witches in some eerie ritual. Not her real mother or father.

So her mother's secrets only became cloudier, more frightening, the more she thought about them—the opening of a drawer, the fitting of a hidden key into a lock, the quick glimpse of a hand behind a shutting door, the ciphers of muffled telephone calls. I am missing something important, Arlinda thought.

But the truth was, no one seemed to know what Arlinda's mother was supposed to be. She had heard her grandma, her father's mother, whisper to a friend: "Pauline is a hillbilly, you know."

Her father's two sisters, Aunt Sharon and Aunt Beth, speculated on the subject often enough, when they came for a visit. Arlinda would hide and listen as they smoked their cigarettes and sipped coffee.

Aunt Sharon, the pretty one, with her big blonde hair and her black lashes and fingernails that hurt when they broke, said that Arlinda's mother was just a "loon. It's all that inbreeding down South."

"I guess Harvey really must be a saint," Aunt Beth said. "To put up with that. He's so good to her. How did she ever get him?"

"Oh, I know how she got him," Aunt Sharon said, and snorted. "It's how she keeps him that I wonder."

And Arlinda had seen strangers on the street turn to look at her mother—maybe it was the quickness with which she walked, almost stumbling fast, or the angry hardness of her face. Maybe they thought, from the way she held Arlinda by the arm, that her mother was a kidnapper. She's not my real mother, Arlinda wanted to tell them, not really, she doesn't belong to me.

But despite what Arlinda would have liked, she was bound to her mother by so many webs that she could never break free. Not only did she have her mother's face, hair, eyes, she also had the name, the awful name her mother had branded on her. She heard her grandmother once, laughing: "For the longest time I thought Pauline was saying 'Our Linda' and I thought, 'Well you don't have to keep telling me, I know she's your Linda,' and then I found out that this was actually the child's name. Where Pauline came up with it I'll never know." I have the name of a crazy woman's daughter, Arlinda had realized then. The memory still made her ashamed.

But worst of all, Arlinda was her mother's accomplice. She was the one who knew all about the secret trips. During the summer, or when she was on vacation from school, Arlinda would go on her mother's drives; and she knew that when she was in school, her mother went alone. Sometimes, Arlinda would be sitting in class, and the teacher's voice would just fade away, and she would picture her mother driving, all the windows rolled down, her scarf flapping in the wind. She could picture the yellow dotted lines of the highway flickering through her mother's sunglasses, her mother's lips in a tight line.

They would always leave after her father had gone to work in the morning. They went many places—distant restaurants, doctor's offices in faraway towns, no place sometimes, just down the highway for hours then back. Most of the time, though, they went to the other grandmother's place in the country.

It was the second day of summer vacation when Arlinda's father told them he would be going out of town overnight, on business. And although her mother said nothing, Arlinda was not surprised to be awakened as soon as her father was gone.

"Get up," her mother whispered. "We're going to Grandma's house today."

The grandmother's house was several hours away from Arlinda's home, and Arlinda had hoped to spend her day sleeping and watching cartoons. But there was a stiffness in the way her mother spoke, and Arlinda knew better than to protest.

"Hurry up," her mother kept saying, sharply, knocking on the door as Arlinda showered; standing, hands on her hips, as Arlinda pulled up her socks.

"Are you mad at me?" Arlinda kept asking, following after her.

"Of course not," her mother said. But when Arlinda grabbed her around the waist and hugged her, her mother felt like a cat might when clutched against its will, and she closed her eyes as if to hold back a cry.

"God damn it, will you please quit yanking on me, Arlinda? I don't feel good." And then Arlinda backed away, shrugging.

"You're always sick," she said, looking at the floor.

"That's because your father doesn't believe in medicine."

Arlinda slept in the car almost the whole way. Her face was pressed against the vinyl seat, so that, when she awoke briefly, she could feel the indentation of the seat's vertical design on her cheek, like a scar. She looked up sleepily, and she could see her mother's head framed in the car window, and the gently sloping horizon, the telephone poles, the gray sky spun behind her, dizzying, a fog of motion. For a moment there was something terrifying about the stillness of her mother's face, the way she seemed to be hurtling through the rush of the world, the way she ignored the sky and hills and trees grasping for her, falling at her like stones or bullets and then spinning away.

Occasionally, her mother would become lost, and these were the most harrowing times. Her mother would begin to tremble, she would find it hard to hold the steering wheel, and the car would sway between the median and the shoulder, as if seeking escape. When they were lost, her mother would trace and retrace the same miles of highway, or drive around and around the same blocks, as if suddenly a fresh path would appear to lead them home. Then, desperate, she would stop the car and get out. In towns, she would ramble down the sidewalk with Arlinda following, stopping people, old women, leering, dirty men, even small children. She would beg directions from them, cringing as if she were asking for money. Once they had been lost on the interstate, and Arlinda's mother had tried to flag down cars, big semis rushing toward her with their foghorn howls, little bug cars swerving to go around her. Arlinda had screamed, crying, "Mommy, don't . . . Watch out, watch out, watch out!"

But there had never been any problem finding the grandmother's house, and Arlinda felt safe enough to sleep, safe until she woke to see her mother's frozen face against the blur of the passing world, her fingers tight on the steering wheel. Then she sat upright.

"Momma?" she said. "Are we lost?"

Her mother glanced into the backseat and glared. "Don't be ridiculous," she snapped. "What, do you think I'm crazy?" Arlinda looked down, and when she raised her head again her mother's eyes were still staring back at her in the rearview mirror. Finally, she lay down and put her arm across her face. When she sat back up, they were pulling down the long driveway that led to her grandmother's house.

Arlinda's grandmother's place was miles outside any town, and it always looked abandoned. The grass around it was thick and long and the high weeds grew into it on the edge of the yard. At night, the dark trees around the house hunched down, the shadows of their branches scuttling along its walls, along the dusty windows with their coverings of blurry plastic insulation. The only sign of inhabitants was her grandmother's car, a big blue Pontiac, parked in the front yard.

For as long as Arlinda could remember, her grandmother had raised things; not normal animals like chickens or hogs but rather exotic creatures—hives of bees, peacocks, guinea hens, horned white goats, which she kept so she could sell their thin, sour-tasting milk. Arlinda had heard her Aunt Sharon talking in low tones about her mother's parents: "From what I hear, they were like gypsies, they just moved from one odd job to the next, one con game after the other." Arlinda asked her father, after that, what Grandpa Bickers had done for a living. Her father had given her that teasing, secretive smile: "Oh, anything," he said. "Like what," she'd wanted to know, but he just shook his head. "That woman reminds me of a witch," Aunt Sharon once whispered to a group of her cousins and their husbands, as the grandmother drifted past them at a Christmas gathering.

There weren't any exotic animals around the house this time, though, as they stepped up the walk to the front door. And when the grandmother opened the door, there didn't appear to be any animals in the house either.

"Hi, Mommy," Arlinda's mother said, and they embraced.

Arlinda did not hug her grandmother, and she was glad that she wasn't expected to. Her grandmother had a dull, sweaty smell, like old clothes, and her arms were wiry and muscled, like an old man's, with blue veins that stood out above the skin, tracing across it like the branches of a gnarled tree. Arlinda merely took her grandmother's hand.

"I've got something special to show you, Princess," her grandmother said, and didn't release Arlinda's hand, though Arlinda pulled vaguely away.

"What?" Arlinda said. But the grandmother only smiled.

"I'll show you," the grandmother said, and she led them through the smoky house, down the hallway.

At first, Arlinda thought they were birds. She could hear them behind the closed door, rustling and chirping, the whisper of wings in cages, of clawed feet against wire mesh. It was a sound she had heard behind doors in dreams, a sound that stopped suddenly when in the dream she opened the door and found it empty. Her grandmother took a skeleton key out of her sweater pocket. This is something secret, Arlinda thought, and she held back, letting the two women enter first.

"What is it?" she whispered.

"Chinchillas," her grandmother said, and it sounded like a magic word.

The chinchillas looked like little squirrels. They were all in cages that lined two walls of the room, cages no bigger than a birdcage, stacked high to the ceiling. They were all quiet, staring with their dark, glittering eyes at Arlinda and her mother and grandmother, their noses twitching, their whole bodies quivering with the quickness of their breath. In the closet, Arlinda could see a large sack of food pellets, a pitcher of still water.

"Chinchillas for coats," her grandmother said to Arlinda. "Beautiful, warm ladies' fur coats."

"Ugh," her mother said. "They look like rats."

"These 'rats' are going to bring in a lot of money," her grandmother said. "They'll all be yours, someday."

"They're filthy," Arlinda's mother said. "Mom, they'll stink up the whole house. Look, they're pooping all over everything."

Her grandmother shrugged, put a cigarette in her mouth. The flame of the cigarette lighter made the grandmother's eyes glint. The grandmother breathed in deeply, and then the smoke came curling from her nose, wisping through the bars of sunlight that slanted from the windows.

"They've got to be kept at room temperature," the grandmother said. "Cool in summer, warm in winter."

The room they were in had once been a bedroom. Arlinda could recall when she and her mother had slept in a big, quilt-covered bed in this very room. When her mother was a child, this had been her room.

"Do you really think it will smell up the house," the grandmother asked. "Even if I keep the door shut?"

"It smells like a barn," Arlinda's mother said. "You might as well have a house full of goats."

"Well, I don't care. It doesn't hurt anyone but me. I'm the one who has to live here, and I can't smell a thing."

Arlinda's mother shook her head. As she always did when she saw someone else smoke, she put a cigarette to her own lips and lit it.

"They're so soft," her grandmother said. "Do you want to hold one? They're tame as rabbits."

Her mother wrinkled her nose, exhaling a stream of smoke.

"Arlinda?" the grandmother said softly, as if something magic were about to happen.

Arlinda looked at her mother, then at the chinchillas with their bright, sharp, waiting eyes. She shook her head.

"I don't care," the grandmother said again. "I'm the only one that has to live with them."

The grandmother locked the door to the chinchillas' room, and Arlinda watched as she carefully slipped the silver key into her sweater pocket.

The grandmother made coffee. Arlinda got to drink some, too, with cream and three sugar cubes. Everything in her grandmother's house seemed to happen in the kitchen, and her grandmother was almost always there. After the grandfather had died, she had even moved the small couch and the television into the kitchen. Nowadays, when Arlinda and her mother came to the house, the grandmother would be in the kitchen on the couch, with her legs drawn up, her knees almost touching her belly. She was always wearing sweaters or coats in the house, draping herself with blankets.

The grandmother and the mother talked in secrets. Arlinda could sometimes guess what was being said, though the meaning always drifted just beyond a certain edge of clarity.

"Went to see O'Connor," Arlinda's mother said, "like you said."

"What did he say?"

"He didn't give me anything."

"Why?" The grandmother cupped her hands over her coffee, as if to gather warmth. Arlinda, pretending not to pay attention, swung her legs gently, fascinated.

"Harvey goes and talks to them," Arlinda's mother said, giving the name a sharp twist, as if it were dirty. "Don't they think I know when it hurts?" She gave Arlinda a glare, as if she were about to protest. "I know when I'm sick."

"I've got something," the grandmother said, and Arlinda's mother cast another sharp glance at Arlinda.

"Little pitchers," she said, and the grandmother, too, looked at Arlinda.

Arlinda felt her skin prickle. Were they speaking of the little pictures she'd found in her mother's drawer? She stared down at her swinging legs, as if she hadn't heard, and she saw her grandmother take a pill from her sweater pocket, passing it quickly under the table to her mother's hand. Her mother brought the hand nonchalantly to her mouth, and then took a swallow of coffee.

So that was all, Arlinda thought. She already knew that her mother and grandmother shared their pills. She scorned them for thinking she was too dumb to notice. She had decided that they had the same illness. She could tell this by comparing them to women she knew to be normal. Her Aunt Sharon, for example, had breasts; most women did. Aunt Sharon's breasts were large and round. They were not like lumps of fat, which was what her mother said breasts were made of; instead, they seemed like a part of Aunt Sharon's body, like an elbow or an ear. Arlinda's mother's breasts were not fleshy—her chest was almost as flat as Arlinda's, except that her mother had two pointy, purplish nipples, hard and angry-looking. The mother in the dirty pictures had real breasts, but that was one of the things Arlinda found frightening.

Also, she knew that her mother and grandmother had babies that died. The grandmother would go on Memorial Day to lay flowers on their three tiny graves, but her mother's baby had no grave. Her mother did not like to talk about it, but Arlinda pressed her, once, and finally the mother had snapped: "Oh, for Christ's sake, it wasn't a real baby. It wasn't developed. It was like a fish." Most women, Arlinda knew, did not give birth to such things.

The mother and grandmother sat for a long time in silence, their hands folded on the table like closed wings. The coffee cups sat in front of them, untouched. After a while, Arlinda began to wonder whether they were somehow talking without her hearing, making signs with their eyes, reading one another's minds. When her mother breathed in, she closed her eyes, and then opened them as she breathed out, a kind of sleepy rhythm that seemed to mean something important. Finally, after trying hard to see what they were saying, Arlinda got up and left the kitchen. "I'm going outside," she said, and her mother mumbled under her breath.

Arlinda walked around the side of the house, peering in through little tears in the plastic-covered windows. She stared for a long time at her mother and grandmother, and she pretended that she was a girl who was going to steal a magic potion, and that they were the witches that guarded it. They sat there like stones, casting their spells. After a time, Arlinda crept back around the house, imagining she was following an ogre that would lead her to the hidden entrance of their den. But as she slipped along the wall, sliding around corners, it began to seem that the ogre she was following was now behind her, watching. The idea so startled her that she stopped making believe immediately, half afraid, almost wanting to run. The grass in the yard looked dense and wild, jungle green, and the branches of trees suddenly seemed to be snatching the birds from the air, rather than the birds alighting on the branches. She shivered, and hurried inside.

Her grandmother and mother were no longer in the kitchen. She called out nervously, walking through the living room, down the hallway, peeking in the doors. She found them in the grandmother's bedroom. They were sitting on the grandmother's big double bed, and didn't look up when Arlinda came to the doorway. They were sorting through a drawerful of things dumped on the quilt between them. They touched letters as gently as feathers, smoothing their fingers across the faded handwriting. Her mother held up a dull-golden earring, her eyes closing as if she were falling into a dream, and whispered "Oh!" as if it were a butterfly.

But when Arlinda approached them, the spell was broken. She picked up the earring and saw that the gold paint was cracked and peeling off, like the shell on a boiled egg. "What are these?" Arlinda asked, and her mother just shrugged.

"Old junk," she said.

"What's this?" Arlinda asked, lifting a letter.

"Oh, why don't you go play," her mother said, her voice slurred and tired.

And so Arlinda went back to the kitchen and turned on the TV. All that was on was the news, and she quickly fell asleep.

When she awakened, it was dark outside, and the phone was ringing. The sound of the phone had reached into her dreams—at first just a distant echo, but growing into an alarm that made the dream people freeze, looking into the air above them as if something were swooping from the sky.

The phone kept ringing, and when she went into the living room, her grandmother and mother were both asleep. Arlinda picked the phone up herself. "Hello?" she said.

"Arlinda?" her father's voice said. He sounded far away, his voice just a tiny, angry hiss of static.

"Hi, Daddy," she said.

"Is your mother there?" He spoke in his lowest voice, as if he were going to spank her. She set the phone down quickly and went to the couch where her mother was sleeping. Arlinda shook her, and she opened her mouth as slowly as a fish, lifting her head, her eyes squeezed shut. "What the hell do you want now?" her mother slurred, as if her tongue was hard to move.

"Daddy called," Arlinda said, and backed away.

Her mother sat up suddenly. She was hunched, breathing hard, looking as sluggish and furious as the mole the dogs had caught in the garden and pulled to the daylight, where it hissed and bared its teeth, circling around and around. "Tell him I'm not here," her mother hissed, and Arlinda went hesitantly back to the phone.

"Mommy's not here," she told her father.

"Arlinda Sue!" her father barked. "I'm not fooling around. Now, you tell your mother to get on the phone right now. I've been calling everywhere and I'm very worried and very angry."

"She's not here," Arlinda said again, dully. Her throat felt like it was closing up. She watched as her mother rose like something ancient and heavy from the couch. She stumbled down the hallway toward the grandmother's room, where the other phone was hooked up.

"Arlinda," her father said, low and menacing, "you can tell your mother that if she doesn't come to the phone right now, I'm going to drive out there myself. Tell her that." Arlinda heard the click as her mother picked up the phone in the other room. "Has your mother been taking pills, Arlinda?" her father asked. Arlinda could hear her mother breathing on the other line, and she said nothing, knowing her mother was there, waiting, hidden. Did her father know she was there?

"I asked you a question, Arlinda," her father insisted. "Has she? Has she been taking pills?" Arlinda could hear her mother's sharp intake of breath, could almost feel the heat of it.

"No," Arlinda said. "Yes. No."

"Arlinda . . . " her father said, and suddenly her mother broke in, her voice rising up like a shape out of the fog.

"So!" her mother snapped. "You're turning Arlinda against me, are you?"

"What the hell do you think you're doing?" Arlinda's father roared.

"Arlinda, get off this goddamned phone," her mother cried, and Arlinda slammed it down—startling as her mother's voice leapt from the receiver to the bedroom on the other side of the house, shrinking away. From where Arlinda stood in the living room, her mother's shrill voice became abruptly tiny, her shouts and denials and accusations like the curses of a genie shut up in a bottle. Then, they stopped.

Arlinda stood very still, listening. Everything was quiet, and then the door to her grandmother's bedroom slammed open. Her mother appeared in the hallway, slumping toward her, holding the walls and still swaying.

"So!" her mother said, in a mincing, mock-sweet voice. "I hope you're happy now, Liar!"

"I didn't do anything," Arlinda cried. But in an instant, it seemed as if everything she'd done—all the jewelry she'd taken, the pills she'd buried, the pictures she'd seen, all of it was suddenly clear to her mother, who could see it in Arlinda's eyes.

"Do you like to tell your daddy lies about me?" Her mother tried to grab at her, but Arlinda slipped away. "Good!" her mother crowed. "Now you've done it! He's never going to come back! Are you happy now!" Her mother caught her by the edge of her shirt and she screamed. Her mother's fingers clutched her shoulders and Arlinda was shaken from side to side, wailing. Her father was gone, she would never see him again. "Oh, you've done it now, you brat!" her mother screamed. Arlinda tried to pull away, and as she did her shirt ripped and she toppled back. Her mother fumbled to catch her, but she slipped through her fingers, her chin striking the floor. "Oh," her mother cried in alarm. "Honey, are you okay?"

"You pushed me down!" Arlinda cried. She could feel herself beginning to heave with tears. "You hit me!"

"No—Liar!" her mother said, but her expression was confused, as if maybe she wasn't certain of what had happened. "You fell yourself. I never touched you!"

Arlinda curled herself into a ball, pulling away from her mother's touch. "I hate you!" she screamed. "I'm going to tell Daddy all about you!"

"Fine!" her mother said. But she was wincing, moving away, and Arlinda could see how her eyes suddenly sparked with hurt, then narrowed. "Good! You hate me? Why not, just like everybody else. So tell your precious Daddy, see if I care!"

Her mother sat down on the couch and closed her eyes. Arlinda watched her furtively, thinking she might suddenly spring up and strike her, but her mother merely put her head in her hands, and Arlinda hurried past her, arcing as far away as possible as she neared her mother, then running down the hall and into the scary bedroom, the one where her grandfather had slept before he died. It was full of boxes of his belongings.

She stopped crying even before she closed the door. She felt numb and trembly, as if she were hollow and her body might collapse, like a paper bag filled with air. She could hear, as she sat on the bare bed, the scratch and rattle of the chinchillas in their cages in the next room.

She wondered what would become of her. Had her father really abandoned her? Or would he come and take her away, so she would never see her mother again? How long would she have to stay here? What would happen to her dolls and books at her real home? Did her mother hate her? Did her father?

For a long time, she just lay there, her eyes open. She was afraid. The dusty-smelling cardboard boxes crouched around her, circled the bed. The shadows of the trees shook and trembled against the walls, thin and crooked pantomimes of lurching figures, of people dancing. Beyond the wall, the sound of the chinchillas was like voices–tittering, whispering, telling secrets.

It was late; she had been vaguely asleep, vaguely dreaming, when her mother came in. At least it was a woman who looked like her mother, in her mother's nightgown, which was transparent in the moonlight, so that she could see the outlines of the woman's body, like branches behind a thin curtain.

"Arlinda," the mother whispered, as tender and gentle as a real mother. "See how pretty. See how soft."

There was a chinchilla in the mother's hands. Arlinda could see its eyes glistening.

"Momma," Arlinda said, softly, as her mother sat on the edge of the bed. There was no way of knowing that this would be the most gentle moment she would ever remember passing between them. There was no way of seeing that her parents would fight again and again in the coming months, that in two years she would have a new mother, a mother like the ones at other children's houses, a mother that baked cakes and went dancing with her father. There was no predicting how little she would see of her crazy mother when they moved away, or how she would come to hate and dread visiting her. She couldn't have foreseen that her mother would live on in the house with the chinchillas even after the grandmother had died, even after Arlinda and her father had gone far, far away. All Arlinda knew then was that, for a moment, she had the key to all those secrets.

She felt her mother's hands on her own, felt the softness of the chinchilla pressed against her palms. It was its shivering, it was the heaving of its lungs, it was the quick muffled beating of its terrible heart.

transformations

The first time I saw my brother Corky in women's clothes, I was eleven and he was fourteen. He came out of my parents' bedroom in my mother's good dress, the one with bird of paradise flowers patterned on it, and her high heels and lipstick. I thought he was kidding. He chased after me, talking in a Southern accent, and I ran off laughing. Corky was always pretending to be someone else, dressing up in clothes he'd bought at the Catholic rummage house or found in the garage, imitating the mannerisms of his math teacher, or Uncle Evan, who drove semi trucks and stuttered, or some disc jockey on the radio. I didn't realize then, not for years and years actually, that he was gay and all.

He is still your brother, my father told me when he showed me the picture. This was the second time I'd seen Corky in women's clothes. In the photo, he was wearing a big red wig, a blue-jean skirt, pumps, and a blouse with fringe. He looked like a country singer. My father asked me: "Do you know who this is?" All I said was, "Yes," and "It figures."

My father shook his head at me. He liked to pretend that he didn't care what Corky was, just so long as he was happy. That was the official line. But I'd seen the kind of cloudy distance that came into his eyes when he talked to Corky on the phone. I'd noticed him, once, studying an old Polaroid of the three of us, pheasant hunting, examining it as if looking for clues. I'd seen his expression when one of his buddies from the electrician's union asked: "So how's that boy of yours doing back East?" My father shifted from foot to foot. "Oh, fine, fine," he said quickly, and looked down.

But he looked me sternly in the eyes. "He is still your brother," he said. He folded his thick hands, staring glumly at the glossy black-and-white photo.

"My sister, you mean," I said.

He frowned. "You're getting pretty smart-mouthed," he said. He laid the photo on the kitchen table between us, like some important document I was supposed to sign. "He does this as entertainment," my father said. The words "CABARET BERLINER, New York," were printed on the bottom of the picture.

"I'll bet," I said.

My brother worked at a bar in New York City. We'd known that. We also knew he was gay. He'd told my parents over the phone after he'd been away for a year. I wasn't sure how they reacted at first, though they seemed calm by the time they got around to telling me. Corky had come to a decision, my father said, and my mother nodded grimly. For a long time afterward, my father wouldn't refer to it at all except as "your brother's decision," though he also pointed out to me that the words "fag" and "queer" were worse than swearing as far as he was concerned.

Corky was going to college in New York at the time, but he dropped out shortly after to audition for plays and work in bars at night. He hadn't been home since he told them. Instead he sent clippings, pictures, lists of productions he was trying out for. "One thing about Corky," my father remarked to me as he looked through the packets Corky sent. "At least he knows what he wants, and he's not afraid to go after it."

It was my senior year in high school, and my father thought I had no ambition. Maybe that was true. In any case, I wasn't like Corky had been when he was in high school. His senior year, there was always something about him taped to the refrigerator—a certificate of merit, or a clipping from a local paper about a scholarships he'd won. He pinned the acceptance letters from colleges in neat rows on a bulletin board in our room, as if they were rare butterflies.

That was why I was surprised when he called to say he was taking some time off to attend my high school graduation. I went to the Catholic school as Corky had, but there was no chance of me ending up valedictorian like him. For a while maybe people wondered whether I'd be a teacher's pet like Corky, and in the beginning they even called me by his name. But it didn't take them long to figure out that I wasn't going to leave any brilliant reputation in my wake. My father always said I didn't "apply myself" like Corky did. Out of ninety-six seniors I was ranked forty-ninth. I would just be a vague, doughy face in the middle of the third row. There was no great cause for celebration. I hadn't found a job or a college to attend in the fall. But at least my parents had a son who could give them grandchildren, they could appreciate that. And as for that fat, mustached drama teacher, Sister Vincent, who continually remembered Corky's beautiful singing voice and his performance in *South Pacific*, well, I wished she could see his new song and dance at Cabaret Berliner.

Corky came home two days before graduation. My mother and father and I went to pick him up at Stapleton Airport in Denver. The whole way there I worried. I couldn't help but imagine Corky appearing to meet us in a feather boa and an evening gown or something, trotting down the ramp to meet us with a big lipstick grin. I told myself I was being low-minded and ugly, but that image of him kept popping into my mind. My face felt hot.

Meanwhile, my parents acted like everything was wonderful. The full moon reflected off the early May snow that still lay on the fields, and my father kept howling like a wolf. It seemed to amuse my mother, because she chuckled every time he did it, and laughed aloud when he grabbed her around the waist and growled.

I was sitting in the backseat, watching the car drift toward the center of the road while they horsed around. "I hope we wreck," I said.

The three of us stood there in the waiting area, watching the planes land. We didn't recognize Corky when he approached us, but at least he was wearing normal clothes. He'd dyed his hair bright red–it was shoulder-length, tied in a ponytail. When he was close enough, I noticed the little crease in his earlobe that meant it was pierced, but he didn't have an earring. He hugged my mother, kissing her lightly. Then he turned and kissed my father. My father always kissed us on the lips, and wasn't even afraid to do it in public. He puckered up like a cartoon character, and it would've been funny if he wasn't so earnest about it. Here he was, this big, middle-aged construction worker, smacking lips with his son. He didn't even hesitate knowing Corky was gay, though I looked around to see if people were staring.

When my brother turned to me, I stuck out my hand. I didn't want him kissing on me. "So," he said, and squeezed my palm, hard. "The graduate!"

I shrugged. "Yeah, well," I said. "I'm just glad it's over."

He kept hold of my hand till I pulled back a little. He grinned. "Congratulations," he said.

"Congratulations to you, too," I said, though I didn't know why.

As we drove back to Mineral, I watched my brother suspiciously. Ever since we were little he'd always been the center of things, and I doubted that he'd come all this way just to congratulate me. I kept expecting him to take over at any minute. I remembered how, when we were young, we had a place behind the house, an old shed we'd furnished with lawn chairs and cinder blocks and such. This became the plantation from *Gone with the Wind*–Corky was Rhett and Scarlett, I was the slaves; or a rocket–Corky was the captain and alien invaders, I was the crew that got killed. Once, when I was eleven and he was fifteen, and he was going to play the lead in *South Pacific,* he got me all excited about trying out for the part of his little Polynesian son. He gave me the music and then made fun of me, standing by our bedroom door and warbling like an old chicken.

Yet maybe, I thought, Corky had changed. It had been a long time since I'd really spoken to him. It had been several years since I'd seen him, and I seldom felt like talking to him on the phone. Even when my father did put me on the line, I couldn't think of what to say. "What's new?" Corky would ask, and I'd shrug: "Nothing." Maybe he'd become a totally different person, and I hadn't known.

But I couldn't tell. He was so motionless as we drove that he hardly seemed real. He just stared, like some stone idol, out toward the passing telephone poles and fields and the grasshopper oil wells nodding against the moonlit sky. His hands remained in his lap, except once, when he suddenly touched his hair with his fingertips as if adjusting a hat. When my parents asked him a question he leaned forward, smiling politely: "What? What did you say?"

It was late, nearly one in the morning, when we got home. Corky went to the bedroom to unpack–our old room, my room now–and when I came in he was already stretched out on the upper bunk. It used to be that I slept in the bottom and he slept in the top, but since he'd left I'd been using the lower bunk to store papers and laundry and stuff. He looked down at me and smiled.

"That's my bed," I told him.

He sat up and his bare feet dangled over the edge,

swinging lightly. He was wearing silky-looking pajamas. We'd always just slept in our underwear, and I
imagined that this was what he wore when he lay
down next to another man. "That's rich," he said.
"You know, all these years I wanted that bottom
bunk. I suppose you always wanted the top."

"I didn't care one way or another," I said. I began
to take handfuls of dirty laundry from the bottom
bunk and put them on the floor. "You can sleep there
if you want."

He nodded and lay back. "It's been a long time
since I've heard any news from you."

"Yeah, well," I said. "My life isn't that exciting."

"You've really changed the room around." He gestured to a poster of a model in a white bikini who was
holding a six-pack of beer. "She's sexy," he said.

"Yeah," I said. "I guess."

He looked from the poster to me, his lips puckered
out a little. "So," he said at last. "Do you have a girlfriend, Todd?"

"Yes," I said. "Sort of." I didn't. I had friends that
were girls, and one of them I took to most of the
dances. But I wasn't like some of the guys in school
who'd been going steady with one girl since eighth
grade. All the girls I liked had either paired off or
weren't interested. The furtive gropes and kisses after
dances hadn't amounted to much. I was afraid that
even if I got a girl to do more, I'd be clumsy, and I
couldn't stand the thought of her laughing, maybe
telling her friends. "You know," I told Corky. "I date
around and stuff."

"Good for you," he said. He pulled his feet up onto
the bed the way a fish would flip its tail. Then he
laughed. I could feel my ears warming.

"What's so funny?" I said.

"Nothing," he said. "Just the way you said it." He
deepened his voice to a macho swagger. "'I date
around and stuff.'" He laughed again. "You used to be
such a little high-voiced thing."

48   *transformations*

"Hm," I said. He leaned back and I turned off the light. I moved over near the closet, where it was darkest, so I could undress without him seeing me. The hangers made wind-chime sounds as I brushed them.

"It's so weird, being home," he said. His voice floated from the top bunk as I took off my shirt. I decided to sleep in my jeans. I didn't have any pajamas. "You can't believe how strange it is."

"Well, nothing has changed," I said. I groped across the dim room to my bed. I could see the lump where he was lying, a shadow bending toward me.

"No," he said, "no." And then, slowly: "So did you see the picture I sent?" The house was still. I could hear water whispering through the pipes in the walls. I could hear him breathing.

"I saw it." I tried to make my voice noncommittal. I sighed deeply, like I was already almost asleep.

He didn't say anything for a long time, and I thought he might have drifted off. When he spoke out of the dark, finally, his voice sounded odd, twittery, not like him, and it made my neck prickle. "Sometimes," he said, "I'm glad I sent it and other times not." I didn't say anything. "Todd?" he whispered.

I waited. I recalled the way we used to lie in our bunks when we were little and tell jokes and make up songs. I remembered how I used to go to sleep to the sound of his murmuring, crooning.

"What," I whispered back finally.

"How did Mom and Dad react?"

"How should I know?" I mumbled. "They don't tell me anything."

"What did they say?"

"What did you expect them to say?"

"I don't know," he said. "It's hard to explain."

But I didn't want him to explain. I didn't want to keep picturing him in that outfit, swishing and singing, maybe kissing a member of his audience, leaving a bright parenthesis of lipstick on a bald forehead. "They didn't say much of anything," I told him. "They don't care what you do in your personal life."

"Do you?"

"Why should I?" I whispered. I rolled over, pretending to be asleep.

When I woke, my brother was already up. I could hear him talking in the kitchen, and the sound of eggs crackling on a skillet. I went to the bathroom to shower and when I came back to dress, I couldn't help but notice Corky's suitcase. It was expensive-looking, dark strips of leather bound around brick-red cloth. Through the walls I could hear the vague whisper of conversation and I bent down, running my hands along the sides, finding the zipper.

Most of the things had been taken out. He'd put them in dresser drawers my mother had cleared out for him. But there was a compartment along one side, and when I opened it, I found what I figured I'd find. It gave me a fluttery feeling in my stomach: a skirt, a flowered blouse, pantyhose, a box of make-up with the colors arranged chromatically. Beneath that were more photos—Corky gripping a fireman's pole, his shaved leg sliding along it, his eyes looking seductively away; being lifted by a group of men in tuxedos, his head flung back, his arms open wide, jeweled necklaces in his clenched fists. There were two clippings of advertisements for Cabaret Berliner: a drawing of a man's hairy leg with a high heel on his foot, and underneath, in small letters: "Corky Petersen and Sister Mary Josephine/After Tea Dance Party." Another had a photo of Corky in his cowgirl outfit. I wondered if he was planning to show us a sample of his act. I closed the suitcase quickly.

They didn't look up when I came into the kitchen. They were sitting at the table, eating toast and scrambled eggs. Corky was telling my father that New York City was in a state of collapse, and had been ever since Reagan took office. He said the homeless filled the streets, that a bag lady had died on his doorstep. My father kept nodding very seriously, frowning, "Mm-hmm," as if he were talking to a grown-up. He never spoke to me that way. Then Corky began to tell about the semis that parked outside his apartment at night, and how his whole place filled up with diesel fumes. He was afraid to light a cigarette. In the middle of this, he looked up and saw me standing there. "Well, hello, Sleeping Beauty," he said, and cocked his hand on his hip.

I glared at him. "Mornin', " I said in my deepest voice. I slid into the chair at the far end of the table.

"You hungry, Punkin?" my mother asked brightly.

I looked sternly at her. I wanted to tell them that my name was Todd, not Sleeping Beauty or Pumpkin. But all I said was "Nope." Then I looked at Corky. "So how come you live in New York if you don't like it?"

Corky shrugged. "Frankly," he said, "there's no other place I could stand." Then he leaned toward my father and lowered his voice. "I'll tell you what's really scary," he said. "This AIDS thing. Out here I'm sure no one realizes, but it's really terrifying."

My father blushed and we were all silent. "Well," my father said, and cleared his throat. "I hope you're being careful." He picked at his eggs.

"Careful?" Corky said. He gave a short laugh. "I can't even tell you. The other night I was out with this guy." He stopped. All of us were sitting stiffly, and my father had a pinched look on his face. He touched his eyelids, as if to clear away the image of Corky and this man, this lover.

"Well, anyway," Corky said. "He didn't even want to kiss. He goes: 'I don't know you well enough yet.'" He took a bite of toast, nervously, then looked over at me and winked. I kept my face expressionless. He winked again.

"So, Todd!" he said. He spoke my name as if it were some ridiculously cheerful exclamation, like "gee whiz," or "wowza," the kind of thing he used to say with mocking relish when he was in high school. "Tomorrow's the big day!" he said. "Graduation! Commencement! The beginning of a new life!"

"Right," I said. I didn't like to think about it that way. I couldn't imagine myself working a regular job forty hours a week, or leaving home for college or the service; it seemed amazing that anyone could live alone, pay their own bills, get up in the morning without their mother waking them.

"Yes, Toddy," my mother said quickly. "We haven't seen you in your cap and gown."

"Yeah, and you're not going to either," I said.

"What's the matter?" my father frowned. I could see how it was going to go: They'd do anything to escape more information about Corky's sex life. "Are you ashamed of your cap and gown?" my father said.

"I just don't feel like putting it on, that's all," I said. "What's the big deal?"

"Oh, come on, Todd," my brother said. He grinned, enjoying himself, and I shook my head at all of them. It figured—even with all of them looking at me, the focus was still on Corky underneath.

"I feel like a dancing dog," I said. I pushed away from the table.

When I went into my bedroom, I just stood there for a moment, staring at Corky's suitcase, then out the window. The morning was warm and clear. Outside, the grass was a sickly yellow-green in the patches that appeared where the snow had drawn back. It made me think of a horror movie I'd seen where the smooth, pale skin of a dead woman peeled away to reveal a monster's face. At last, I went to the closet and took the box out. The cap and gown were still wrapped in plastic, and I tore it away roughly. I slid the gown over my head, the silky cloth slick against my bare arms, my neck. I fit the cap over my hair, and it fit snugly. It made me think of a wig.

When I came into the kitchen, Corky began to hum a jazzy "Pomp and Circumstance," snapping his fingers. The gown billowed around me, the cap tilted against my line of vision, and I shambled forward, trying to imagine how Clint Eastwood would walk in a cap and gown.

"You look real nice," my father nodded.

"Stand up straight," said my mother.

It would have been nice to say that I was going out that night with a group of friends to some party on somebody's farm where everyone was singing and carrying on around a keg an older brother had bought. Some of my classmates were doing that, but not my friends. Jeanine's grandparents were coming in from California that night, Craig's family was taking him out to dinner, Brad and Janice, both of them too good for their own good, were going to a special Mass or wake or whatever it was for graduating seniors. I remember Corky and the other seniors who were in plays had a formal dinner for themselves. They'd sent out calligraphied invitations, and dressed up in coat and tie. At the party, they'd put parts of Corky's valedictorian speech to the music of *My Fair Lady*. He'd come home late, singing in a Cockney accent at the top of his lungs.

And what did I do? I sat around. Corky was busy providing the entertainment. As I sat after breakfast and read a horror book, my brother helped with the dishes and told my mother about Jacek, a Yugoslavian man he'd dated, a man who made independent films and had done a music video for a rock group. Actually, Corky didn't say they'd dated. That was only implied by the careful, wistful description he gave. My mother drew various dishes out of the soapy water, nodding as if she didn't quite understand what it all meant.

After lunch, we went for a drive. Corky seemed excited. He wanted to drive by Rattlesnake Knob, he said, and take pictures to show his friends in New York. I pictured him laughing about it at a cocktail party, showing his photos to a group of lithe, smirking gay men, as they stood on the terrace of some penthouse, surrounding Corky, looking at the bleak landscape in the photos and then, thankfully, gazing at the city lights that blurred to dazzles, at the Statue of Liberty with the moon hanging over her head. "How quaint," they'd murmur.

The four of us squeezed into the cab of the pickup, with Corky and me in the middle. We drove out toward the hills, and when we passed the rock house, Corky made us stop.

The house stood in the middle of a field. It had been built by pioneers, and the sod roof had long since collapsed. The walls had been built of pumice rock that the pioneers had gathered from the hills, and from the smattering of trees they'd found by the creek and cut down. It was still recognizable as a house, there was still the frame of the doors and windows, though the wood was mostly rotten and even the stone walls were crumbling. My father used to take us out here when we were little and tell us about pioneers. Corky wanted to take a picture.

He got out of the truck and strode through the ditch to the fence. We followed after. Corky stretched the lines of barbed wire apart so he could squeeze through, then paused on the other side and looked closely at the wire. "Hey, Dad," he said, as we came to the edge of the fence. "Look at the strands of this wire. It's really intricate. Is that rare?"

My father bent over to look with Corky, so that their foreheads nearly touched, so they looked like mirror images of one another, leaning over, hands on their knees. "No," my father said. "No, not rare. Just old." He sighed, straightening up. It used to be that, wherever we went, my father would be pointing things out, explaining things. As we'd drive up into the hills, my father would tell us how the trickle of creek we'd passed a mile back had made them; over millions of years a valley was created with hills on either side. I remember imagining the gray hills with their jagged lace of pumice cliffs, rising up on either side, pushing slowly out of the flat prairie like mushrooms. My father taught us trivia that seemed amazing back then—how to tell a rattlesnake from a bullsnake; types of barbed wire. Maybe he was remembering the same thing, because he just stood there, touching his fingers to his eyelids, as Corky clicked his camera at the barbed wire.

"So," my brother said to me as we walked across the pasture to the rock house. "Am I going to get to meet one of these girlfriends of yours? Is one of them going to stop by the house tomorrow?"

"I don't know," I said. My parents looked at me. They didn't say anything, but it still made me feel like a failure. They knew I didn't have a girlfriend. Even in the one thing I had over Corky, I was a flop. Corky stood out in front of the rock house, which was surrounded by tall dry weeds, and put his hands on his hips. He looked over his shoulder at me, and I sighed. My parents looked at me curiously, and I stared down at the ground. "They're not really girlfriends," I said. "They're just friend friends."

When I looked up, my eyes met Corky's. I couldn't tell what he was thinking. "Hey," he said. "Why don't you all stand in front of the place? That'll make a nice shot."

We arranged ourselves—my father stood behind my mother and me and pulled us close to him so he could hide his potbelly. He and Corky were the tall ones in the family, and I'd inherited my mother's shortness. We pressed together. "Smile," Corky called, and I set my lips into one of those smiles that I knew was crooked and dopey, but I couldn't stop it. "That's great," Corky said. He aimed the camera at us. "It's one of those pictures you'll keep forever, you know?" We separated from our cluster. Corky took another picture.

As we walked back to the car, Corky put his arm

around my shoulder. I stiffened, but I didn't shrug him off. "I think just plain friends are the best kind," he said.

"Yeah, right," I said. He tilted his head as if a cool breeze were blowing.

"I sing this song in my show called 'We're Only Friends.' It's really great. I've got this sort of Dietrich look, and the tune is a 30s German thing, you know." He began to sing softly, his voice raspy, deep, but strikingly like a woman's. His voice carried, wafting into the open air.

I didn't know what he was trying to prove. Maybe he was trying to get us used to the idea. Maybe he was just needling my parents. Maybe he was showing off. But whatever he thought, the Subject kept coming into our conversations. He had given a man my mother's recipe for fried chicken. He used a song my father liked, "Someday Soon, Going with Him," in his show, and the closing number was a song my mother had loved when she was younger: "Where the Boys Are." He sang a bit for us. He kept at it, through dinner, then after, while we were trying to watch TV, tossing little comments out for our consideration. My father got a glazed look, as if he could hear someone far away calling his name. My mother looked more and more bewildered.

As for me, I found myself thinking about the clothes I'd seen in his suitcase. I wondered if he was planning to put them on.

When he came into the bedroom late that night, I was lying on the bottom bunk, reading my book. "Corky," I said. He was bent down, searching through his suitcase. "Do you–" I cleared my throat. I watched him collect a toothbrush and dental floss from his bag. "I mean you normally wear normal clothes, don't you?"

He looked up at me, not smiling. "Are you asking if I'm a transvestite?" he said. He stared me down, but I didn't say anything. "I only dress for my act, if that's what you mean," he said. "For my job."

I nodded. I took a deep breath. "So . . . how come you packed women's clothes?"

His eyes narrowed. I remembered how he used to have his secret box of stuff, a scrapbook full of old clippings and things, the way he'd come in and found me looking through it. "Keep out of my stuff, Toad!" he'd shouted, and started punching me.

"What do you mean?" he said softly. He was looking me up and down, appraising me, and I watched him set the items in his hand back in the bag. He unzipped the compartment and pulled out the make-up kit, the photos. "This stuff?" he said fiercely. For a minute I shrank back, as if he were my older brother again and he could beat me up. He stared at me until I looked away, and then he suddenly chuckled. "Todd," he said, almost affectionately, as if he were remembering some other brother that wasn't me. "I thought maybe someone might have wanted to see my show." He sighed. "People pay money to see me perform, you know." He put the blouse to his face. "Here," he said, and threw it at me, hitting the book I was still holding in my hand. "Smell it."

It must have been the look on my face that made him laugh. I held it and sniffed. I had dark thoughts about what I was supposed to smell.

"Old Spice," he said. "For the manly man." It was my father's brand of cologne. "It's a joke," he said. He picked out the bunch of pictures and clippings and walked over to the bunks with them. He put them on top of the blouse. "If you want to look at this stuff, you can," he said. "I'm going to brush my teeth. "

Before he got to the door, he turned. "Jesus, Todd, what did you think?" he said. "Did you really think I was going to run around your graduation party in drag or something? Did you think I came home for the sole purpose of embarrassing you?"

I looked down at the pictures of him. "Why did you come home," I said.

He put his back to me. "Because I was stupid."

At my graduation party, my relatives drank and gave me money. Commencement was as long and dull as the past four years of high school had been. In her speech, the valedictorian kept referring to the future as a train, and I imagined myself standing on the railroad tracks, watching it bear down on me.

The party made it even worse. There I was, in the middle of the living room, holding a paper plate–melting ice cream, a slice of chocolate cake–dabbing the frosting from the base of the little wax graduate that had been in the center of the cake, which my mother had insisted I take as a memento. When my uncle Evan came up and handed me an envelope, and asked what my plans were, I tried to tell him that I had a lot of options I was considering. But after that, I gave up. The next time, when my aunt Susan handed me a card and asked me the same question, I just shrugged.

Which of them had futures that were so wonderful? I watched Great Aunt Birdie, already drunk before noon. She'd been married twice, and now was living with some man in Denver. Or my cousin Russell, who'd just gone bankrupt. Or Grandpa Mitch, who a few months before had a heart attack, who had to crawl from the bedroom, down the hall to the phone. "Oh, he looks so thin, so pale," they whispered behind his back. "He shouldn't be in that old house alone." Soon he'd be in a nursing home. My parents sat on the couch near my grandfather, looking nervously at Corky. It was sickening. They'd spent the better part of their lives raising us, and look where that got them.

Corky was across the room, sitting on a folding chair with his legs crossed at the knee. He was right on the edge of the kitchen. People had to walk past him to get to the food or the beer. I watched my relatives file slowly by, their eyes fixed on him. They asked how life was treating him in the Big Apple, and tightened their smiles.

I stirred my ice cream and cake together. Even I couldn't help noticing him. Aunt Birdie came weaving up to me, fiddling with the tab on her beer. A napkin was stuck to her shoe, dragging behind her as she sidled up to me. "Congratulations, Precious," she said, and pushed her lips to my forehead, leaning against me for support. "What's in your future?" she asked, and pushed a crumpled bill into my jacket pocket. I shook my head. "Nothing," I said. Corky had lit another cigarette and was saying: "You know, that sounds an awful lot like a film I auditioned for." Aunt Birdie kissed me on the eyelid, and I slid away from her grasp. I decided I needed to go outside for a while.

The wind was blowing hard, and it was cool for late May. I bunched my jacket together at the neck, staring out past the yard to the driveway, which was crowded with my relatives' vehicles. I breathed slowly. For a minute I'd imagined I was going to spin out of control. I might have broken free of Aunt Birdie, lisping and sashaying, cooing: "Ooo, a film I auditioned for. Ooo, how wonderful I am." I might have denounced my parents in front of everyone, what hypocrites they were: "We're so proud of our Corky! How nice it is to have a son who's a successful drag queen!"

Corky came out a few minutes later. He exhaled smoke as he poked his head out the door. "Todd," he said. "You're missing your party."

He kept his body inside the house, so it looked like his head was a puppet, moving along the doorframe. He bent so he could look at me upside down. It was an old game from childhood. We used to practice miming around the edges of doors, so that from the other side it looked like we were floating, or being lifted by an invisible force. "Todd," he said, in a mock-solemn, British actor voice, like they have when they recite Shakespeare. "Why are you so glum, Todd?" His head vanished then, as if it had been yanked from the stage. He came out of the house and stood beside me.

In the house, someone had turned on music, my father's Patsy Cline tape. It drifted mournfully in the stillness, wisping through the walls.

I sighed. "Did you ever," I said, "wonder what was going to happen to you?"

There was a flicker in his eyes–I had caught him off guard, and he thought of something, remembered something. His smile wavered. "No," he said.

I considered this. Maybe he'd always known. "Well," I said. "What do you think will happen to me, then? Because I wonder. I wonder a lot."

He stared at me for a long time, then he put another cigarette to his lips.

"You'll probably be miserable," he said. "Like everybody else."

Our eyes met, and we both looked down. His words hung there– as if he'd dropped a cup or a bowl at my feet and we were both considering it, looking at the shards of broken glass. In the house, I could hear my father laughing.

"Thanks a lot," I said stiffly. "Sorry I asked."

He shrugged and pulled a folded bill out of his pocket. He pushed it into my hand. "Maybe I will go squeeze into that dress," he whispered.

"Don't," I said through my teeth. I looked at the piece of paper in my hand. A hundred-dollar bill. "I can't take this," I said. "That's too much."

He lifted his eyebrows, and I watched him put it back in his pocket. His hand slid out of his pocket holding a nickel, which he flipped toward me. I fumbled, caught it. "There," he said.

"Very funny," I said. He dragged deeply on his cigarette.

We stared at each other. "Go ahead," my brother whispered. Smoke curled around his face as he breathed, and he pushed his hands through his dyed hair, loosening his ponytail. "I know you're dying to. Say 'faggot.' Say 'cocksucker.'" He smirked at me. But then as I watched, it seemed that some awful transformation was coming over his face. It was trembling and contorting like there was something beneath it trying to escape. For a second I imagined that he must be seeing something terrifying, a dark shape lunging at us, and I turned quickly. But there was only the empty yard.

"Say it," he whispered. "Say it."

fraternity

Cal used to be president of the fraternity. But then he was in a car wreck. Cal and Hap and a group of boys from the fraternity house had been out to the bars, and they were on their way home. Afterward Hap often pictured Cal dipping his hand into a cooler of beer, letting the water run off the can, popping the tab. Cal's head was tilted back, Hap could see him in the rearview mirror, and it was when he looked back to the road that he saw the parked truck. Hap remembered, or thought he remembered, someone screaming, "Mom!"

John wasn't hurt that bad. He was in the hospital for a few weeks, but then he didn't come back to school. He was still at home, working in his father's auto parts store. He didn't drink anymore, he didn't go out. Talking to him, Hap remarked to people, you'd think he was middle-aged.

Stephen wasn't injured at all, but he graduated early–finished up his major and got out of school and their fraternity as quietly as possible, packing up like a swindler without even saying goodbye.

It was Cal who got the worst part of it. He'd ducked down at the last minute and covered his head, but it was his side of the car that was crushed. They had to cut him out of the wreckage, where he was pinned between the car door and the seat.

Cal was in a coma for nearly a month, and all that time they were expecting him to die. He woke up one morning, but he wasn't the same person. There was brain damage and he had to go to a rehabilitation clinic.

Hap had been driving the car. He wasn't drunk, and in fact he took a Breathalyzer at the site of the accident. All he could remember were the faces peering out of the slow-moving cars, and the whirlpool of red and blue lights from the police cars. He passed the test. He'd had a beer or two, of course, but he was definitely within the legal limit. It was an accident. And it wouldn't happen again: he didn't drive anymore.

Not that anyone ever blamed him. Still, he sometimes noticed how their eyes darkened sidelong when he reached for another beer. He noticed how their faces suddenly tightened when he was in a good mood and got to laughing. It was as if, he thought, he'd turned for a second into something unclean.

Hap had tried to put everything back in order. They'd held an emergency meeting when they found out Cal wouldn't be returning, and since Hap was vice president at the time, they told him the presidency was his if he felt up to it. And so he'd stood there, with bandages on his head and hand, talking in nervous circles, saying how life had to go on, how Cal would have wanted it that way.

A few months after the accident Hap began to pass out in unusual places. The first time it happened was for real: he woke in the hallway, with no idea how he got there. Magic Marker was scribbled across his face and belly, as if he'd been trying to write himself a message.

After that first time it became an act. On mornings after parties, his fraternity brothers began to find him in the foyer, curled up among the discarded advertisements and catalogues, or in the shower fully dressed, with the water running, or outside under a tree, his hands caked with dirt as if he'd been digging. At first they thought it was funny. They joked that

Hap ought to have bells tied to his heels before he was allowed to drink a beer. Some of the incidents became amusing anecdotes.

He planned things in advance, considering which place might be most surprising, most ridiculous. One night he'd squeezed onto a shelf on the trophy case, twisted around gold statuettes of basketball players and wrestlers and the engraved plaques. Even in that precarious position they couldn't tell he was faking. He opened his eyes with a start, and sat straight up. One of the trophies fell clattering onto the living room floor.

Often he'd wait a long time before anyone found him. He'd get frustrated, sometimes, and decide he was just going to forget it and go on up to bed. But then he'd hear voices and his heart would pound and his mind would begin to whir like a fan. He could feel the shape of them as they moved closer, slow, hovering, and he'd open his eyes to find them leaning over him like surgeons. Once this pre-med named Matsumura reached down and took his pulse. The pressure of his finger had run through Hap like an electric shock. He jerked up, and everyone laughed, circled around him, shaking their heads.

But the novelty began to wear off. "Oh brother," he heard Charlie Balbo say one morning. "Look who's passed out again." Balbo pulled on Hap's arm. He was in ROTC and always woke up early to do exercises. Hap could hear Balbo sighing through his nose. "Rise and shine, buddy," Balbo said, and when Hap fluttered his eyelids and moaned, none of them were smiling. Hap figured they were all thinking about the accident.

Cal's mother called. Cal was back home, she told Hap, and she hoped some of his fraternity brothers would come for a visit. It had been six months since the accident.

Hap wondered how she'd gotten his number. He

hadn't met her, really, just shook hands with her once during parents' weekend when Cal pointed them at each other and said, "Mom this is Hap he's one of my best pals," or something like that, quick and stilted; that was the way he talked. Later, after Cal had gone to the clinic, Hap sent a get well card to his home. He'd never visited the hospital, though he told people he had: "Cal's doing real good," he said. He'd called the hospital a number of times, and that's what they told him. "Under the circumstances," they said, "he's doing well."

As the visit approached, Hap would feel a wave of panic pass over him. and he was desperate to call Cal's mother and make some excuse. But what? He couldn't think of any excuse that wouldn't provoke disbelief. He would think of it from time to time, when he wasn't expecting to. That Saturday, a week before he was to go, it was like a rushing at his back.

There was a party that night, and Hap had been downstairs long before anyone else, organizing guys to clear the furniture and push it against the wall, directing the football players to lift kegs of beer into ice-filled trash cans, hurrying to get the tap or the strobe light. There were certain things Hap did that he felt no one else could do quite so well. He was the one who liked to put up decorations and make up themes for parties–putting red lights in the windows and taping up orange and yellow poster board in the shape of flames, so the house looked afire; lining the dance floor with old mattresses and balloons; setting up elaborate spreads of dips and vegetables and so on. He played the music, building up to the best dance songs, urging the crowd into a kind of frenzy. He'd stand on the window ledge and look out over their heads, calling out chants which the crowd would repeat. It was almost as if this was his fiefdom, for one night at least.

Cal used to shake his head. "Geez," he used to say. "Take a Valium." Hap remembered one night they'd gone to this place, Elbow's Room, where they didn't card. It was a dim, hazy bar, with country music on the jukebox, and they went in before a party. Hap was anxious to get back, he didn't want to miss anything. But Cal was in no hurry. Hap was telling him that he was going to miss the fraternity when they graduated, that it was one of his main reasons for staying in school, and Cal stared at him. His face was lit by the fireplace glow of neon, made spooky and dark by it. Hap was hoping he'd say, "Me, too," or even, "Yeah, when we go that place is dead." But all he said was, "Christ, I can't wait to get out. You're crazy, Hap." He shrugged, and Hap felt something clench inside him; it was like Cal was abandoning him.

That was one of the things that stuck in his mind that night. The dancing had died down early, and Hap was making his way upstairs to his room. There were four girls on their way up to the ladies' room when they saw Hap rubber-legging up the steps. He nearly fell over them, and they caught him, laughing. It was what he did, sometimes, he wasn't sure why. He liked to act more drunk than he was. The girls wrapped their arms around his shoulders and guided him toward his room–someone in the hall directed them. Hap kept his eyes closed, and shortly he felt one of the girls sliding her hand in his back pocket to get his keys. "I can't believe I'm doing this," she said breathlessly, and another whispered, "Is he out?" He wasn't, of course. But when their grip loosened he slumped to the floor, and another girl said, "I guess he's out." They carried him in and put him on the bed, but he didn't sleep. The more he lay there, the more awake he became, listening to the music pulsing through the floor. A couple stood outside his door, thinking they had privacy, and murmured urgently– he couldn't tell if they were arguing or making out. When he was sure the party was over, nearly five in the morning, he went downstairs. He planned to pass out again, this time sprawled on the pool table.

It was a gray morning: it could have been dawn, or dusk again. When he passed the window in the stairwell a heavy bird lifted from the sill and blurred into the fog. It startled him, and he felt suddenly that there was someone watching him. He wondered if the house was all closed up. Often after a party he found the front door hadn't been bolted or one of the fire exits was slightly ajar, or a window on the first floor was open, crepe paper streamers trailing off into the breeze. Sometimes it was hard to feel safe.

Everything seemed to pause, waiting. He peered in on each floor. All the doors were closed, lined up as still as motel rooms. Long shadows stretched in the dim hallways. He felt as if the place had been abandoned.

When he went downstairs the living room seemed thick with haze. No one had cleaned up after the party. The furniture was all cleared out still, and there were plastic cups cluttered on every surface. From across the room he could hear the wind blowing through an open window. He squinted in the pale half-light. For a moment he was certain he saw the shape of someone standing there, a figure by the window, with the curtains fluttering around him.

"Hello," he called, and his voice rang hollowly in the empty room. "Hello? Is someone there?"

And then he turned and ran up the stairs to his room. He bolted the door and put on the radio. He wanted to wake someone up, just to prove he wasn't alone in the house. He kept turning the stereo louder, until at last Doug Cohn in the next room began knocking heavily on the wall between them. Hap turned off the stereo and sat there in the bed until it was light enough to sleep.

There were times, lots of times, when it seemed like everything was back to normal. Hap would go downstairs before dinner to find a group of guys standing around the pool table, tapping balls into the pockets with the palms of their hands, and the talk was all easy jokes and gossip. Mornings, he'd walk into the bathroom, where a line of people from his floor were all at sinks shaving, and move in beside them without a hitch. Even the day after the party, when he woke, there was a moment when he imagined himself shrugging to Doug Cohn, he heard himself chuckling, "Hey, thought I saw a ghost last night, Doug. Scared myself shitless."

But later, when he saw Doug Cohn on his way out the front door with his bookbag, it seemed that the things he planned to say were frivolous and artificial. He drew back, acting as if he hadn't noticed Doug, and he decided that it was probably best not to mention anything at all. After that, the day didn't seem like it would cruise along so easily. There was always some little snag to send him spinning.

The early evenings were the worst, after everyone had gone off to the library or their girlfriends' rooms. He flipped through channels in the television room, one after the other so the voices and music and yelps of white noise melted together in a collage, an abstract code he could almost recognize. Or he'd end up back in his room, listening for someone to come down the hall. He made lists: party ideas; things he planned to do tomorrow; friends, in ascending order of closeness. He'd number things from one to ten. It was calming to mark things down.

Sometimes he thought he would just give in, that he would let himself spend the whole day brooding about Cal. But he found he couldn't. He tried to remember something specific about Cal, some significant conversation they had, the special things they used to do together. But his mind would go blank. Or rather, he'd remember how once someone spray-painted ELIMINATE GREEKS on the outside of their house.

They'd circled the A in ELIMINATE, and there was a picture of Cal in the campus newspaper, standing in front of the big red A in his Greek letter sweatshirt and grinning. He recalled the time he and Cal came up with a way to combine philanthropy and partying. They planned to get a bunch of organ donor cards from the Department of Motor Vehicles and use them as admission tickets to a huge bash. They were going to have T-shirts that said: Lose Your Liver–donate an organ/have a beer!

It seemed to Hap that all these memories were grotesque, like the old photos he'd found once in his basement at home, pictures half-eaten by silverfish. He wondered if something was wrong with him. He believed that if things were the other way around, Cal would remember him better–that Cal would have fond stories of the night they pledged or the time they were both elected officers of the fraternity; some recollection that would make everyone laugh.

He didn't know what the others were thinking. At the chapter meeting on Monday night, he announced as if effortlessly that "a group of brothers will be visiting Cal Fuller this Sunday," and then went on with the other items on the agenda. When he scanned their faces he couldn't read anything. Even the other three guys who planned to go to Cal's house didn't seem to respond. Eric sat staring at the textbook he'd opened on the table in front of him; Charlie Balbo rocked back in his chair, balancing on two legs; Russ, Cal's freshman-year roommate, traced his index finger across his palm.

He didn't know what he expected. But he didn't like it when Balbo patted him on the back, and said, "I hear you made it to bed Saturday night, for once." He didn't like his own reply: "Yeah, your girlfriend showed me the way." He gave a short laugh, and the sound of it made his face feel pale.

There was no party that Saturday and the house was unnaturally still. Yet he felt too edgy to go out. In the distance, up and down the fraternity quad, people were calling and laughing, on their way to other parties. Any other Saturday night Hap would be out there with them, on his way somewhere to unwind. He'd melt into the heat and flex of crowded rooms, nodding at acquaintances, easing into casual conversation with girls, just letting the smoke and alcohol work through him. There might even be a moment, late at night, when everything seemed perfect–like the time he and Cal had sung "Papa's Got a Brand New Bag" on their way home, very slowly and with melancholy, and there had been a few bars of clear harmony, echoing against the walls; or the time an enormous raccoon had regarded him from a rain-soaked lawn, standing on its haunches, holding an apple. Heavy clouds of steam were rising from man-holes, drifting low to the ground, all the way down the sidewalk.

Hap could see his reflection in the window, staring in at him. The ivy was thick across his window so he couldn't see who was laughing outside. All he could see were twisting vines, the shadows of leaves showing through his reflection like an X-ray of something, he wasn't sure what. This was what it was like for Cal, he thought–floating as people passed below you, as if you'd levitated out of your own body.

When Russ knocked on the door, Hap was staring out the window and feeling as if he could lift out of his skin. He hoped there wasn't an edge of desperation in his voice when he said, "Come on in, buddy. Have a beer with me."

"I was just stopping by to let you know when we were going to leave in the morning," Russ said. He glanced around as if he were entering a room full of strangers. When Hap handed him a beer, he sat there considering it. For a moment, they sat not saying anything, both moving their heads to the music that Hap had playing, constantly.

"So anyway," Hap said at last. "It'll be good to see Cal again, huh?"

Russ shrugged. "I guess," he said. He moved his mouth as if to say more, but then took a sip of beer instead. He swallowed. "I mean, you know," he said.

"Well anyway, they say he's doing pretty well," Hap said. "It'll be cool. We'll just sit around, shoot the breeze for a while. No big deal."

They nodded at one another. Russ had never been easy to squeeze conversation out of; some people used to say that if he hadn't been roommates with Cal freshman year, he never would have gotten a bid. He'd still be in the dorms, studying his Saturday nights away.

Yet it used to be easier to talk, even to Russ. Hap used to believe he could connect with most any of them, that they would all get together in twenty years, like the old paunchy alums who came back every spring to drink together, to tell old stories and sing songs. Hap had seen that as part of his future. He used to imagine that his fraternity brothers would think of him from time to time for the rest of their lives. Some little thing—an old song on the car radio, a face glimpsed as an elevator closed—would startle them, and they'd think suddenly: Hap! What's he up to these days?

Russ lifted the beer to his lips; when he set it down, a droplet of moisture trickled slowly down the side of the can. Russ seemed to be waiting for him to say something. But all he could think of was small talk, trivia: sororities, classes, sports teams. It made him cringe. Outside, the wind came up. Hap could hear the muffled buzz of a motorcycle speeding down a faraway street, someone showing off.

"I don't think it will be so bad tomorrow," Hap said.

Russ nodded slowly. "Yeah," he said at last. "It should be okay. I mean, I'm sure you'll do fine."

Hap said, "Hey, I'll be sober at least."

Russ looked down and shook his head. "Yeah," he said softly.

"No big deal," Hap told him. "It won't be any big deal."

Cal's home was in a new development called Stone Lake Estates. It was at the far edge of the suburbs, and some of the streets weren't marked clearly on Russ's map. No trees had been planted yet, so the rows of houses stood bright and unshaded against the clear sky.

The boys were all still as they circled through Stone Lake, so quiet that Hap could hear Charlie Balbo in the backseat, breathing through his nose. Every time they passed a street sign, Russ slowed and gazed at it uneasily. At last, he pulled into a driveway. "This is the place," he said. Hap saw him cast a quick look at Charlie Balbo. None of them seemed to look at him, though if they had he would have simply smiled firmly.

Cal's mother came to the door, but she didn't open it right away. She peeked through the curtains, and they waved at her uncertainly. Hap could hear the bamboo wind chimes that hung from the porch, the deep hollow tones as they rustled in the breeze. Then they heard the lock being turned, and she stared at them through the half-open door.

"Hi boys," she said.

"Hi," they echoed. They stood for a moment on the threshold, and she took Russ's hand. He'd stayed over with them one Thanksgiving, and she spoke lightly: "Good to see you again, Russ," she said. Then she turned expectantly to the rest of them. Eric and Charlie introduced themselves quickly, and they shook their hands, too. "Welcome, Charlie, Eric," she said. Then she smiled at Hap.

"I'm Hap," he said. "We talked on the phone."

"Of course," she said. "I believe I met you once at a reception."

She had dark eyes. They seemed wet and glittering as Hap took her hand. Hap thought maybe she was wishing the same thing on him, wishing him crippled or dead, though she held his hand for a long moment, tightly. She was always angry with Cal, Hap remembered, she always complained that he spent too much time socializing and not enough preparing for his future. Hap wondered if she thought it was he who led Cal astray. He wished he could tell her that everything, everything had always been Cal's idea.

"You're very lucky," she said softly, and dropped his hand.

She ushered them past several framed photographs of Cal: as a baby; as a long-haired high school boy; another that Hap recognized as the one Cal had taken for the fraternity composite when he was elected president. They walked into a living room, and it was then that they saw him. He was sitting cross-legged on the floor, watching an old black-and-white television series. He didn't move. He had his face turned away from them, and his mother seemed not to notice him.

"Can I get you anything to drink?" she asked, and it sent a shiver through Hap as if it were an accusation. "Coke? Milk? Water?"

As she went toward the kitchen, Cal looked up, and Hap lifted his hand hesitantly, as if to wave, or to shield his face. But Cal let his eyes drift shyly over them, then turned back to the TV. He didn't recognize them, Hap realized. Their stares made him shift bashfully. He leaned toward the television as if to be swallowed up by it and vanish. None of them looked at one another, or spoke. Hap just watched the screen, thinking that all of them were sharing the same images, at least.

The curtains had been drawn, so the TV was

brighter. The sleepy dimness of the room reminded Hap of winter, of childhood sicknesses. Everything was muted. In the next room, beyond the cheerfully artificial voices of the TV characters, he could hear ice cubes being cracked from their trays.

Mrs. Fuller came in, carrying their drinks on a tray. Cal continued to watch television until she said, "Cal, honey," very firmly. Then he looked up at her impatiently. Hap tried not to glance at him. He held tightly to his glass, staring down into it.

"Do you see your friends?" Mrs. Fuller said. "Look who's come to visit you!"

"Hi," Cal sighed, and Hap's hands began to throb. He wasn't the same person, Hap thought. He tried to put on a polite smile, but he knew it looked false. All he could think was that Cal must be in that body somewhere, but sleeping, or maybe only vaguely aware, like someone drugged; he imagined the real Cal was submerged somehow, curled up like a fist, struggling to break out.

"How's it going, Cal?" he said brightly, and Cal gazed up at him. Russ and Eric and Charlie were lined up on the long sofa that faced the television, and Hap was a little apart from them, in a high-backed easy chair, his hands clasped tightly in front of him. Everyone was watching him. "Good to see you!" he said, but Cal didn't answer. He glanced back at the TV show.

"Cal," Mrs. Fuller said, in her calm, stern voice. She got up and shut off the TV, and Cal's head turned as she went, noting each movement wistfully. "Look, Cal," she said softly. "Who are those boys?"

He hung his head. "My friends," he whispered.

She was close to him, avid, bright-eyed. She lifted her finger suddenly and pointed at Hap. His heart leapt. "Who's that boy, Cal? Who is that?"

Hap caught his breath, stiffening, but Cal was silent. The quiet stretched out like a long shadow, and Hap felt that all of them were waiting for him to do something. He stood up. For a moment, he just wavered there, awkwardly, as if he'd been asked to give a speech, but at last he began to move forward a bit. He nodded encouragingly at Cal. "Who am I, Cal?" he whispered, so soft he could barely hear himself, and Cal closed his eyes. He slumped down, and for a moment Hap thought he'd fainted. But then his eyes snapped back open.

"I don't know," Cal said.

The room seemed to darken. Hap kept inching forward, holding out a hand to shake, though he could see that Cal didn't quite trust him; he drew back a little, the way a child would when a stranger's friendliness seemed false. "Hey," Hap said. "It's me, Cal." He raised his voice. "It's me—Hap."

Cal sat there on the rug, his legs tucked carefully under him, and Hap just hovered there, looking down on him. He thought maybe he ought to crouch down on the floor, too, so that Cal could see him face to face, but before he could Cal stood up and walked over to his mother. He sat down next to her, leaving Hap alone in the middle of the room. He faced all of them.

Mrs. Fuller put her arms around Cal, and he leaned his head against her shoulder. "When he came out of the coma," she said—Hap standing there helplessly, as if surrounded—"When he came out of the coma, he didn't even know who I was." She smiled ruefully. "He was like a baby again: couldn't dress himself, feed himself, anything. But he's come a long way." She couldn't look up. They all watched her, hypnotized, as she spoke in a slow, sweet voice, as if to Cal. She told them how happy she'd been when he'd drawn a circle on a piece of paper, when he played a game of Chutes and Ladders with a nurse. "Who knows what he remembers?" she whispered, her mouth close to Cal's ear. "He'll look at those pictures from your fraternity for hours. He's just fascinated. And sometimes he'll say something and he'll sound almost like himself."

She sighed. "But you can't think of it that way," she said. "He's a new person now. And we have to love him in a different way than we used to. Not any less," she said. "Just different." She laid her hand on Cal's cheek, and he nuzzled against her. There was a long silence, and at last, the spell broken, Hap edged back to his chair. That was it, he thought. Cal was gone. He imagined a sudden bright flash burning the person who had been Cal away, leaving only a blurry whiteness, a hiss of static. He saw it so clearly that for a minute he felt as if the chair were tilting underneath him. He held to the arms, tightly.

"Of course, he'll always need to be taken care of," Mrs. Fuller said at last. "Like a little boy." Then she was quiet again, stroking Cal's hair, watching the movement of her hand as if mesmerized.

"Do you see how his forehead is scarred?" she murmured finally. A kind of thrum went over Hap's skin as she brushed Cal's bangs back to reveal rows of reddish, rounded strips. "It's hard to believe, isn't it? That's the pattern of your car seat. And he was pushed forward with so much force that the imprint is still there." She was moving her hand slowly through his hair, as if thinking of something far off, but her eyes were fixed on Hap. He couldn't meet her gaze; he could only look at Cal, who was enjoying the touch of his mother's fingers over his brow. He had his head tilted back, his expression relaxed, staring up as if he were stargazing. And for a moment, Hap felt as if they were seeing the same thing, up there in the distance, a meteor shrinking into the stratosphere, layers sloughing off in fiery husks until it was just a speck, plunging into the dark. They stared up toward some distant point and it seemed, it was almost as if Hap or even Cal himself were about to remember something important. Something he'd forgotten. But then it was gone.

No more than a few words passed between them as they drove home. They each took a corner of the car, each tilted in different directions. Russ held the steering wheel in both hands, staring out at the signs, the road. Eric turned his face away from Hap, resting his head against the window, pretending to be asleep.

It was almost as if it were late at night, and the world was calm and dark. But it was still daylight, and when Hap closed his eyes, orange flashes beat irregularly against his closed eyelids: the sun, flickering through the trees.

On the very edge of sleep, Hap could feel the shape of a dream. It was a party, and Hap had just joined the fraternity. He could see someone moving toward the dancing crowd, clapping, shouting. Everything began to stop: the music faded, the lights came up. One after another, the dancing couples separated, began to clap in rhythm, and the men from the fraternity emerged out of the dark. Then he felt himself being lifted. He was up above their heads, carried on a rippling of dozens of hands. Their chanting echoed beneath him as they poured out into the open air, under the night sky. He was floating, and when he looked down he saw a boy waving at him, at the end of a long tunnel of people. Cal! he thought.

He started up with a laugh.

sure i will

Here in the heart of the country, the trees are all in lines and patterns. There were no trees here before the pioneers came, I'm told, and when the cottonwoods and elms and spruce were finally brought in, they were planted so they conformed to the edge of a road or a field; they were organized into regiments to protect houses from the sun, or land from erosion. It seems to me that people must have forgotten how trees grew in forests, or even that trees were a natural phenomenon, not something they could erect like sod houses or barbed-wire fences. They were hypnotized by the flatness of the landscape, by the unyielding conformity of everything in their lives.

My paternal grandmother's house was a perfectly symmetrical place, set in the middle of miles of wheat fields and lined on either side with elms. When I was small, there had been a tire swing in one of the trees. One day, while I was playing on it, the rope had broken and I dropped to the ground and got a concussion. My grandmother never put the swing back up, but on one of the highest branches, the knotted rope that held the tire remained. Years later, when I came to live with my grandmother, I found the rope there, with the tree trying to grow over it. The rope had cut deeply into a branch, and in the summer the tree would bleed brown sour-smelling juice from the place where the rope wounded it.

My grandmother had been on a slow, erratic decline for some months when my parents suggested she go to a rest home. They hated the unpredictability of it. They wouldn't hear of her staying in that big house all alone, where anything might happen. But my grandmother didn't want to leave. The compromise was that I would go to stay with her.

It was the summer after I'd graduated from high school, and my parents, I think, were looking for ways to get me out of the house. They were happy people and had found it hard to understand me when, in the months following commencement, I'd become distant, introverted; I was easily obsessed. For a while, I'd been interested in genealogy. I spent a full week poring over family trees, old Bibles, obituaries. At one point, I'd written down the ages at which all my relatives for the last four or five generations had died, and averaged them; from that, I was able to predict that I would be most likely to die sometime in March 2050. I'd also thought for a while that I might like to be a doctor, so I went to the library to check out medical books.

In one of the books, it showed a cadaver that students were dissecting. I hadn't been able to resist turning back, again and again, to stare at it. It was an old woman, but there was something inhuman about her: the claylike, immobile face; the yellow-grey flaps of skin pulled back, the uterus, the womb divided. I'd been amazed and sickened to imagine that an infant had once come from that place. But I couldn't help looking; looking again.

My parents wanted to know what had made me so morbid, but I couldn't tell them. I'd always thought that they read me better than I read myself. Once my mother called me into her room and asked me to sit on her bed. "Do you," she wanted to know, and then she hesitated. "Do you ever think about bad things?"

"What do you mean?" They had never given me The Talk, and I was always expecting it. "Do you mean sex?"

"No-o," she said, and she closed her eyes as if trying very hard to remember something. "I mean do you ever think about death? About doing yourself in?"

"Not really."

"Well, you know that is the worst thing, the most evil thing a person can do."

"Is it?"

"I hope that you would never do that to your father and me. And you should know that if you ever have thoughts like that. Bad thoughts. We are always here to talk to. We are always wanting and willing to help."

It's terrible to realize that your parents think you are crazy. That was why I agreed to go, and why it was so easy to put on a show of happiness when they were around.

I sometimes wondered whether I really was insane. There was a path I'd been on, a path that started when I was born and then moved along nicely–taking my first step, saying my first sentence, going to kindergarten, moving up grade levels; then I turned sixteen and I was able to drive, and then high school ended. There was a big chasm where the path should have been. That was the worst thing. And everyone thought I was weird when I told them this. Maybe I was.

I guess that, without really thinking about it, I'd been expecting that I would die any day. It wasn't a suicidal impulse at all. It was just that it was impossible to imagine myself in the future, at thirty or forty–I couldn't believe that I would ever reach those ages. Even twenty was obscure and cloudy enough to seem like a dream.

So, I expected it. The day before I moved my belongings to my grandmother's house, I cut the grass at home, and I couldn't help thinking of the story of how one of my friend's cousins had a long stick thrown at him by the mower, how it pierced him right through the belly. I put my hand to my stomach, imagining my own look of shocked surprise, the green sweet smell that bleeds off each blade of cut grass all around me as I fall to the ground, my parents running toward me, their voices swimming in the roar of the mower–my mother's hand on my forehead: "Honey, it'll be all right . . . "

I took off my clothes that night and I noticed that there was a small lump on my inner leg. I lay awake, just breathing.

The room I was to stay in had that sweet, dusty smell that seems to hang over old people and their belongings, but otherwise it was empty. She brought in her old roll-away bed, and the rest, she said, was up to me.

She was an enormous woman and apparently had been for many years–when I was small I called her the "big grandma," to distinguish her from my mother's mother. She always had loose, fat upper arms. As I child, I'd ask to hit them, lightly, because they'd wobble. "Those are my muscles," she'd say, and grab me. I was always surprised by her strength.

It was hard to imagine that I was supposed to care for her. She still looked strong enough to arm wrestle with me, like we used to do. After I'd gotten the few things I brought unpacked, she came in, moving slowly, precisely, carrying bedding.

"I know this must be a burden on you," she said. "Having to live with some old woman." She said it in that loud, ironic voice, the one she used for witty comments–"Call me 'Bubbles,'" she used to say when introduced to my father's friends. But her voice had less of an edge now.

"No, Gram, I don't care," I said. "It'll be fun staying. Like a sleepover."

"Right," she said. "But you know it may be longer than a sleepover. Maybe."

I shrugged. "I'm glad to stay," I said.

"I just want you to know that I don't care what you do while you're here. I know about boys your age. Come and go as you please. Come in as late or as early as you want, don't mind me."

I nodded, smiling. But I thought she was wrong about boys my age, or at least me–there wasn't much likelihood of me going out carousing anymore. I hadn't really spoken to my friends since graduation. They were all different now, headed off to college or the army or jobs or marriage–and I just let them go. It would never be the same.

"Like a beer?" my grandmother asked.

"Sure," I said.

I was working nights at the St. Bonaventure radio station, six to midnight. I'd sign off the air at twelve, saying the last words of the night in my clearest, most noncommittal voice: "This is Kip Dubbs, on behalf of the entire staff and management of KBOV, wishing you a happy tomorrow and a very pleasant goodnight."

I'd sit there, sometimes, in my swivel chair, staring at the microphone. There was such a silence. I could imagine all those radios out there, the click of stillness and then the steady brush of static, and it was as if I were presiding over a suddenly empty world. Outside the window everything was dark, none of the houses had lights, there were no cars on the streets.

And then I'd get into my car and drive home to my grandmother. Sometimes she'd be waiting up for me, the radio static still whispering out of the little red transistor by her bed. "You sounded good tonight," she'd tell me, or she'd ask me some question about the news. I'd always go to her room and stand by the foot of her bed, even if she was asleep. "I'm home, Gram," I'd whisper, and if she was still awake she'd open her eyes. Otherwise, I stood there for a while, until she rustled or mumbled or sighed–that would reassure me, and I'd go on to bed.

My grandmother moved with exaggerated slowness, and in the morning with her big housecoat billowing around her, she seemed like an aquatic being, moving through water rather than air. She made huge, hearty breakfasts–eggs, toast, bacon, hash browns, applesauce–as if they could fill the atmosphere with robustness and good health. Neither one of us ate much.

We never talked about the future. She never asked me about my plans, and of course I couldn't ask about hers.

Instead, she told me that they really did call her "Bubbles" when she was young, but she couldn't remember why, and she felt funny about it. She told me that she was once at a bus stop and hit a man over the head with her high-heeled shoe. She didn't recall who he was, or what he'd done. But it knocked him out: she could see that clearly. In a quiet voice, she told me that the cruelest thing she'd ever done was to my father. He'd taken a dollar from her purse and she caught him. As punishment, she'd pinned an index card to his shirt that said "I STEAL FROM MY OWN MOTHER," and made him wear it to school. Now, she was sorry; she wondered if he'd ever really forgiven her. She told me that she didn't have her first beer until she was fifty, when her husband died. She bought a case of Miller and sat there, alone, and drank it. It was the type of beer my grandfather had liked.

"I still like the taste of beer," she said.

"That's really funny," I told her. That's the kind of thing I'd say when we talked. I never said anything personal about myself. Her stories seemed as disembodied as trivia–the nickname without any reason behind it, the drinking alone in the house, told with irony but no pain. I couldn't rattle things off so easily. Once I wanted to tell her about the graduation party I'd been to with my high school friends. I got drunk and hid from them. Something someone had said hurt my feelings, and I wanted them to all worry a bit, to hunt for me. But they only called my name for a short while. Before long, they were dancing again, and I sat in the closet watching them from a crack in the door. The beat of the music made them happy, and they were singing, flapping their arms. I was too embarrassed to come out then: they'd see how child-ish I was. So I just sat there, and finally I fell asleep. When I woke, everyone was gone. I was alone in the dark living room of someone else's house, and I had to sneak away into the early morning.

But I couldn't tell my grandmother such things so easily. I just smiled and listened. It was embarrassing to hear myself repeat over and over–"That's really funny," or "That's really cool"–in my cheerful radio voice, empty-headed, as if I wasn't even in the same room with her.

I went home once or twice during the week, and my parents' first question was always, "How is she?" I didn't want them to worry. I didn't tell them that she drank beer, because that would trouble them; I didn't tell them that she washed a whole bottle of pills down the toilet because they were too big, she said, to swal-low. I felt like she was a disreputable friend I was covering for.

Then they asked about me. Had I thought about what I wanted to do in the fall? My father wanted me to talk to a friend of his, an army recruiter.

"You may not believe me," he said, "but I think the army would be very good for you."

"You never know," I said.

I told them I liked my job at the radio station. Then my father suggested I look into a communications college.

"We only want you to do something you like. It doesn't matter how much money you make, so long as you're happy."

"Yeah, I know," I said. "I know."

Looking out to where the trees lined the yard, I smiled for them. "I'm working on it," I said. "Believe me."

"We're here to help you," my mother said. "Use us as a source of information. We can advise you."

"I will," I said.

Jim called me on the phone the day before he left for college. "But what are you going to do?" he kept saying. When I didn't answer, he'd offer some inane suggestion. "Why don't you . . . " Finally, I just told him.

"Look," I said. "I guess I really don't give a shit about anything, anyway."

He was pretty quiet. He didn't call back.

I asked myself: Why does everybody care so much about the future? I never understood what made them think it would be better. How long before they all forgot me, I wondered, how long before the house and my parents and my grandmother grew distant and faded in my mind's eye. I wished things could stay the same; I hated the future.

We sat on the sofa one afternoon drinking beer out of cups, because she didn't like to drink out of cans and there were no clean glasses. We closed the shades and watched soap operas, stacking the cans on the coffee table.

"All the women on these programs smoke cigarettes," she said. "Do you smoke?"

"No," I said. "I tried once, but it made me cough."

"I could never smoke," she said. "I tried many times. I wished I could. I used to think it looked so sophisticated." She looked at me for a moment, and then laughed.

"I also wanted to be a WAVE or a WAC or something in World War II. A heartbreaker in a uniform." She laughed again. "I was married, so I couldn't go, of course. Your grandpa was already too old to go. I married such an old man, you know." She finished her beer and then bent down to pour more into her cup. She didn't laugh this time.

After the soap opera was over, we listened to records. When I played a song on the radio she liked, she'd have me bring it home so she could tape it. She liked Aretha Franklin. It reminded her of the blues, like in Chicago.

She got out her photo album to show me pictures of herself in Chicago. It was as if she wanted to prove that she wasn't lying, that she really was once the person she remembered. There was a photo of her standing in front of Union Station with her feet carefully posed, like in ballet position. It was taken by some old man she'd stopped as he was passing. She looked like Betty Grable, I told her.

"How come people don't look like that anymore," I asked.

"Because they all look like me now," she said, and laughed.

When I came home from work that night, all the lights were on. She'd usually go to bed long before I got home. Maybe, I thought, she'd fallen asleep in front of the TV or someone had come for a late visit unexpectedly.

But when I walked in the house, I heard her voice, loud and angry, and I thought she was arguing with someone.

"Goddamn it!" she was yelling. "Goddamn it!"

I took a tentative step, walking toward her voice. "Gram . . . ?" I called out hesitantly. "Gram?"

She was lying on the floor of the bathroom in her floral nightgown, on her stomach. The nightgown was pulled up, revealing her bare legs and her panties. She looked up at me, and her eyes were wet and raw-looking from tears. "Kip," she said. "God . . . damn . . . I slipped . . . I've been trying . . . Oh, I . . . "

I didn't know what to do. I opened my mouth and shook my head. "I'll call an ambulance," I said weakly.

"No!" she cried, and her voice was ragged. "Just help me up! Please."

I bent down and pulled her nightgown so that it covered her legs again. "I don't know how to do this," I said softly. I grasped her under the arms and she flailed, struggling.

"It hurts!" she shouted, like a little girl. "It hurts me!"

I was able to get her into a sitting position, and we rested for a moment. She was breathing hard, tears falling onto the lace around her neck. "What am I going to do?" she said, stuttering, small hiccuping sobs breaking into her words. "What's going to happen to me?" I touched her hair. I didn't know how to help her. "Some nights," she whispered, "some nights I wake and I can't move. And one night . . . I wet . . . and I couldn't get up to change . . . But then I was better in the morning . . . I was all right . . . but what's going to happen to me when I can't?" Her voice was drifting off, and then, slowly, the sobs drifted off as well. She bowed her head, and the whole house was quiet.

"I think I can make it now," she said at last. She held my arm tightly, leaning, pulling, and then, with terrible slowness, and with my arm around her waist, she was able to stand.

"Will you be all right?" I asked. "Should I call a doctor?"

"Let's go to bed," she said quietly.

I dreamed that I got out of the car when we stopped along the road; we were going on a long trip, she and I–passing through miles of wheat fields on a dirt road. Something had fallen out of the car and I had to get it. I waded knee-deep in grass, hearing it hiss around me, and then I turned to see the car was gone, a red blur through waves of heat. I ran, waving my arms, but the weeds were as thick as water. And then I was running along the middle of the highway, calling after the car, which always seemed on the verge of disappearing over a hill. The shadow of an airplane passed over me. I looked up, and that was when the car came from behind, blaring its horn. I covered my face with my arms and the car hit me. A dull thump. I could see my shadow arcing over the asphalt, and then I landed on the ground. My grandmother was bending over me, and I could feel my spine moving around loose inside of me. I wanted to tell her not to move me, but when I opened my mouth there was no sound.

When I woke, the sheets were knotted around my lower legs, and I kicked at them, then finally had to reach down and untangle them with my hands. The house was silent, and I got up and walked in the dark to the living room. The moon gave the room a pale glow.

The photo book was lying on the coffee table where she'd left it that afternoon. I turned on the light and picked the book up.

All those pictures, pictures of people waiting. I shook my head.

When I looked up, my grandmother was standing there, with her housecoat billowing around her, her hand moving like something gently swaying in an underwater current.

I turned to her. "You'll be all right," I said softly, "won't you, Gram?"

"Sure I will," she said.

I sat there for a long time, looking at the trees outside the window, then down at the rows of photographs in the book. For that night, anyway, everything was still in order.

my sister's honeymoon: a videotape

PM 12:19:46
9-11-91

There is a moment or two of vertigo in the beginning, that kind of cinema verité thing that all the young future filmmakers back at school were so crazy about for a while–a blur of color and darkness before the camera comes to rest on the motion of the landscape passing outside the car: the silver stream of an interstate guardrail sliding past, impressionistic dapples of green and yellow vegetation, sky. Part of the dashboard rises up and we see a map. One of my sister's red fingernails appears hugely in the corner of the frame.

We hear her voice: "Do you think this is working?"

She is not very steady. The camera jerks and bobs–the window frame, the glint of the rear-view mirror, her feet, barely recognizable in the dimness below the dash. She points the camera at the map, focuses.

Colorado.

PM 12:59:03
9-11-91

My sister's husband's grip is firmer. He makes a clean sweep over an orchard of apple trees, an orderly orchard made quaint and picturesque by its many boughs of bright, heavy fruit. A red van crosses in front, obscuring the view for a moment, and then my brother-in-law arcs slowly over the trees again.

"Old apple orchard," he murmurs solemnly, as if reading aloud to himself, as if narrating for a blind person. "Along the side of the road. Lots of apples!"

He zooms in for a close-up of a particularly bountiful branch. Another red van, or the same one, drives across the picture.

PM 1:18:32
9-11-91

Deer are eating grass by the side of the road. The couple doesn't say anything.

It is about one in the morning, and I lean back, taking a slow drink from my beer. I don't know why I'm watching this—out of boredom, maybe, restlessness, insomnia. I'm not sure why I've come here at all, to my sister and brother-in-law's new house, not far from the small town where we grew up. I guess one has to be somewhere at Christmas, and I am single, unconnected, and we used to be close, my sister and I. You haven't seen your new niece yet, my sister said to me. You've got to come. But she goes to bed at ten every night, and the night seems to expand and expand, radiating out from the new and silent house. In a nursing home five miles away, my mother lies in her bed, her thumb and forefinger moving against each other in her sleep, the late early stages of Parkinson's. Across miles, in a distant city, my empty apartment sits in darkness. The faucet drips slowly into a pot I didn't have time to wash before I left.

On the screen, the camera tries to zoom in on the head of a doe who is now lifting her head suspiciously, but the picture won't focus properly. High weeds obscure the view of the suddenly alert animal, the frame is mottled with blurs of leaves.

"They're sure not scared of people, are they?" my sister says at last, in a stage whisper.

Here are my sister's thick bare legs walking along a
narrow asphalt path. She is wearing sandals, her toenails are dull red, a polish that is almost wood-colored.
Other legs can be seen in front of her. The camera rattles, the microphone jostles hollowly as they march.

You have to wonder about a shot like this, especially when it continues on and on like it does. Has
my brother-in-law turned the camera on accidentally, or does he completely lack imagination, any sense
of aesthetics? Can we read this as a representation of
his mental process, some secret symbolic system that
isn't clear? Maybe it's merely his sophomoric sense of
humor—the camera lingers as she tugs at the back of
her shorts, which have ridden into the crack of her
buttocks.

Everyone else in the house is asleep. My sister and
her husband are spooned together under the com-
forter in their king-sized bed; their baby is motionless
in her crib. The living room is dark except for the
slow-blinking colored lights on the Christmas tree my
sister has erected. The shadows of wrapped packages
extend under the blinking lights, expanding and con-
tracting in a creepy way, like something breathing.

It's a larger house than I expected, more nicely furnished. There is a plush beige sofa, new; glass coffee
table, big stereo, wide-screen TV. "Thirty-eight inches,"
my brother-in-law informed me, and I was like,
"You've got me beat, buddy."

He finally takes the camera off her backside. We
move upward, and there is my sister, turning her
head back to say something I can't catch—the sound is
turned very low, so as not to wake anyone, and I'm
already so close to the screen I can touch it. It seems

my sister's honeymoon: a videotape 93

like she says, "Nice one," but what is she referring to? She laughs after she says whatever she says, that old edgy, cynical chuckle I'm familiar with, though it's more polite than I'm used to, tempered by something—by love? By the fact that this is her honeymoon and the weight of the "fun" and "romance" she is supposed to be portraying is pressing down? Is it simply that the camera makes her self-conscious? My brother-in-law turns the camera from her laughing face abruptly, revealing a railing with a magnificent, high-cliffed vista beyond. There is a river far, far below: we zoom in and back.

PM 2:18:17
9-11-91

The Royal Gorge: that's what it is. We see the words on a historical marker, in large capital letters, underneath which is a brief text explaining the gorge's history and significance.

The camera doesn't move. Unbelievably, we pause before the placard and stay there. I watch as a minute clicks by, and then another—the video camera has automatically superimposed the time and date of the taping in the lower left-hand corner of the screen. Even the seconds seem to crawl by. The focus is adjusted obsessively.

I refuse to read it. There is something irritating about having this thing thrust on you, the camera's dull, plodding insistence that we take it all in, every last word. It says a lot about my brother-in-law, I think; you can see how pushy and oblivious he is.

I don't really know him that well. We've only just met. But this reminds me of the way he directed me on a tour of their house, each room with its specific, invariable focal point of something he had to fix or something he'd recently purchased. "Here's our new bathtub. We've had big plumbing problems here so I had to go into that there wall," and etc., etc. "Here's the baby's room. We put up the wallpaper ourselves, and that crib's the one my Mom just bought us. This is the toybox I built, and as you can see it's full of toys. She's got a lot of them, doesn't she?" And then the minute he was done talking he'd say, "Moving right along."

I think he bullies her. I noticed right away when I got here that there was something subdued, some-thing submerged about her now. I noticed little things: the night I arrived we were sitting down to dinner, after my sister had put the baby to sleep. She'd prepared the meal, set the table, even poured his beer into a glass for him, but the minute she lifted her fork, he said: "Is that the baby?" We were all silent. Nothing. The conversation started again, but before too long he raised his finger. "Shh," he said. "I think she's crying." Again, we heard nothing, but I watched as my sister got up from the table and went to check. He got his way.

Four full minutes of screen time pass before we are allowed to turn from the historical marker. I wait, feeling a bit bullied myself, wondering if it had really taken my brother-in-law that long to read the text. At last, we get some views of the scenery, the gorge from various angles, and even–for a moment–my sister herself. She stands at the railing and smiles at the camera he's pointing at her. The wind lifts her long hair. She looks down, over the edge, and he comes closer. We stare down at the rushing of the rapids, see a raft, bright orange, whisk past.

"It doesn't look that deep, does it?" my sister muses. "But I guess it is."

PM 3:20:56
9-11-91

More scenery. My sister's shaky hand gives the frame an unpleasant edginess–I am reminded of reading newspapers on microfiche at the library, and the vague queasiness that comes from too much of it. There are views of mountain roads seen from the moving car. We pass high cliffs, walls of sediment-layered stone that have been gouged through by the highway. We pass beautiful drop-offs, mountain passes gilded by silver highway railings.

I guess she trains the camera on this because she is moved, awed by the beauty of it. She wants to record it. But it's odd how little videotape can catch. In our old photo albums, it's not the background but our own faces I notice now–us, as children of eight, eleven, thirteen, posed before the Space Needle in Seattle or the Grand Canyon or some cactus we drove by in Arizona. This is us, we seem to be saying. We exist, even in this strange landscape. And the photos that are without people are as anonymous and inexpressive as postcards. No one is capable, at least in my family, of framing a view so that it expresses anything beyond the fact of its obvious grandeur.

Although–there is a photograph my sister once took when we were growing up that has something to it. It's a photo of a train wreck that happened near our house, when I was twelve and she was eleven. She rode her bike over there, our mother's pocket camera tucked under the waistband of her shorts, the hard plastic casing nudging her belly as she peddled.

It's not a morbid photograph. At the very center of it, framed perfectly, is a plume of blue-white smoke, rising in a column and spreading out in that familiar cauliflower shape at the top, like a cumulus cloud. At the bottom of the photo, clustered around the trunk of smoke are the derailed boxcars, piled together as if arranged. It's a mysteriously calm picture–no hint of melodrama or sensationalism. It's almost romantic, in its way, like those solemn and stirring photos of thunderstorms over the prairie which sometimes appear in magazines like *Life* or *National Geographic.*

Of course, I don't know if that's the way she really saw the thing. But I am one of those who can't help but see a relation between style and soul. I can't avoid imagining this eleven-year-old girl, her bike tipped beside her, her gangly bare legs shifting as she steps back–this child standing before a great disaster and slowly, with a purity of self-possession, arranging the scene in the crosshairs of the camera. That is what she was; what she could have been.

PM 4:01:37
9-11-91

My God, more panoramas. They've stopped the car–this one has really impressed them. But I'm not really paying attention. I take another long sip of beer, thinking that this one will be the last, this one will put me to sleep. I lean back and close my eyes. I keep thinking of sex.

I've masturbated twice since I've been here. Once, the second day of my visit, I kneeled in the basin of the bathtub with the shower running hot on my back; the next night, I did it in bed, surrounded by fistfuls of toilet paper which I used to clean away the snotty evidence of my passion. How embarrassing.

It bothers me now, thinking of it–considering it again, actually. Ten years ago, I would have been disgusted to learn that I'd still be jerking off at age twenty-five, thwacking away at myself while playing some blurry mental pictures of a girl I'd seen at the airport. I haven't had a steady girlfriend in over a year. The pathetic twitch of my stocking feet makes me feel less horny.

I wonder if I seem pathetic to my sister, or to her husband. When I wake in the morning, the baby is already taking her morning nap, and I slouch through the kitchen in my T-shirt and sweatpants, headed for the coffee. I feel like a brother-in-law–smelly, shiftless, liable to steal a few towels when I leave. I can feel it as I cross the room: she is showered, brushed, dressed in some bright color. She is still on maternity leave from the photo-developing store where she works. Picture Palace, it is called, nestled in a mall on the outskirts of the town where we grew up. She will turn to look at me from some corner of her clean kitchen, and at such times she's nothing but a righteous little wife and mommy in the center of her ranch house. She could be anybody. She listens to Whitney Houston tapes, and sings along with them.

You'd think that after two years at the Picture Palace she'd at least be able to hold a video camera with some competence. But when I look back at the TV screen, the image is wobbling helplessly. It's had more beers than I have, it seems.

This is the bridegroom's first appearance. She has trained the camera on him at last, and he seems to be posed in front of some great view. He straightens, grinning broadly, as if the majesty of the backdrop has conferred a mantle upon him. But we can't see the background. She has pulled in too close, and all we can see is my brother-in-law, from the waist up—a typical medium shot. "I think you're too close," he says. "You're not going to be able to see anything." He waves his hand at her, and she begins to step back, slowly, hesitantly. We can hear the crescendo and decrescendo of a car passing on the road behind her. She keeps stepping back, the frame jiggling, and I can't help but imagine that she will back onto the highway just as a car comes up the hill. We'll hear the screech of brakes, her scream, and then the screen will go black. It would be a good scene in a thriller, especially since he keeps directing her to go farther, farther. "Keep on going," he says. "You're okay. Keep on going." His eyes narrow as he waves his hand at her.

Of course, nothing happens. She stops at last, and he is framed in what I remember from a film class as a *plan americain,* a full body shot. There is the mountain range he wants so much to appear in front of—jagged peaks coated by a pale haze, like a picture seen through a sheet of onionskin. He shifts; he waits for his presence there to be recorded.

PM 5:24:11
9-11-91

So many gaps! Over an hour has passed since they last turned the camera on, and you know that so much has happened in the space between one jump cut and the next. They talked; moods shifted; subtle plays of interpretation and intent have been calculated as their conversation in the car ambled on, whirring smoothly and then slowly. Their minds wandered through miles of memories, associations, abstractions.

But all this has passed. It has evaporated, like steam or smoke, so that all that remains are atoms and molecules, untraceable and free-floating, combining at last with other detritus to form dust, or rain. Who remembers what they were thinking twenty minutes ago? What was the last thing you thought before you fell asleep last night? Who knows what motivated a certain choice of words, or why the expression of a listener, a certain eye movement or flicker at the mouth, was interpreted in the way that it was? None of that remains.

And yet a tape such as this one is saved—these images, always ruined by the inescapable self-consciousness of the performers, by the camera's moronic lack of subjectivity. This, which says nothing about who my sister was or what's inside her, this—is permanent.

They've set up a tripod, or perhaps they've merely balanced the camera on the hood of the car. In any case, they both appear in a frame which is obviously not hand held. My brother-in-law leads. He glances back at the camera, then stops. They are at some scenic turnoff again; it must be fairly high up because there are patches of snow on the rocky slopes in the background. They stand there for a moment, facing each other, both in profile.

And then he starts to sing. It isn't clear at first, but slowly his voice grows bolder, and his thin tenor strains distantly from the speakers.

"I'm on top of the world," he sings, "looking down on creation . . . "

He lowers himself uncertainly to one knee at the second chorus, spreading his arms wide, like some old vaudeville actor rehashing the *Al Jolson Story*, a sweep to his gestures. For a time he holds an imaginary microphone in his fist, then forgets and spreads his palms, letting it fall to the ground with what would be, I imagine, a clatter of feedback.

I watch my sister's face. It expresses the usual sort of pain we feel when someone sings to us. How are you supposed to react at such a moment, especially if you know that it's being recorded for posterity? How do you hold your posture, what expression is appropriate? You can see these questions pass over her as he sings. She tries at first a polite attitude of attention, her arms limp at her sides; then a more responsive pose, smiling or nodding or putting a flattered hand to her throat as he goes through his various mimelike maneuvers. She's mortified, though. You can see that in the furtive flicks of her eyes toward the camera.

The person I grew up with, the one I knew, is in there somewhere. I press pause as she looks sidelong, and there she is–this is her, really, I think–though the image trembles as it is held there and thin white static lines blur across her face. That's my sister.

There was a time, about five years ago, when my sister was once wholly the person that I must now use the pause button to locate. Which is to say that she, the former she, or my construct (if you don't mind that term) of what she was, has slowly disintegrated. This sidelong glance, for example, exists here

ing and the toilet-papered and tin-can-dragging car with its "Just Married" sign, even the tour of beautiful, exotic sights. Everything points the way toward this climax. Here is the motel, the bare, simple room, the intimation of consummation.

My sister was not a virgin, of course. There had been several men—perhaps more than a dozen—before my brother-in-law, and she had almost certainly been sleeping with him for some months before they even began to consider marriage. Neither one of them is being initiated into some great mystery.

So why (one might ask) does the film pursue this line of thought with such obsessive—even fetishistic—insistence? Why does he move slowly from the motel sign to her face, lingering, following as she turns and begins to walk across the parking lot to the glass doors, toward the motel's office. And you have to remember that the camera is her husband, so that, given the lexicon of film and the expectations of point of view, we, the viewers, become the husband as well, strolling a few paces behind her, focused on her body as she leads us toward the marriage bed. Given the context, you can't help but look at her in a sexual way, you can't help but imagine the act that waits beyond, as she reaches out to open the glass door and enters. Why else would you show this sequence in detail if not to titillate, if not to pique our expectations?

It would be one thing if there was some real reason for excitement and anticipation. But there isn't. Why should intercourse as a married couple be any different from the intercourse that occurred a few days or weeks before, or that will occur with (presumably) some regularity in the future? Why make it into this big moment?

What I am trying to get at, what I am trying to express is simply that they are worshippers of empty ritual. There is some ideal, some model they want to ape, as if their life was like the build-it-yourself furniture they buy at department stores, with easy-to-assemble instructions. I never would have guessed that this is what she wanted.

She used to write me long, sad, bitchy letters, full of furious observation–when she first started dating him, she dissected him completely in a letter she wrote. She said that he had a face "like kneaded dough," and that he talked too much. "He is extremely tiresome, besides he is only thirty and has big bulgy varicose veins right behind his knees. I almost gagged when I saw them." This was around the time that she was very depressed, even (I thought) slightly suicidal. She seemed to think she'd missed something in life, or that she wasn't going to get what she wanted. She dropped out of college her freshman year, for no apparent reason, moved back in with our mother. In that same letter, she wrote: "It is hard to see the point to most of what I'm doing. I have been told by several people that it is all attitude, that I seem like I would rather see the negative that the reasonably good things but the truth is that when I look at a flower I would rather shove it down some certain people's throats than sit and contemplate how pretty it is . . . "

Less than a year and half later, she was writing me postcards. "Just a quick note to let you know all is well. John has been spending a lot of time remodeling the baby's room. It is a lot of work, but it will be worth it!!"

If this is happiness, I want no part of it. Look at her! Following some mechanically romantic dough-face into the lobby of an anonymous motel, her shoulders stiffened by the weight of the camera pointed at her back. The attendant at the front desk glances up as she enters and (there is a nice moment here) his look is so "Candid Camera." His mouth goes a little slack, and he stares directly into the eye of the video recorder, utterly taken aback for a moment. As she approaches the desk, the attendant does a quick double-take, his eyes shifting between her and the man holding the video camera.

"I'd like a room," she says, and he looks down uncomfortably, his shoulders hunching like a person who is unsure of whether or not he is the victim of a practical joke. His face hardens: "Uhhh . . . sure . . . " he says. He bends down, shuffling a few papers, and brings up something that he huddles over, pointing with his pen. He mumbles as the camera draws nearer and nearer.

My sister glances back at us, smiling. We are drawn into a close-up of the exchange with the poor desk clerk; he, too, is sucked into this vortex of artificiality, pinned there and forced to "act." My sister signs the credit card voucher, and the desk clerk grins helplessly as he gives her the key to their room.

For a moment I wonder whether we'll see what happens next. Will they actually set up a tripod in their room and record the consummation of their wedding night for posterity, as, more recently, they have recorded the birth of their baby (which I refuse to watch).

No. They don't. We cut from a close-up of their motel room door (102) to the next morning: AM 10:03, 9-12-91. Another day of innocuous scenery begins to unfold, and I hit the fast forward button. Behind a thin membrane of video static, I can see beautiful sights hurtling by, my sister and her husband flitting in the foreground, their speeded-up movement making them twitch like epileptics. Their happy mouths chew the air as rapidly as insect mandibles, their heads nod and bob. I finish my fifth beer.

Her life will pass like this, I think. It will shoot by her in a blur, and she will hardly see it. I watch her jerk like a puppet through landscape after landscape, and then I imagine the the same girl, the same woman asleep in the next room, falling heavily through some sad dream.

Oh, Honey, come back to me.

I press stop. Stop––stop. Eject––eject––eject.

rapid transit

The night he got mugged, Alan Lowe had stolen his manager Mr. Dugan's long, hide-colored trench coat, which had been thoughtlessly left on the coat tree outside Dugan's office. Alan knew he was doomed, it was only a matter of time before Dugan fired him, so he thought: "Why not?" He'd been the last to leave that evening, and he'd taken the coat off the hook as if lost in thought, swinging it casually over his arm. Afterwards, he'd gone to a bar where he was sure he wouldn't see anyone he knew. He felt impressive and elegant in the coat. But by the time he left the bar, he had begun to worry again. He had to find some way to make Dugan like him. He had to find some way to hide how much he hated working at Pete Preneta & Co. He needed his job. He was thinking all this when he was thrown to the ground.

He didn't have any money on him. In fact, he'd awakened that morning in a cold terror over it. Apparently, he'd been dreaming of his bills, because they were on a circular track in his head, like an image from a nightmare he'd been startled out of. Even before he'd showered or brushed his teeth, he found himself at his desk with all his bills piled in front of him, calculating. It was the first time in his life that he saw no escape from his own irresponsibility, and he panicked.

There were utility bills and rent that would be due in a few days. There was a government loan from college that was several months past due, but he hadn't really looked at it carefully. DEMAND FOR PAYMENT, it said. He had three credit cards that had already reached their limit, and a few days before a waitress came slinking back to his table to inform him that VISA had instructed her to retain his card. He saw that even if he sent in the minimum payment each month, the balance wouldn't change very much. The rate of interest was too high. That morning he'd sworn to do something. But that evening, after he'd stolen the trench coat, he used a credit card to buy some drinks. One last time, he thought.

In the comic version of the story, Alan was a typical, wide-eyed Nebraska boy, and it took him a long time to register what was actually happening. The men grabbed him around the neck and waist, and as he was thrown to the ground he was aware of his arms and legs waving languidly as tentacles. "Wait a minute," he shouted. "Hold on, I'm slipping." That was when he struck the pavement and one of his attackers kicked him in the head.

Afterward, when he described the mugging to his co-workers and to his family back home, he found himself leaving out a good deal of what had really occurred. For example, he kept the part where the muggers found his wallet empty, and began to kick him over and over, shouting "Where's the money?" But he didn't mention that, as the men continued to kick him, he'd cried "Momma," and "Oh, Mom, please help me," with each blow. The character he played in the story had a certain dry wit, enduring the attack with a startled, dignified innocence. When, in the story, the men shouted: "Where's the money?" the narrator responded: "I spent it!" He didn't want anyone to picture him as he often saw himself: squirming through the bits of garbage on the sidewalk, weeping, calling out for his mother. He didn't want them to imagine him playing dead less than two blocks from his apartment, his cheek pressed into a pool of his own vomit, staring at the things scattered in the patches of scrubby winter grass: a chicken bone, cigarette butts, the neck of a broken ketchup bottle. Every time he thought of himself this way, it made him actually dizzy with humiliation.

He wasn't seriously injured, though he looked terrible the next day, his face covered with bruises and scabs. His ribs and head were sore from being kicked, but he was sure nothing was broken: it would have hurt more if there was, he thought. The policemen who'd come to his apartment later, after he'd managed to run the few yards to his door and call them, had suggested he go to the emergency room, just to be safe. But he refused. He didn't have any insurance, and he knew how much those things cost.

The truth was, the policemen were somewhat annoyed with him. He wasn't able to tell them what the men looked like, and he wasn't even sure in what direction they'd run off. The policemen kept exchanging ironic looks.

"You gay?" one of the men had asked him, and when Alan exclaimed, "Of course not," the man had shrugged.

"That's who they tend to go after," the policeman had said pointedly. "Fags."

"I have a girlfriend," Alan told them.

He and Sandy hadn't dated in almost six months. But he *did* consider calling her that night. It would have been nice to have someone sleep over. There was a telephone pole outside his window, with rusty metal stakes driven into it so someone could climb up. In the next few days, he began to dream that he woke to find a face peering in his third-floor window, a grimacing man with a knife clenched in his teeth like a pirate. And when he was outside, even in a crowd, he often felt as if the space around him were shimmering, as if at any moment the people nearby might grab him and throw him onto the cement, kicking him with their sharp shoes.

At least it was a good story, one he could tell exceptionally well. The morning after he was attacked, Alan was the center of attention, and the older secretary, the one who always called him "honey" and "sugar," was very concerned about the neighborhood he lived in. When she first saw his face, she'd let out a small cry of shock. Even Dugan had listened to Alan's story, and Dugan, who was white, was reminded of the time he himself was held up on the el platform by five Puerto Ricans with knives. Dugan pulled up his shirt to show them a pale, leech-like scar above his left nipple. They'd tried to stab him in the heart. "Luckily," Dugan said, "I don't have one."

As they all listened to Dugan, Alan found himself wondering what Dugan and his co-workers were thinking of him. There were often times when he would feel as if he were lifting out of his body and observing himself from above. He could see himself clearly at this particular moment, standing there in a business suit he'd bought from a secondhand store. Though it was a Brooks Brothers suit, it was ill-fitting, and he was certain that everyone could tell that it was used. They were polished, had gone to fancy schools, had rich parents. They were going to be wealthy and successful, and Alan wasn't. Though he was twenty-two, he looked younger: big and gangly like a teenager who hadn't yet grown into his body, with a round freckled face, cheeks that would not grow hair. His smile was broad and simple. He looked like he was from Nebraska, people told him; a redneck, as someone had once unkindly put it. Standing there, he was aware that each of his co-workers had probably developed an unflattering version of him in their minds.

The co-workers were generally cordial, though, even if they weren't friendly. They kept their opinions to themselves, unlike Dugan, whose advice to Alan had the jovial, insulting edge of a football coach. "Lowe," he'd said once. "Get another aftershave. You smell like a teamster. What the hell is that, Old Spice?" It was–a Christmas gift from his father, who was, in fact, a teamster. "Lowe," Dugan would say. "Do you own an iron?" Or: "From now on, Lowe, don't bring a brown bag lunch. You want the clients to think you're Bob Cratchit?"

Dugan was a small burly man in his mid-forties; the backs of his hands and fingers were covered with dark bristly hair, and the day after the mugging, when Dugan leaned the ham of his palm against the top of Alan's computer, it seemed the hair had a burnished glow, as if he'd moussed it. "Lowe," he said, in a confidential, fatherly voice. "Look, I don't want to seem insensitive or anything, but you've got to get some more professional-looking bandages, man. We can't have clients coming in here and seeing you like this. You look like 'Welcome to My Car Accident.'"

Alan looked up. He had been staring at the blinking cursor on his computer for well over half an hour, and he didn't want Dugan to see how blank his screen was. "What?" he said.

Dugan told him again. He hated having to repeat himself; he'd take on the expression of a comic who had to explain his punch line. "This is the name of a drugstore on Superior," Dugan said, and handed him a slip of paper. "I'm sure they have something decent. Where'd you get that stuff? Woolworth's?"

"I just had a first-aid kit at home," Alan said, and Dugan nodded, flexing his hand as Alan smiled sorrowfully. The hot core of loathing Alan felt for Dugan was often cooled by the idea that maybe Dugan was right. In his own way, perhaps Dugan was really trying to help him. And everyone else on the floor seemed to like Dugan. Dugan had nicknames for some of the employees, little private jokes, and Alan would watch them laughing together beyond the glass wall of his cubicle. Some of them even called Dugan "Dave."

"I'll take care of it," Alan said agreeably. He gave Dugan a thumbs-up, having seen Dugan do this himself on occasion, and tucked the slip of paper into his pocket. But Dugan just stared at him.

"Good man, Lowe," he said.

When Alan graduated from college, everything had been perfect. He had a good job, an apartment. Three banks sent him notes of congratulations, offering him credit cards so he could buy the things he needed for his apartment, the appliances and furniture he'd always imagined himself owning. "You deserve it," they told him. "We want to invest in your success!" He curled himself up into this new life as a hermit crab might ease itself into a conch.

But within a few months Alan became aware that something had changed, something was wrong. He had been well-liked in college, but suddenly there was something about him that people hated. That autumn a homeless man walked up to him and spit in his hair, for no reason. Apparently the man just hadn't liked his looks. Another time, he'd been by himself in a restaurant, sipping coffee, when a smartly dressed, grandmotherly woman had glared at him from a nearby table. "Please don't watch me while I'm eating, sir," she said coldly. And even his old friends from college called him less frequently. They had jobs they were settling into, new lives.

"Do I seem different to you at all," he would ask his friends when they were all together. "What do you guys think of me? I mean really?"

The friends seemed to answer kindly. But afterwards he felt certain they were not telling him the whole truth.

In the mornings, he always resolved that his day at work would be a good one. Even that day, the morning after he was mugged, he'd tried to imagine himself as a young executive, purposeful, eager, the Pete

Preneta & Co. Person they often spoke of in their memos. He loved the moment when he reached the elevator banks, the brush of shoulders as a group of people moved toward the opening doors, the sudden tingling in the pit of his stomach as the elevator glided upward. This was how he used to imagine himself when he was in high school, when he was riding in the passenger seat of his father's pickup with empty beer cans and twenty-two shells rattling on the floor. He would see himself in a suit and tie, sitting down at a desk on the upper floors of a skyscraper, writing with gold-plated pens in a leather-bound appointment book.

He sat at his desk and took the stack of papers from the in box. He smoothed and straightened them in the center of his desk. But when he looked down, it seemed as if these were the exact same memos and computer manuals he'd gone over the day before. He'd only been working there for six months, but already it seemed as if there were no discernible beginning, middle, or end. Minutes and words began to melt into one another with the hallucinatory tedium of a lava lamp. By ten, Alan would find himself falling into dreams, eyes closed, fingers poised above his keyboard as if in brief, brilliant thought.

He spent a little time applying his new bandages in the shining, brassy bathroom. Dugan had been right: the old ones looked awful–dingy. A crust of blood had appeared through the gauze he'd taped to his forehead. But after he'd finished, the afternoon extended like a dark tunnel in front of him, and he found himself on one of the long errands he often felt compelled to make at this time of day.

That afternoon, he'd gone to the supply closet. He did this usually once or twice a week, and if he was lucky he would kill almost an hour collecting fine-point felt pens and stationery, Post-it notes and erasers. It was very peaceful.

No one seemed to wonder where he was. He always left his desk in a bit of a clutter, as if he'd be returning any minute; but no one, not even Dugan, mentioned it. It reminded him of a spooky television program he'd once seen, where a man went about his business for days and days before he finally realized that people weren't noticing him because he was dead, a ghost.

At home, after he had put away his cache of office supplies, he tried on the trench coat again. He had hurried back to his apartment in the waning late January light, his back prickling as the streetlights began to hum, turning blue in the dusk. He'd jumped when a dour young woman had rushed past him on the sidewalk. Now it was dark, and he pulled down the shades in all three rooms, fingering the black buttons of the trench coat through their holes.

In the mirror, he could see the trench coat had been damaged by the attack. It was wrinkled, scuffed with dirt. The sleeve had been torn a little, and the collar marked like a map with dark islands of blood. He hung the coat back up in the closet, regretfully. He had wanted to wear it when he went out that night. It would have made him feel calm.

He liked to go out to restaurants and bars, or to go shopping in those cathedral-like downtown malls, with their high ceilings and gentle music. He knew it was wrong to do this, actually destructive since his money troubles had begun. But most of the places a person could go for free seemed drab and sad, and he dreaded sitting in his apartment alone.

He forced himself to stay at home that night, and did not even call for a pizza. He had considered it, but when he picked up the receiver he discovered that the phone company had made good on their threats. There was no dial tone.

The next day, rent was due. But he didn't have enough money in his account, and he had even tried calling his parents from a pay phone. "Boy, I know it can be tough financially those first few years out of college," his father had said. "You know we'd help you out if we could, but we just can't." He couldn't bring himself to tell his father how desperate things were. How would he explain where his money had gone when he didn't know himself?

He decided that rather than panic, he would just have to wait a few weeks until his next paycheck. Then he would just go without groceries for a while, that was all. He tried not to let himself imagine his debt rolling over and over, accumulating. It would be all right, he told himself.

He was thinking this, actually whispering it under his breath, when he rounded the corner and bumped into the two boys. They had been walking close together, their shoulders almost touching, and he stepped into them as if into an invisible wall.

"Oh," he said. "Excuse me!" He grinned. They seemed young, maybe seniors in high school.

"You better take care, mister," said the taller of the two. "Your head in the clouds."

"Yes, well," he said, a bit flustered. They were at the mouth of an alleyway, near a liquor store that hadn't opened yet. In the distance, people were striding toward the rapid transit station. "I guess I'm a little spaced out," he said. "Sorry." The boys exchanged glances, and it was then that he began to have a feeling. He hadn't been able to see his muggers–it was too dark and fast–but an image flashed through his mind, like a single frame of film, and he had the sudden intuition that these boys were his attackers. It was the way they looked at one another, as if trying not to chortle; it was the way they had their eyes fixed on him. Yet they were so young and clean cut. He told himself not to be paranoid.

"How much do you want for those sunglasses?" the taller one said.

He was wearing a pair of yellow-tinted sunglasses that made him, he thought, look sort of hip. Sandy had given them to him. He took them off, and he sensed how easy it would be for the boys to pull him into the alleyway. He put his fingers on the grate across the liquor store window. "They're not for sale," he said. "Thanks for offering."

"I'll give you ten dollars for them," the taller one said. The boys smiled, and Alan watched as the taller one took a black leather wallet out of his back pocket. Of course, many people have black wallets, Alan told himself. But it looked very much like the one the muggers had taken from him.

"Those are the nicest sunglasses I've ever seen," said the boy.

"No, no," Alan said. "Seriously. They have sentimental value."

The two boys stood there, and Alan wondered whether he could grab something–a blade of broken glass, a stone–to fend them off. Then they turned. "Stay cool," the smaller one said. When they rounded the corner, walking toward the space of ground where he'd been mugged, Alan thought he heard them laugh.

This was not a story that would amuse people, he thought: it made him sound insane. Often, he would finish relating some anecdote and the silent faces of his coworkers or friends would be like the heavy ticking of a clock. It made him cringe. Once, he'd told someone about the time he had worms as a child. It had seemed comical in his head, but afterward, when he was alone, he was so filled with disgust at himself that he'd struck his idiot mouth with his fist, making it bleed. Once, he was trying to tell Sandy about the Pete Preneta Trainee Week–how the company had shipped them all to Atlanta, where they lived in dorms and learned about firm policy–but Sandy stopped him halfway through. She shook her head. "You know what's weird," she said. "You're not who you think you are." She wouldn't explain what she meant.

Alan gazed out the window of the train. He'd taken this trip hundreds of times now, but nothing ever looked familiar. They could be taking him anywhere. At some corners, buildings slid by only a few feet from the window; walls shuffled past in a blur of colors and textures–grimy red brick or wood or ancient brownstone, the crowns and curlicues and stylized letters of gang graffiti, billboard models with their eyes and teeth blocked out. Then suddenly, there would be a flash of open sky, and an empty schoolyard would appear, or a street, tunneling its way toward Lake Michigan. Then, just as abruptly, the train descended into the underground, and there was only darkness, or in a sudden flicker of light, the crumbling damp walls and shadowy nooks and crannies of the subway. The train conductor mumbled out the names of the stops in bursts of static over the PA system, but Alan could never understand the words. Often it wasn't until he recognized his stop that he was sure he wasn't going the wrong way.

The rent–of course it came back to him in the middle of the day, while he was trying to talk to Dugan. There was this buzz in his head, like interference from a distant station on the radio.

"So–like, my father," Alan was telling Dugan, "is in the unions? An organizer. He's, you know, fairly big." He wasn't sure how this had started, how it had led into this lie about his father.

"What union?" Dugan said. He seemed vaguely interested, turning the heavy gold ring on his finger around and around.

"Teamster," Alan said quickly. "A real old-time progressive, you know."

"The unions are dying fast," Dugan mused. He looked at Alan pointedly, and Alan tried to remember where the conversation had been going before this terrible detour. It had been something about Dugan's parents.

"Well . . . yeah," Alan said. "That's what I tell him. He's always giving me crap about working here, for a corporation and all. But I tell him, you know, this is the nineties." This was one of Dugan's phrases, and Alan waited a moment for some slight acknowledgment.

"Hmmm," Dugan said. This was the longest and most personal conversation Alan remembered he and Dugan ever engaging in. But it was fading fast. "Well, anyway," Dugan said.

"Hey," Alan said. "You know what I wanted to ask you." He hesitated for a moment, but the buzz in his head had grown loud enough that he thought he could risk it. "You know those emergency loans they talk about in the employee handbook?"

"Yeah?" Dugan said.

"How do you get one?"

Dugan considered him, his expression flickering. He looked suspicious, and Alan could sense that the rapport had been killed. So that's why he came to my office, Dugan was thinking. "What's the emergency?" Dugan said at last.

"I don't know," Alan said weakly. "I'm out of money?"

Dugan's face was blank for a long second. Then, as if Alan's voice had just reached him from a distance, he chuckled. "Nice, Lowe," he said. "Very cute."

A few days later, on a Saturday, Alan saw Dugan walking down a street. This was in Alan's neighborhood, far from the Gold Coast condo where Dugan lived. What was he doing here, Alan wondered, and he felt a trickling sensation go through him. He'd never before seen someone from work in the civilian world, and there was something unsettling about it. He saw Dugan come out of an occult book store wearing a thick leather jacket with a fur collar, striding slowly, purposefully away from him. He waited for Dugan to get a bit ahead of him, then he followed.

It was an unseasonably warm day for January, and Alan had been wandering the street all morning, trying to stay out of the apartment for fear his landlord would come looking for him. But he'd felt edgy and vulnerable out in the open, and he'd been trying to stick close to people. For a while, he'd browsed in windows beside an elderly lady in heavy makeup and a fur. Perhaps, he imagined, people passing would think she was his mother, and he tried to look bored and impatient. It wasn't long before he'd made her nervous, however, and she hurried away.

He'd followed Dugan a few blocks when he remembered that he was wearing the trench coat. The realization branched across his skin like frost: it was impossible, but he had actually forgotten that it was stolen. When he paid for the dry cleaning, it had been as if he'd purchased the coat. It felt like he'd always owned it, now.

He stopped and swiftly shed the coat. For a moment, he considered stashing it somewhere. But of course it would be stolen. He folded it a couple of times, and then rolled it up tightly, as his father had taught him to roll sleeping bags on camping trips when he was a child. He bent down and picked up a piece of newspaper that was lying on the street, wrapping it carefully around the bundled coat. When he tucked this cocoonlike creation under his arm, it looked like he was just carrying a newspaper–the Sunday edition, but a paper nevertheless.

Dugan had stopped too. He was peering into a storefront window, absently drumming his thighs with the heels of his hands, as if trying to remember a tune. From a distance, Dugan's mouth looked odd, doll-like. It took Alan a minute to realize Dugan was whistling.

Alan hung back. He knew he should take his opportunity, turn back before Dugan caught sight of him. And yet there was something exciting about this. For once, it was as if he knew more than everyone else on the street, he had his own secret purpose. He was transformed into someone shadowy yet magnetic, someone larger. Maybe this was what his muggers had felt.

Dugan was completely unaware. He walked on, pausing sometimes in front of a store. Where was he going? Alan cruised easily around the little islands of walking people, sometimes letting Dugan drift far ahead, sometimes drawing close enough that if Dugan turned, he would surely see him. But he didn't turn.

At the end of the block, Dugan went into a coffee shop. When Alan got to the entrance, he peered in the doorway just in time to see the hostess leading Dugan to a booth. The angry-looking Greek man at the cash register looked over at Alan as he was watching Dugan being seated. Alan smiled. He'd been in this coffee shop several times, and the man, the owner apparently, was always nasty to him.

"You coming in or going out? What?" the man said to him. "You want me to heat the whole world?" Alan pulled back uncertainly, but then he surprised himself by giving the man the finger. Then he went out quickly, imagining for a moment that the man might come after him. But the man just waved a tired hand at him, making an ugly face from beyond the glass doors. Alan tapped his crotch, as he'd seen disgruntled people do. "Heat this," he said, and then he stepped back a few paces, out of the man's line of vision, and leaned against the wall. He didn't want to get in a confrontation and risk drawing Dugan's attention.

But he was pleased with himself. "Heat this": it was a very urban thing to say, the kind of response Dugan himself might have for such a person. Generally, Alan never thought of quick comebacks until long after the fact; often they would come to him when he was trying to go to sleep, and he lay there with his eyes open.

People walked by and he looked at their shoes. Sandy had once told him that if you make eye contact with people on the street, you're asking for trouble: That was in July, when he'd nodded at a man in a big Russian-style fur hat as he and Sandy came out of a bar. The man had followed them for blocks, asking for money, and they hadn't been able to go to the automatic teller machine until he'd finally given up on them. "What's wrong with you?" Sandy had said afterward. "Do you like being harassed?" But it was hard to avoid looking into people's faces; often he'd find himself smiling and saying "Morning," to those he passed, as his father used to on the streets of their small town.

But now, he didn't look up. He leaned back against the wall, hardening his face, narrowing his eyes as if he was concealing a weapon. It made him smile a little to imagine that some redneck was walking by, trying not to look at him.

When Dugan came out, that warm sensation of menace rose up in him like a rush of adrenaline. It was the opposite of what he'd been feeling on the street for weeks now. The people strolling by seemed as vulnerable and trusting as the pigeons that waddled around statues downtown, moving out of the paths of passersby so slowly you could kick one, if you wanted.

It wouldn't feel bad to kick Dugan, he thought. There was something annoyingly mincing about the way he walked. He was so proud of those dainty, slipperlike Italian shoes, with their ridiculous sheen, and Alan could tell he was keeping an eye on the ground to avoid stepping in something that might mess them up a little. It wouldn't feel bad to take a blowtorch to those shoes.

Nothing bad could ever happen to Dugan: that was

how he acted, that was what he said with his pace and his whistling. He would never lock eyes with a crazy man on the street; such a person didn't quite exist in Dugan's dimension. He never shuddered as strangers brushed past. Not even a knife in the heart could faze him.

Alan's hands were shaking, but it was a good feeling. When he was little, his father imagined he was going to be an athlete and taught him how to box. If he let down his guard, his father struck a good one to his face or chest, and by the end of a session, Alan's hands would be shaking like that. "You got the butterflies?" his father would say, feigning punches. "You nervous?" That was good, his father told him. It meant his body was getting him prepared.

Prepared for what?

He wasn't going to do it, he thought. But then Dugan was slowing down, flexing his shoulders luxuriously, as he always did when he'd made some nasty comment. Nice, Lowe. Very cute, Alan thought, and then he knew he was going to do it after all. They had strolled off the busy street, away from the shops and people, and when he saw Dugan turn down a narrow alleyway, toward a parking lot, Alan quickened.

He felt his hand pull the trench coat from under his arm; he worked swiftly to unravel it as he came up on Dugan, stretching it out, and just as Dugan heard the rushing footsteps and began to turn, Alan pulled the coat over his head from behind.

This muffled Dugan's surprised cry; Alan jerked back on the coat, and he could see the shape of Dugan's face, like a mask emerging on the surface of the canvas. It was easy to knock him to the ground. Alan had once helped one of his father's friends clip the ears of his calves, and this was much easier than throwing a calf. Dugan struck earth, and Alan landed on his back with both knees, knocking the wind out of him.

"Help!" Dugan gasped, and Alan struck him with his fist.

"Shut up!" Alan said in a deep voice. He was trying to imitate a street accent, but it came out more like a Southern one. "I've got a knife, you motherfucker, and I'll use it."

"This is a busy street!" Dugan cried. "Someone will be coming!" His voice was barely intelligible: Alan had tightened the belt of the coat around Dugan's neck, creating a sort of bag over Dugan's head. But when he realized what Dugan was saying, it made sense: he had to hurry. They were kneeling beside a Dumpster, and he maneuvered behind it with Dugan still beneath him, shoving toward the blackened back wall of the building as one might push off from a dock. Dugan's hands clawed the cement, and Alan picked up a long shard of broken glass and pressed it against Dugan's back.

"You think you're so great," Alan said through his teeth. "You really need to suffer a little, man." His accent wavered, and he knew he shouldn't talk; Dugan would surely recognize his voice. Alan pressed the glass harder against Dugan's back, and Dugan let out a small shriek, though he wasn't cut.

"For the love of God," cried Dugan. "I've got money! Credit cards! Take them! Take them!" And Alan did reach into Dugan's pocket and draw the wallet out.

But that wasn't what he wanted. He didn't know what he wanted, really, or how this could have possibly happened. He could feel the adrenaline ebbing away, and he felt as if Dugan was a raft he was kneeling on, adrift on the open sea.

He *did* want Dugan to suffer—but there was nothing he could bring himself to do that would hurt him enough. He wished he could think of some word, something that would go straight through Dugan's heart as no weapon could.

"You . . . " he said, and he hoped his voice boomed. But he couldn't think how to finish the sentence, and there wasn't time to ponder it. "Say 'Momma," Alan said at last, and Dugan paused for a moment, then did.

"Momma," Dugan said woodenly.

Alan wanted to make him repeat it with more conviction, but his stomach was beginning to feel heavy, and all he could think was to reach down and pull off Dugan's shoes. He wasn't wearing socks, and his pale feet lay there like beached fish. Alan slipped his belt off and knotted it tightly around Dugan's ankles. That would give him time to run, he thought, and he could picture himself melting into the groups of people on the distant street, walking lightly in Dugan's shoes, off toward where the train was pulling into the station, waiting to bear him away.

accidents

Charlie got his first car while his mother was still in the clinic. If it hadn't been for that car, he was sure that the dread of her eventual return would have driven him crazy. He might have just locked himself up in his room and never opened the door.

But driving was like a fever. After school, he would leave St. Bonaventure in a rush, passing trailer courts and truck stops that were clustered on the edge of town, pushing past each changing speed zone sign, out toward the country. Everything took on a kind of jittery excitement—the skittish horses along the fence, nipping each other playfully; the sudden yellow-green of the ditches and the shimmering green rows of winter wheat; even the ghostlike, uneasy stares of white-faced Hereford cattle. His father's farm was about seven miles west of town, and by the time Charlie was out on the highway, he would have to keep glancing down at the speedometer, and, finding himself going 70, 75, 85, slow with effort back down to 55. While he was driving, all those thoughts about his crazy mother in the clinic could be brushed over while Charlie concentrated on enjoying the speed and his own vague recklessness, racing until the landscape blurred around him.

His red Mustang was a wreck. There was a spidery-thin crack that ran the length of the windshield. Shallow valleys of dents sloped their way across its body. The gas cap was missing, left in one of a dozen possible gas stations and never retrieved. He had been in several small accidents with his car in the four months that he had had his driver's license. He'd bumped into a lamppost and knocked it over, and quite a few times he'd backed into other automobiles. He could remember his father's icy, understanding voice, as he stood trembling into the pay phone after he had missed the entrance to an alleyway and hit the side of a building. His father had pulled up in front of the courthouse after Charlie had filled out the accident report. Charlie had run out and got in on the passenger side. When he remembered this, Charlie felt almost sick—the way his father just glared, not saying a word all that drive home. His father had turned up the radio, and humming, looking straight ahead, had pretended his son did not exist.

On the day that his mother was to come home from the clinic, Charlie had another small accident.

He was driving home as fast as he could, having succeeded in putting any thoughts of his mother out of his mind—it was the first genuinely beautiful spring day, and the smell of the air, the taste of it, had Charlie quivering. It felt as if a storm were coming. It brought back fond memories of other summers, memories of early childhood. He could remember watching the combines move across the long stretches of yellowed wheat as he stood along the dirt road by the mailbox, waiting for his father to come and pick him up, to take him in the truck or the cab of the combine. He remembered running a few steps, waving his arms over his head as his father rushed past him in the pickup, pulling a plume of dust around him. In the distance, he could see thunderclouds gathering.

Everything was being drawn into sharp vertical and horizontal lines: the cut wheat met the uncut; the road met the field; the horizon met the sky.

Then the sky grew dark. Great blue-black clouds

rose like smoke, up out of sight. The thunder boomed once. A breeze rushed across the stillness with a drawn-out hiss. The wheat rippled, seemed to fatten. The combines looked as if they were rising, roaring, like sea monsters from a yellow water. Far away, Charlie remembered seeing what looked like a gauzy curtain billowing toward him; but before he could move the hard rain and then the hail began hitting him–and then he was running, covering his head at first but then just holding his head up and squinting his eyes, laughing–there he was, he could remember the feeling, out there alone, the world moving fast, almost out of control.

It was disappointing, he recalled, that the hail-storm passed as quickly as it had arrived. Everything in the landscape was left quiet and noncommittal, even more than it had been before.

What he had forgotten, while he was thinking of all this, was that his father's car was parked at the end of the long driveway. When he looked up again, he realized too late that he was going very fast–he stepped on the brake, and heard an involuntary cry come from his mouth as the car impacted on the rear fender of his father's Buick, making a "whumph" sound that seemed horribly loud despite the fact that he was sure that he didn't hit it that hard. For a moment, it seemed to him that he was outside his car, looking in, for he clearly saw an image of himself tipping forward and then lightly back, like a dancer.

But the worst part, the most dreadful thing, was that his father was coming out of the barn just as it happened. He could hear, even as he stepped on the brake, his father yelling: stop, Stop, STOP, *STOP!*

Charlie's mouth hung open, and he sucked in breath. He tried to put the car in reverse, and then he realized the car had stalled. He turned the key and heard a grinding sound.

"This is the last time you ever sit behind a wheel,"

he heard a voice say. He looked up and startled when he saw his father peering through the window at him. He nearly fell out as his father yanked the door open.

"Just what are you trying to prove?" his father breathed.

"Nothing," Charlie said. Already he was probing his mind for an excuse. "Dad, I didn't even see the car there, I don't know I think there's something wrong with the brakes because I really wasn't going that fast and I was trying to stop."

"Back it up," his father said, his voice hushed with rage. Charlie turned the key several times and only got a grinding sound. I've broken it, he thought. His father scowled in at him. "I don't know what's wrong with it," Charlie said, shaking his head at his father. Then he noticed that the car was still in reverse. He pushed the gear stick back to park, smiling and trembling and stuttering: "Oh . . . uh . . . hm . . . " He started the car and slammed into reverse. The quickness with which the car sped backwards, toward the ditch, surprised him. He slammed on the brakes again, flushing when his father called after him: "How in the hell did you get your driver's license?"

His father stared down at the Buick's fender, looking from it to Charlie as if Charlie would suddenly attack it once again. Charlie ambled cautiously toward him, nodding his head as if to shake excuses out of it: "I'm sure it's okay. It was just a little tap, you know, I guess I wasn't watching, you know, I must've just turned my head for minute . . . "

"Here's the scratch," his father said.

"I'll pay for it," Charlie said. "I'll pay to have it fixed." He looked eagerly at his father and received a cool smile. His father's calm withered him.

"Pay with what?" his father asked politely. "With your good looks?"

"I'll get a job!"

"Oh, really," his father said. He took a step toward

Charlie, showing his teeth. "And how do you plan to get to this 'job'?"

"In my car," Charlie said lamely.

"Charlie-O," his father said, "I wouldn't trust you with a tricycle, let alone an automobile!"

The excuses started to slip out of his mouth again, uncontrollably. "Dad," he said, "I was distracted. Just a minute. It could happen to anyone."

"But it always seems to happen to you," his father said. "Now I wonder what could have distracted you? The scenery, maybe?"

"I was thinking," Charlie said, and then a sudden flash of brilliance came to him. "I was thinking about Mom, and her coming home and all."

It was almost a pleasure to watch the smile on his father's face droop. "Oh," his father said.

Eventually, the damage evaluated, his father went back into the house. As the screen door closed, and his father disappeared into the house, Charlie had the sinking realization that another lane of communication between his father and him had been permanently closed.

He stood for a moment, staring out at the interstate that divided their property. Sometimes, it was hard to imagine the world out there beyond except as lines upon lines, the rim of sky underlining the flat stretch of horizon. He could stand at one point, and out there in some other place was another point where he could be standing, and in between those two points was an infinity of points which were places he might have been. So why was this place, out of a million possible choices, where he had to be? Some days, he wished he was going away; not driving off to school again, but out onto the interstate, headed off toward one of those points, or all of them.

Nothing ever changed. There was something maddening, hopeless in the sameness–the miles of flat horizon, the endless drift of his father away from him. Every time, it seemed, that there was a chance for them to finally be close, another door would shut, and his father would be as far away as ever.

And then there was his mother. She would never change. And it wasn't even that she was crazy—there was something unpredictable about real crazy people. But with her it was just that determined glaze, tracing over the same routines until they didn't mean anything to anyone. How many times did she think she could run off to the Greyhound depot with her grocery bag full of hastily packed clothes and expect them to go trailing after her? She would never really get on the bus. He could remember how she kept calling and calling, one night when she had left, his father had gone out searching for her and Charlie was alone in the house. Every time he picked up the phone, it was that nasal, uninflected, insistent voice: "You'd better say what you have to say to me now, because you'll never have another chance." He would just let the phone fall back onto its receiver. Then it would ring again, and after a while he would know it was her even before she opened her mouth, he'd hang up before she said a word. When he woke up the next day there she was, wearing the same clothes she'd had on the night before, smoking cigarettes and letting the ash grow so long that it dropped off and lay like a caterpillar on the table, on the rug, on the stove. It was that look of dull triumph—as if she expected him to run and catch her in his arms, as if she expected him to be happy—that made him hate her.

The second time she came back from the clinic, she told them never again. "Oh, I'll never let that happen again," she said.

And now she was going to be home again. But he could still remember that puckered smile as she told him, mornings before school, that he better take a good look at her because she wouldn't be there when he got back. She was always smirking, as if she was about to get some kind of well-deserved revenge, holding her long-ashed cigarette between her fingers like a movie star with a long cigarette holder. So what could he say to her now? "Of course I still love you," he would tell her. But the real thought was the one that kept turning over and over in his mind: "You'll never change. You'll never be any different."

Trust, Charlie thought, watching his tennis shoe toe the gravel. We should have never taken her back. No more chances. He watched as cars rushed by on the interstate, passing through their plot of land, becoming dots in the distance. I wish I were leaving, Charlie thought, I wish I were going somewhere, just like them. Then he turned and went into the house.

"Charlie-O," his father said as he came into the kitchen. "What do you want for supper?"

"I don't care," Charlie told him.

"Hamburgers okay, Charlie-O?" he asked.

"Fine." His father always called him Charlie-O or some other nickname. There were dozens of them– Chip, Chas, Charles, Broadsides (after he started wrecking his car), Chally, Char, names that no one but his father called him. Sometimes Charlie thought it was because his father really wished that he were a different person; by calling him by a different name, he could somehow change Charlie himself. He knew well that his father tired quickly of people. His father had lots of friends, and they would come over almost every weekend for beers and cards, but the friends were always different. It was mysterious that he had remained so constant toward Charlie's mother.

"You don't know anything about me," Charlie had once said, when his father, trying to get Charlie to mow the lawn, had gone into a calm, smiling tirade about how irresponsible Charlie was.

"I know all I need to know," his father had responded. That had stuck with him, as if it were an accusation, proof that his father had found that bland sameness in Charlie himself.

"Dinner's ready," his father said, and Charlie looked up.

The argument came easily during dinner, in between small talk about the weather and football. "How many minutes do you give her before we have to ship her off again?" Charlie asked his father. One of those calm discussions ensued; Charlie was a smart-mouth, his father told him, it never failed, he was always disrespectful and he should take a moment to be thankful for what he had. Count your blessings, his father advised, and Charlie, by this time so worked up that he wasn't even afraid of his father or worried that his father would suddenly quit loving him, looked into his father's face and counted each blessing: "Zero," he said. Then he got up and walked out.

He sat in his car, with the doors locked, and the exhilaration of telling his father what he thought wore off quickly. He began to wish that his father would come outside and say: "Charlie-O please come back inside, let's talk this through, please, Charlie," but he was becoming more and more sure that his father wouldn't come outside at all. In fact, he was beginning to think that his father didn't care whether he came in or not. He felt as if he might start crying.

Why did you do that, he kept asking himself. So often, so often, he just kept his mouth shut; all those wrecks, with their subsequent discussions in which his father told him over and over: "You've got a lot of growing up to do, Charlie-O," or "I think you are the most irresponsible person I have ever known." Charlie had been quiet, penitent. "I'm sorry, Dad," he kept saying. "It won't happen again."

Charlie looked out the windshield. He could see the dark shape of the barn, hunched indifferently against the sky, as the last orange glow of sun disappeared behind it. He could see the blinking lights of an airplane moving across the surface of the sky, and below it, the red taillights of autos passing in the distance. It's her, Charlie thought. If it hadn't been for her coming back, I wouldn't have gotten so worked up, I wouldn't have said those things. I wasn't yelling at him, I was yelling at her. Oh, Dad, you've got to believe me, he thought, I won't be a smart aleck anymore. It's her. Don't you understand that you can't trust her?

He pictured his mother's face in his mind. I hate you, he thought, but the image kept smiling at him, and he felt suddenly very sad. He could remember a time when they used to be close. When he was little they would spend hours alone together—she would read to him, or they would stay up late watching scary movies. She'd laugh suddenly at the climax, so he wouldn't be frightened. Even after her first time at the clinic, they remained close. When she would ride over for her weekly visits with the doctor, he would go with her, to keep her company on the drive. But after the second time, they had drifted apart. I love you so much, she would say, even though you really couldn't believe anything she said. After an argument, she would go to him with the same stories: "So and so is talking about me behind my back, this person is rude to me for no reason, that person is sure acting funny lately. But you wait. I won't be around much longer, and they'll be sorry." Then she would stroke his hair. "You are my very special one," she would say, as if she were talking to herself. He was irritated by the way she still sometimes touched him as she would a baby. "You're just like the rest of them, like all of them," she yelled at him once, when he didn't feel like going to the doctor and waiting in the waiting room all afternoon. He had ridden away on his bike, leaving her standing in the driveway, those words "all of them" lingering as he peddled past the trees and the mailbox, to the road.

Charlie got out of the car and stood for a moment, regarding the yard and the house, lost in the twilight shadows that reached across the grass, creeping along the circle of light made by the porch lamp. The living room was lit with the pale blue light of the television. He could see his father in his easy chair, staring toward the television's dim glow.

Charlie raised his head and looked out toward the elms that lined the driveway. The rustle of branches and leaves mixed in a sudden gust of wind with the rattle of paper skittering along the sidewalk. A storm is coming, Charlie thought. Then all the sounds stopped, as if they had been startled. In the distance, he could hear a car approaching. The flicker of headlights moved briefly through the trees, and Charlie shrunk up close to the house, out of sight.

The headlights swept against the side of the barn, two circles of light that pinned the shadows of trees and weeds starkly against the surface of the barn. He glanced around the corner and saw that it was his mother's car. He heard the motor die, and then the headlights went out. He heard his mother's footsteps on the gravel. The screen door banged.

Charlie hurried around the side of the building, stopping short at the edge of the kitchen window. He could hear their voices through the glass, and he peered nervously over the rim of the windowsill. Maybe they're talking about me, he thought. He was startled suddenly by a flash of lightning in the distance.

His parents were embracing. His mother was kissing his father, and then his father was telling her how glad he was that she was back, how things were going to be better from now on.

Outside, the rain appeared, and beat on the windows. Charlie wasn't sure why he had suddenly turned and run to his car, or why he had roared the engine and driven slowly down the road to the mailbox and then out onto the highway. There had been a sudden rush inside him—he had to get away, just to clear his head. Maybe this would show them, he thought. Why aren't they following me? he wondered.

At first, just a few drops of rain hit the windshield at random points, but soon it was coming down faster and faster, until it was not separate drops but a single sheet of water across the window. The wipers thrust apart, endlessly sweeping back the water, but it just kept coming. He felt like the rain was burying him. He couldn't see. The wipers were fluttering like big black wings, and he couldn't see anything but the dark beyond the hazy curtain of rain, no road, no trees. Even the headlights only illuminated the tangled lines of falling rain. There was a static hiss around him that grew louder and louder–Charlie felt first a bump, and then the slow tilt as the car began to spin. It was almost an afterthought, realizing that he'd gone off the road. And then he just let it go, a slow, inevitable release as if into a dream. He closed his eyes lightly, feeling the car lift and him with it, rising, nothing outside but darkness. There he was, he knew the feeling, out there alone, the world spinning around him, almost as if it wasn't there, as if it had blurred and disappeared.

Then, everything was quiet. He kept his eyes closed, hearing the approach of a car, and then footsteps running, and finally a voice that called to him through the cracked windshield. It doesn't sound like my father, he thought. It could be anyone.

"Son?" the voice kept saying, but Charlie wouldn't open his eyes. "Son? Son? Are you all right?"

do you know what i mean?

O'Neil had come at last to the town where she lived. The bus rose up over the crest of a hill and Bedlow, South Dakota appeared below him in a blur of falling snow. One of those houses, he thought: She was inside it.

But as the bus pulled into Bedlow he just sat there, as if he might not move. They stopped in front of the bus depot, which was part of a truck stop on the edge of town. Heavy flakes of snow were falling onto the cars in the parking lot, and O'Neil was reminded of the furniture in a house that has been closed up, all draped with sheets. Everyone was silent. A few people in seats near him shifted fitfully, perhaps troubled by a dream. "Bedlow," the driver called impatiently. When the driver called again, O'Neil realized that he was the only one getting off. "Are you Bedlow?" the driver asked as he teetered to the front, and O'Neil nodded. He knew he was doing the wrong thing.

She didn't know he was coming, that was the worst part. As he stood alone in the parking lot under the high, brightly humming Shell sign in his trench coat, he imagined that he must look like an assassin in an old movie, someone who would make the music turn ominous and dissonant. He didn't like to think of it that way, to picture her unaware of the trouble that was bearing down on her–innocently going about her business, fixing her dinner or balancing her checkbook at her kitchen table, or snug in an easy chair, placidly reading a book.

He had always tried to think of it like this:

he'd come across a doe in the clearing of a forest, and it was still, its hide shivering, its ears pricked up; any sudden movement would cause it to bolt. Only the most subtle, graceful approach would allow him to step closer, to put out a hand. And then? He didn't know. It wasn't, he thought, a very accurate metaphor.

From a strategic standpoint, **and** from a moral one, all the books warned against surprising them. They were very pious about honesty, these books, with their talk of the evils of secrecy and closed records, with their stirring passages about the "right to know." But the truth was, the only way to get information–birth certificates, court documents, etc.–was to lie and connive, to fake everything. For a year now, O'Neil had pretended to be the father of a dying child, in urgent need of medical information. He forged letters from an invented pediatrician on stolen hospital stationery. He wept into the phone, into the embarrassed silence of some clerk or another, and after he got what he wanted he almost laughed with the exhilaration of fooling them, even while his eyes were still blurry with real tears.

He had her address for a long time before he did anything about it. Three months before, on his birthday, he sent her a rose. There was a card attached, with his name and phone number.

There was no response. He waited a month, and then he sent another note. "Did you receive my rose?" it said. He enclosed an envelope for her reply. The answer came at last, two weeks later. It was a little white card with the words "Thank You" in gold script on the front. Inside she'd printed, in careful block letters: SORRY. She underlined this three times.

Perhaps she really thought that this would be the end of it, but O'Neil had to believe that she knew better. She had to have doubts of her own, and deep down she was expecting him, he thought. For weeks now, every time her phone rang, every time she locked her door at night, a shadow of dread, anxiety, even vague eagerness would pass over her. Or so he imagined. It might even be a relief for her to have it over with.

In the phone booth outside the truck stop café–EAT GAS WELCOME–he dialed information. His plan was simple: He would take a taxicab directly to her house and ring the bell. There would be no way for his uncertainty to get the best of him if he was standing there at the edge of her yard, and he found it practically unimaginable that she would close the door on him after she'd opened it and he began to speak.

But there was no taxi service in Bedlow. He knew he should have guessed as much, since it was a small place, but he had let himself become too pleased with the directness of his plan. Beyond the interstate, the town itself–the dazzles of streetlights that were beginning to glow in the dusk, among the dark tree-tops–looked to be several miles away. By nightfall, it would be below zero. Walking seemed out of the question.

He pressed his hand to the glass of the phone booth, watching the snow fall onto the barren lot. Once, in Chicago, he'd answered a randomly ringing pay phone and a husky male voice had said: "I can see you, Mister. I'm watching you right now." He'd looked up: rows of windows, dotting upward like endless ellipses, almost into infinity. The rest of that day he'd found it hard to shake the sense that some-one was out there, watching.

Remembering this made him edgy. Something inside his stomach shrunk a bit, and he couldn't help but think again that he was making a mistake. He stepped out of the phone booth, walked around it once, trying to consider his course. Then, feigning nonchalance, he turned and went inside the café.

For a moment he'd let himself imagine that he might meet someone there, maybe hitch a ride into town.

do you know what i mean? 139

But it wasn't that type of place, he realized. It seemed to him that everyone looked up when he crossed the threshold, and he felt as if silence fell over the room and everyone was staring as he lurched into the unfriendly, greasy-smelling brightness. The cowboys and truck drivers threw a glance at his trench coat, the red and gold scarf tucked carefully into his collar, and he put a hand through his hair, combing out the snow with his fingers.

There was a little area by the cash register where trinkets and novelties were on display, and he walked over and looked at them, folding his hands in front of him as if he were self-possessed and untroubled, a man with a bit of free time to kill. Tiered within the glass case, jewelry and belt buckles made of Black Hills gold and turquoise were lined up; below them, metal figurines of forty-niners, cowpokes with lariats, Elvis, an Indian on a horse, his arms open wide, with the inscription: "Great Spirit/Teach me to criticize another man not/Until I have walked a mile/In his moccassins!" Staring at this, he half-considered just staying, sitting down and drinking coffee until the bus back to Chicago showed up. He lingered over a revolving rack of postcards, trying to sort out his thoughts, flipping through the pictures of Mt. Rushmore and Reptile Gardens and Wind Cave. He couldn't help but imagine himself and this woman, his mother, visiting these places, seeing the sights of the world she lived in. He pictured them slowly beginning to tell their stories, to become friends. It wasn't so improbable.

O'Neil had always felt sure that it wouldn't work over the phone: it was too unreal, too easy for her to simply hang up. But why not call her, he thought now, just to hear the voice, the brief, hesitant "Hello . . . hello . . . Is someone there?" Then hang up, go home.

Or say something, he thought: "You don't know me, but . . . "; or "Mother, this is your son"; or "You can't hide from me anymore"; or even "I love you."

O'Neil whispered all of them under his breath, testing the feel of each on his tongue. None of them worked. None of them got past a few lines before he imagined a click, a dial tone.

When he looked up, he could see an elderly man staring at him from a table near the window. The old man's mouth was turned up in a tiny crescent smile, and O'Neil shrugged his shoulders at him, as if to say: "Well, we all talk to ourselves once in a while, don't we?" But rather than turning away, the old man began to nod his head, still smiling and watching, and O'Neil could feel the friendly expression on his face tighten into a mask.

No one in the world knew where he was. He'd managed to keep it secret, though sometimes he felt as if he could hold it back no longer. At work, poised over his computer, O'Neil would catch the girl in the next cubicle glancing at him, and he'd feel a quivering inside his stomach. For a moment, O'Neil imagined he was going to tell. And when he called his parents, his adoptive parents, he could sense it, moving beneath the talk of health and weather like a fish below ice. He spoke into the hiss of long distance, imagining that his words disintegrated to travel through the wire and then came together at the other end, but not in the same pattern. Who knew what they would hear him say?

So he told them nothing. He didn't want to hurt them. He didn't want his mother to ask, after a long pause, "What can she give you that we haven't?" or even "Why?"

O'Neil couldn't answer that. For years, he hadn't even thought about it. His parents had told him at an early age that he was adopted, and he'd grown up taking it for granted. He was his parents' son, he told those who asked, an O'Neil 100 percent. The nameless lady who had given birth to him didn't matter.

But slowly, it had crept up on him. Sometimes, it

do you know what i mean? 141

was just little things—a face seen closing a door, a certain smell of wood, a woman's laugh heard from across a restaurant. Sometimes, on a busy Chicago street, all the bodies passing around him would suddenly have histories—pasts, futures, secrets. It was a mundane realization, he knew, except that he was aware that any of them—a woman stumbling down his street at midnight, singing in a high clear voice; a lady vanishing into the doorway of an elevated train; a businessman in silver sunglasses, cruising slowly past in his convertible—any of them could belong to him. He sensed mothers, fathers, siblings in the faces that passed. Once, at a bar, O'Neil had been drawn to talk to a man who looked like him. A little drunk, O'Neil found himself pushing the conversation, asking the man about his family. "What's your mother like?" O'Neil had said, leaning forward, as the man shifted uncomfortably.

And O'Neil wondered what had happened to her. Did she look at him, after he was born? Did she cry? He couldn't picture her face, though sometimes if he concentrated he could almost catch a glimpse of some aspect—the set of the eyes, the shape of a finger. Occasionally, he would indulge himself, pretending she might be someone famous. He'd even clipped out photos that had caught his eye in newspapers and magazines, actresses or experts of some sort, society-page ladies. He liked to imagine her as someone with quick things to say, a party-giver. Perhaps she was known for her moods. He tried not to construct a rape, the natural father pulling her onto the dirty ground, the heel of his hand against her mouth. He tried not to imagine her smiling as she left the hospital, free of an annoying burden and nothing else. He'd read a book about a home for unwed mothers, and this was where O'Neil most often saw her. For months, the pregnant girls lived separate from the rest of the world. Once, when the nuns took them to town for ice cream, they were given wedding bands to wear. There were white corridors, crisp pages of forms she had to sign, the movement of O'Neil's unformed limbs inside her.

He didn't know whether this would make sense to his adopted parents; probably, it wouldn't. He could see his father shaking his head, frowning, looking down at his hands. And late at night, when he was alone in the guest room, his old bedroom, his adoptive mother would come to him. Or so he imagined. She'd sit down on the edge of his bed, he imagined, and look at him sadly. "You're lonely," she'd say. "That's what it is, you know. You live in that big city by yourself and you're having a hard time finding a direction." She'd touch his hair, push it gently back from his brow. For a long time, they'd stay like that, in the dark, in silence.

"Whatever's missing in your life," she'd say at last, "whatever that is, you're not going to get it from her."

O'Neil wasn't sure that she would say this, of course. It was possible that his parents would be encouraging. Maybe, if he'd tried to explain his reasons to them, they would have nodded sympathetically. "Do you know what I mean?" O'Neil would ask them, and they would say, "Yes, we understand, we support you." But even then, the other conversation, the negative one he'd imagined, would be right there beneath the surface. After all, the questions he put in their mouths were the same ones he'd been asking himself all along.

He walked back out to the phone booth. None of those imaginary conversations mattered, O'Neil told himself. He was here now, there was no turning back. He was going to talk to her, see her, and after that, maybe all the answers would fall into place.

He felt light-headed. Out in the distance, semis and cars nudged toward the exit, the interstate underlined the flat stretch of horizon. For a long while he just stood there in the glass box, his hand on the phone. As he watched, the lines of wheel tracks, the dots of footprints casually disappeared in the accumulating snow. His hands felt disembodied when he dialed the number.

O'Neil had imagined that this moment would be dizzying, that the air would hum with electricity. But the phone seemed to ring and ring, and the air seemed suddenly thin, and his stomach tightened as if he'd been running a long ways. At last he heard the receiver being lifted. And then her voice, tired, somewhat impatient, said: "Hello?"

"Hello," O'Neil murmured. "It's me. I'm calling to find out if you received the rose I sent you." His voice sounded as he imagined hers would, soft and sensual.

There was a long pause. All O'Neil could hear was an echoing hallway of static through the wire, muffled voices and computer sounds mumbling as if from behind shut doors. He gripped the telephone tightly, could feel his body straining forward as if he could somehow catch hold of her words and pull them to himself. "Yes," she said finally. "Yes. I received it."

"Did you like it?" he whispered. His heart was pounding. In his mind he was already rushing through the conversation, exchanging life histories and breathless, emotional phrases. He thought of her hands, shaking right now as his were.

"It was nice," she said. She cleared her throat at the same time O'Neil did, and he laughed a little, because they thought alike, they really were alike.

"Really?" O'Neil breathed. "I thought you'd like it. I knew you would." He was unrehearsed, speaking quickly, and he sensed himself picking up momentum. But before he could continue, she sighed heavily.

"Listen," she said, as if O'Neil were an eager salesman and she wished he'd come to the point. "What do you want? Why are you calling me?" She spoke stiffly, and the half-swoon he'd been in dropped away. He was intruding.

"I want to meet you," O'Neil said at last, and she nearly cut him off.

"But I don't want to meet you," she said. "I don't want to correspond with you, I don't want to know about you." Her voice sharpened and grew more deliberate as she spoke. "I'm sure you're a very fine person, very smart, very nice, very handsome. I'd be proud of you. But I don't want to know you."

O'Neil opened his mouth. "Please," he said, and his throat tightened, "I'm here. I came here to meet you." Outside, things were beginning to distort and double and he wiped his hand across his eyes. "What if we just met once? Then I'll be gone away and I won't bother you. I won't call you anymore. I just want to see you, we don't even have to talk."

"What good would that do?" she said flatly. It was what O'Neil always thought his other parents would say, and he felt the question sink heavily inside him. He sighed into the phone, the sound amplified, huge against the mouthpiece.

"I don't know," he said. He paused, but she made no sound. He thought he could hear her breathing. "I want to just because you're my mother."

"I'm not though," she said. "I'm just someone who made a mistake a long time ago. And I've been punished enough for it, I think."

O'Neil didn't say anything—he couldn't speak. And after a long silence she said: "I'm going to hang up now. I'm really very sorry."

"Wait!" O'Neil blurted out. "I've come a long way. I'm here now. Couldn't I just see you from a distance? Couldn't I maybe stand outside your house, or across the street, and then you could step outside for a minute. A minute."

"Don't come near my house," she said sharply. "You're not listening to me. No."

do you know what i mean? 145

"Please," he said, and he could hear himself repeating, softly, anything to keep her on the line, "Please please please. I don't want to cause problems. You understand, don't you? What could it hurt?"

There was no sound coming from the phone, and for a moment O'Neil thought she'd hung up. Then he heard her sigh. "Look," he said. "What about this. I'm at the bus station now. I'll stay here, I won't come to your house if you'll promise me. If you could just walk by–walk by here and give me some sign so I know it's you. You wouldn't have to see me at all. You wouldn't even have to look at me."

"Why are you doing this?" she said tiredly.

"What can it matter to you," he said; his voice had hardened. "Just to walk by? It would mean everything to me." She was silent. "Is that really too much to ask? In the next hour or so. I'll be in the window of the café. Walk by and just wave, so I know. Then I wouldn't have any reason to go to your house."

"Don't come to this house," she said.

"I won't," O'Neil said. "If you'll just do this for me, you'll never hear from me again." And then he startled himself, the coldness that crept into his own voice. "But if you won't," he whispered. "I'll have to come to you."

She was silent. Dead air.

"Will you do that," O'Neil said. "Mother?"

That word felt poisonous as it left his mouth. There was something ugly about the way he said it, he thought, though he had once practiced whispering it, the exact right inflections, the exact right moment. It seemed to stun her.

"All right," she said. She was frightened now, O'Neil thought, and he felt her doubt in the space between words.

"All right," she said, and hung up.

He didn't know whether to trust her, but for her sake, as well as his own, he waited. He told himself that if she didn't come, he'd go straight to her house, he'd bang on the door. He'd force her to call the police. The thought surprised him a little. He hadn't realized how close he was to the bottom of his life.

Still, he couldn't believe that she really wouldn't come. She had to be curious, deep down, even if he was a "mistake." O'Neil thought of her, at twenty, at thirty, the years passing. Childless, watching toddlers in the park, the bright parkas the color of balloons, looking away as the mothers caught her staring. He pictured her, alone for years now, listening to the creak and groan of an empty house, mumbling to herself. Or flipping through an old photo album, a picture of herself as a child, her round face gazing solemnly at the photographer. She must think of that child she gave up. It would only be natural.

It stopped snowing, and the temperature began to drop. O'Neil went inside again, and took a seat near the window. The waitress came up at last.

"Help you?" she said sternly.

He looked up at her. Sometimes it seemed so attractive, that phrase–may I help you?–and he wondered what people would do if someone took them seriously, if someone really needed help. "Coffee, please," O'Neil said, and she wrote it glumly on her pad.

"That be all?"

"Yes." She reached down to turn over the cup on his table, and her hand brushed his. It gave him a funny feeling: sometimes it was easy to forget that there are other people thinking thoughts, maybe off in some daydream like you. All those minds, talking in people's heads. And when you feel their skin on yours, you realize it. That was what O'Neil thought.

He waited. After a while, the waitress stopped filling his cup, and still he just sat there, his hands shaky, his mind whirring. There weren't very many people at the café by that time, and whenever someone approached, his body tensed. He waited for a sign as they rounded the corner, each one a possibility at first, not even the most unlikely could be easily discarded. He stared as an old lady in a scarf hurried past; stretched forward when a red-haired girl in a cowboy hat came sidling along, on the arm of a wiry, squinting man. O'Neil watched them take a booth at the back of the café. The girl leaned over the table to whisper things to her companion. No—too old, too young, not right in some way. In the end, O'Neil knew that when she passed, he'd be certain.

Almost two hours had gone by when he finally saw her. He was staring impatiently at the face of his watch. Outside, the red taillights of cars were tiny points.

Then he caught sight of the woman. She came around the side of the building and entered the lighted area outside the café, hesitantly, in a bright blue ski coat and a red stocking cap. He saw the cap first, bright and forlorn against the white-and-black landscape, melting out of the darkness. The figure appeared on the edge of the circle of light, stopping once, looking back, as if she'd forgotten something.

He sat up straight. As he watched, she walked toward the café, toward the window I was staring from, flirtatiously slow, as if coming into a spotlight.

When at last O'Neil could see her face, she stopped. She looked around, scanning the area, her breath coming from her mouth like smoke in the cold night air. She turned her head, gazing one direction, then another. As if hypnotized, she lifted her hand. It was long and pale in the fluorescent light. She pulled off her cap as if drawing back a veil, and the dark hair spilled out, falling over her shoulders, black hair like O'Neil's, that shiny jet color he'd always felt conscious of, adopted into a family of blondes. Perhaps she looked like him too, though in the bright light her features were cold and white as bone, a gaunt face, her lips tight and expressionless. She stared at the place where he was sitting, her eyes both tired and critical. "Careworn" was the word that came to him, a word his adoptive mother might have used. But that wasn't right, exactly—they were the kind of eyes that might stare back at you in the mirror, if you could judge yourself truly enough.

And then he realized. She saw her own reflection in the window he was staring from. She posed, unself-consciously, brushed her hair with her fingers. It was her: he could feel a coldness rippling over him when she cocked her head and tried on a brief smile.

Then she turned away from him, spun on her heel and began walking, trailing that electricity behind her, into the dark.

Without thinking, O'Neil ran after her. He left his coat in the booth, ignoring the waitress who yelled after him: "Hey! You haven't paid your tab!" O'Neil brushed past her as she tried to block his exit, digging a five from his pocket and pressing it into her hand. "Thanks a lot," she said, but he pushed on. He hit the door and the cold air came rushing over him like a premonition. She was already yards ahead.

"Hey!" he called, but she did not turn. "Hey!" He began to run toward her. She whirled, as if frightened, and for a moment their eyes met. She was looking at him, though there was no telling what was registering, really—his clothes? his expression? Did she see him as he appeared to himself in the mirror? Who did she see?

She took a step backward. "Are you talking to me?" she said. Her voice was careful, uninterested.

"I love you," O'Neil said. He started to shiver, his arms cringing from the cold. "I wanted you to know that I love you." His breath came out in foggy gasps, curling out into the night air.

She seemed taken aback—her eyes slanted, and her mouth hardened as she appraised him. It was the face of a bureaucrat, he thought, someone whose job was to turn people away for eight hours a day, the kind of person he'd dealt with all the time when he was searching for her. That was what was in her face. She looked him up and down, and then abruptly gave a sort of sighing laugh, as if dismissing him.

"Oh, get lost," she said. "What are you, crazy? Get lost."

"I love you," O'Neil said again, but the words felt wrong, too small in his throat. She was backing away from him, and he put out his hand. His fingers brushed the slick material of her coat. She screamed.

The cry filled up the empty parking lot, ringing, echoing off the side of the building like a shot. She jerked away, but O'Neil's fingers held to her coat. They swayed: for a second it seemed to O'Neil as if they could have been dancing, held there in stasis. Her eyes widened, and he could sense how thin her body was beneath the heavy coat, sinew, muscle twisting. Her arms flailed, and she screamed again: "Let go! Let go!" The dark hair whipped from side to side. The streams of their breath twined together. He tried to catch at her hands as they flew.

"Hey!" he heard a man's voice shout. O'Neil turned in time to see a short wiry man striding toward him, cowboy boots crunching on the frozen gravel. O'Neil recognized him as the man he'd watched coming into the café. The man's girlfriend, the one in the cowboy hat, was standing off by the door.

"This man bothering you, Miss?" the man said loudly. He put his hand on O'Neil's shoulder, clenching, and she pulled free.

But she didn't answer him. She just nodded her head vaguely, still backing away. O'Neil didn't know what was in her expression, but she didn't blink as she looked at him, and he imagined a softness wavering there for a moment, pity or a kind of apology. He knew from the way she took him in that she wanted to remember his face.

"Son," the man said, "I think you'd better move on

your way." He spoke firmly, and his hand tightened on O'Neil's shoulder. "Tell the lady you're sorry," he said. He gave O'Neil a little shake.

"I'm sorry," O'Neil said, but his voice was hoarse and barely audible. He looked down at his feet, trying to keep himself from shivering, and when he lifted his head, she was already moving away, she had turned and was walking fast, faster, almost running. And then she was gone, vanished into the darkened parking lot. He heard the slam of a car door, the grinding of a key in the ignition. Wheels turned in the slush and gravel.

The man released his grip on O'Neil's shoulder, but O'Neil didn't move. The cowboy observed him, squinting at his face, then shook his head. "You're going to catch cold, son," he said. "You better go on back inside, and don't bother people no more."

O'Neil couldn't say anything. He just stood there, staring out at the rows of snow-covered cars, the glitter of half-revealed chrome winking like eyes, glinting. His mind blurred. And then he heard footsteps as the man, too, walked away. The tips of O'Neil's ears and his fingers ached sharply from the cold.

A little after midnight the bus came. O'Neil stood among others in the snow and waited. They were in a group, each of them facing a slightly different direction. They braced against the wind as the bus doors hissed open.

O'Neil left home on a bus, going east for the first time. For hours he could feel the place on his back where his adoptive mother had put her hand when they hugged goodbye. He'd sat there, watching cars and farmhouses pass, wondering whether the people inside them could sense him, O'Neil, out beyond the range of their living rooms and pickups. He was out there thinking of them, and they would never know the difference.

He stumbled down the aisle of the bus, holding

onto the seats for balance. Searching for a seat, O'Neil hovered over the faces of old women, their coats draped like blankets over them, children curled into balls. And for a moment he paused, standing over the form of a sleeping woman, and he leaned over her, seeing how her feet were tucked under her, how her hair hung loose over her face. Slowly, he held out his hand. He could feel her breath, and for one second he just stared down at those eyes closed tight, the motionless lips; and he touched her wrist.

dread

That summer, just before my father began chemotherapy, I took the bus to Chicago. No one said, "You're leaving just when he needs you most." My brother, Alex, told me, "You've done enough already. You need to get away. This is the best thing for everyone." My father said, "Don't worry. Things will be fine. I've got your mother to look after me."

I'd been living at home for quite a while, helping our parents get the house and farm in shape to sell. They were going to retire and move to Sun City, Arizona. When I suggested that I could spend a few months with my brother and his wife, everyone seemed to think it was a good idea.

I had a job waiting for me. My sister-in-law, Nora, was a supervisor at a small telemarketing firm, and she said she thought I had a good phone voice. Alex was an opera singer. He'd just had his first big break, a part in the chorus of *Tannhäuser* at the Lyric; he'd been attending rehearsals five nights a week since April and giving voice lessons during the day.

As for me, I'd done nothing much since I dropped out of the local community college a few years before. I followed my father on his old rounds, checking fences, lifting bales of alfalfa, helping him decide on good resale prices for his equipment. After the first auction at our house I helped him pack things away. I sat on the floor with my mother, wrapping jars in newspaper, listening to her talk about canning, imagining her hands filling the jars, a sieve raised from a steamy pot. I watched TV with them, ignoring the calls of our horse, made skittish by the auction of the rest, trying not to hear its cries of fear or pain. I recalled my father's fist, knocking against its muzzle. He had it by the harness, and it reared as he tried to calm it. He struck it twice, glancing around in shame at the staring people.

It was one of the few times I'd seen him lose control, and I couldn't help but think of it as the bus pulled away. I stared at my mirror image in the window. Behind my reflection, the wheat fields were black, spreading out like empty, starless space.

Every day that summer I woke to the sound of my brother singing. Some mornings, his voice would be soft, the rising scales fingering into my dreams and transformed—into the call of a bird, or my father's laugh, or a sudden fall that startled me awake. Other mornings, especially when Nora was gone for the day, his voice was loud as an alarm. I thought maybe he sounded a little happier too. I could tell by the sound of his voice that we were going to meet Theodora Redding that day.

Alex had been meeting this woman in secret for some time. He told me about it shortly after I arrived, and I still wasn't sure whether it could really be classified as an affair. He'd slept with the woman once. But, Alex explained, he was drunk at the time, and now he and the woman were just friends. He still loved Nora, he said.

I wasn't sure how I was supposed to react. I could see he wanted to shock me. He watched my eyes, his head nodding vaguely as if to some metronome in his mind. But I just shrugged. I didn't want to seem like the stiff he'd always accused me of being. I often hoped that I could become a different person, that I could erase or cover over what I'd once been, whatever it was. Look at Alex, I told myself. We were from the same place, but he had sophisticated himself; he could talk to anyone with ease. He could see himself without being embarrassed. But when I woke up, half the time I wasn't even sure where I was, let alone who. It was as if I was rising from anesthesia to an unfamiliar hospital room. I was a blank space, waiting to be filled in.

So I would wear Alex's clothes. He must have had fifty sweaters, arranged chromatically: stippled heather, Oxford gray angora, thin cotton summer sweaters of magenta, turquoise, ivory. We'd wear these sweaters and a pair of knee-length shorts. We looked like men of leisure, I thought, pausing before the next game of tennis. Sometimes, passing a mirror, we put our chins to our fists, posing like male models.

Three days a week Nora went to work early, and on these days Alex and I went places. We browsed the expensive men's stores on Michigan Avenue, pretending we could afford to buy ties that cost nearly a hundred dollars. Before Alex got me a fake ID, we dressed up in coat and tie and went to bars in hotels, where they'd serve anyone who looked arrogant enough. We drank Manhattans, imagining that people were watching and wondering how rich we were.

Other times, Alex would take me to places I think were meant to frighten me, streets where there were a lot of punks or gays or bums. But I always kept my eyes straight ahead, nodding briefly at the hairless girl in the doorway who was watching us pass, looking in a storefront window as two men kissed nearby. There were moments when Alex and I were walking–gliding through wide hotel foyers or standing under certain skyscrapers that reflected the sky, a rippling metallic blue; or in a crowd in the rain, moving briskly through a cave of umbrellas, not daring to slow down–I'd become actually dizzy with the wonder and excitement of it. I'd slow, imagining I was walking through the opening credits of a film. It was as if I'd glimpsed, for an instant, the other person I hoped to become.

dread 155

Most mornings, though, we ended up in the little bookstore and coffee shop next door to our building. It was called Ennui, which Alex thought was very funny. We got flavored coffees or espresso or some other exotic drink I'd never heard of, and just sat by the window. We liked to watch the fashionable women pass outside. The ones we admired the most were bohemians, with wild hair and long earrings in shapes of peace signs, snakes, moons. Their thin, hard bodies slid mysteriously in oversized clothes.

Theodora was that bohemian type. Inevitably, she'd show up at Ennui after we sat there for a while. She worked at the Lyric in the advertising department. Alex had met her at a party for the opera people.

The first time I met Theodora, I thought she'd been crying. Ever afterward, when I remembered her, I'd think of that aura of secret melancholy that trailed her, the way she seemed on the verge of telling you something heartbreaking. The pauses in conversation would draw out, crackling with concealed energy. I imagined sitting with her on the shore of a lake, the sound of oars treading depthless water.

Year later, when I'd become more jaded myself, I would come to realize that she'd perfected a pose. I saw her as a recognizable type–but by then I'd become a sort of Theodora myself, staring too long after people asked me questions, looking away when I finally spoke. Maybe Theodora was truly in love.

I was never quite sure what was going on. Mostly they talked about opera things, gossiping about their co-workers, the seedy details of self-destructive divas. They joked about an English translation of *La Bohème* where someone sang, "A muff! A pretty muff!" Alex could make her laugh just by whispering a line from *Turn of the Screw:* "My dear," he sang softly, "you look so white . . . and queer. What happened? Wha-a-at happened?" I sat there, smiling, shifting a little. It was as if they spoke in code. It reminded me, somehow, of the way we spoke to my father. We joked, teased, orbiting around and around his sickness and our own dread–pretending, as Alex and Theodora did, that everything was normal.

After lunch, Alex and I started our day. Alex gave voice lessons in the afternoon before rehearsal, and I went downtown to Stars Telemarketing, where I worked from one in the afternoon until nine at night.

The El train came rising up out of the distance and into the station. It shuffled the light between its windows, bearing down on us. The reflection of our faces, gray poker stares, finally slowed to a halt, like a wheel of fortune, with the mask of my own face directly in front of me. It always surprised me.

I worked on the twenty-ninth floor of a skyscraper. At first it made me nervous to crowd into the elevator. I hated the way the numbers chimed upward, like a machine measuring heartbeats. But I grew used to it. The office for Stars was really just a room, a cluster of tables with phones on them. There were twenty-five of us–students, housewives, unemployed construction workers and so forth. We were paid to sell women's undergarments over the phone. We dialed numbers from a computer-generated list. "Is the lady of the house in?" we asked, and then we read a salespitch off our cue cards. "Extra large?" we were supposed to say cheerfully. "All the more of you to love!"

Nora was our supervisor, responsible for keeping us positive, ensuring that we made as many calls as we could, watching to prevent private calls. She was beautiful. She marched through the aisles in her high heels, her blonde, blunt-cut hair bobbing. She waved her arms like a cheerleader for big sales, gave out prizes of jellybeans, buttons that said, "I'm the BEST, just ask me!" She scolded a towering forty-year-old bricklayer: "Come on Roy! Get with it! Let's hear some excitement! These are lonely homemakers you're talking to, so use that deep male voice. Seduce them!"

I thought Nora liked to believe that her callers loved her. She joked with the middle-aged men, calling them "honey" and "darling." Some of the women brought her gifts, like cookies or things they'd crocheted. But the fact was, Nora told me, few people lasted a month. Some just vanished. Most people, she said, just couldn't stand the rejection.

Still, she'd never fired anyone. Even Roy, who was always late, who sometimes called in sick at the last moment. "Roy," she'd say, "you're putting me in a bind. Promise you'll try harder." The truth was, the only person who'd been there longer than six months was a young black woman named JoAnn, who cursed at people who didn't order from her. "Sugar," I'd heard her say, "you can shove it up your ass." Nora ignored this, just as she let me continue on, sometimes not making a sale for days. At times I found myself just sitting there, moving my lips, pretending to give my pitch, listening to the hum of the dial tone and thinking of my father.

And I'd watch her. Sometimes I'd think of Alex and Theodora, whispering over the phone. Alex hardened his voice to monosyllables if Nora passed nearby. The thought of it ached inside me, spreading silently. Nora looked so innocent. As we were lining up to punch out, the sight of her sent a dull throb through my arms and legs. She'd slipped off her heels and was sitting cross-legged on her chair, rubbing the soles of her feet with her thumbs. Her hair made a tent around her face. I thought that life was sad for her, even if she didn't know it yet.

I usually called my parents when Nora and I got home from work. Alex didn't think it was such a good idea. "What's going to change in a day, for Christ's sake," he said. "You just get yourself all worked up and depressed." But I couldn't help it. I wanted to do things, to enjoy my life while I was still young and single, like Alex said. "You're not doing Dad any good by moping around," he told me. But thoughts of my father seemed to shadow me everywhere.

Once I walked into the apartment and Alex and Nora were sitting on the sofa. For a moment, I thought Alex was crying. They were hugging and their voices were low. I thought something terrible had happened to my father. And then I realized that it wasn't sadness: they were kissing, nuzzling each other.

But Alex was right. Nothing much changed from day to day. That night, Dad was still too sick from his second session of chemo to talk to me.

"He can't keep anything down," my mother told me. "He's slept most of the day. I'm just sitting here, reading a book. I hate to go back to the motel." They were in a hospital in Denver, and my mother was afraid to go out after dark. It was a bad neighborhood, she said. She'd seen people lying in alleyways, and once, a man with one leg had limped along behind her for blocks, his crutch thumping, calling, "Lady! Can you do me a favor?" Now, my mother had one of the security guards escort her to her room. He was a veteran, she said, and he'd offer her his elbow to lean on.

Everyone else seemed to know what to do. Nora was able to flirt with my father over the phone, talking about anything but his illness. She made him laugh. Alex would send comic, slightly off-color get well cards or flowers, the little things I wished I'd thought of. I just kept calling without anything to say—I'd pause, the sound of throat clearing would go tipping end over end through the wire like an asteroid. Then I'd say something stupid. "So what's new?" I'd ask, and feel myself pulling back, distant, just a tiny speck.

I remembered when we first found out, and my father had surgery. I sat in the hospital room on the radiator. I could see the entire room's reflection in the big picture window. My mother and father and the furniture were like pieces of colored glass, and I saw the outdoors through them: the dark boughs of treetops through my father's white bed, tossing across his hands and face; the parking lot through my own head and chest. "You're looking good," I said. I put my hand on the blanket, right by his fingers: waiting, motionless.

The three of us went out to bars when Alex got home from rehearsal. There was a strip of them a few blocks from our apartment, on the other side of the El tracks. They all had different themes: fifties, new wave, jazz–and it often seemed like they were full of the same people in different costumes. The place Alex liked best was a blues bar called Fibber McGee's. Once, drunk, he'd sung so loudly and soulfully that Koko Taylor had pointed the microphone at him for a moment. "She's the queen bee," Alex wailed, and Koko took it from there.

The way we walked was always the hardest part. Sometimes we'd walk single file down the street, and I thought this was really the most honest way, when we were like small planets, each in our own circles, millions of miles of space in between. Other times, when we were happy and the sidewalks were clear, we could all walk together, three across, and I would almost always be in the middle, my arms around both their shoulders. Otherwise, the two of them went on and I walked in front, always turning to make sure they hadn't disappeared, or in back, dragging after them like a beggar.

It was Tuesday night, so there was no band at Fibber's. Nora said she was grateful. She had a headache, she said. We had the place almost to ourselves, a dark corner by the window where we could see the El passing on its high tracks. I liked to try to make out the silhouettes of people framed in each window of the train.

Alex got a pitcher of beer and set it down in front of me, trying, I guess, to turn my attention from the window. Alex hated it when he thought people weren't paying attention. "Liquid cheer," he said. "That means you, Buster."

Alex and Nora were always trying to perk me up, even when I felt happy. They'd sit on either side of me, doting—correcting the slump of my shoulders or the way my hair fell over my forehead. "What's wrong?" they'd ask, even when I was smiling. They were very concerned about my love life.

In the beginning I tried to explain that finding a girlfriend wasn't the first thing on my mind. I told them I'd always believed that when the right girl came along, I'd know it, and I'd always expected, someday, to marry. But Alex said I had to get out there and work at it. So I tried to play along. Nora would tilt her head toward a girl I was watching on the dance floor, whispering "She's good-looking, isn't she, honey?" and I'd have to nod and agree. On weekends, they took me to singles bars and abandoned me, hurrying off to the dance floor. I guess they hoped they'd come back and find me locked in deep conversation or a passionate kiss, instead of alone, turning my drink nervously in my hand. I felt, I told Alex once, like a horse taken to a stable to breed.

But Alex would look at me as if I hadn't understood him. The more he drank at these bars, the more insistent he became. His grin grew rigid, and he'd begin stopping women who passed us, pointing at me: "This guy thinks you're really sexy and he wants to dance with you." Sometimes these women were dazzled by Alex and they'd sit down, exchanging phrases like punchlines. When this happened, Nora and Alex kept trying to turn the conversation back to me. "Oh, Josh does a really hilarious imitation of a blues singer. Do your imitation of the blues, Josh. Come on." Alex and Nora leaned forward, but the girl was always as annoyed and impatient as the women I called at work.

When Theodora Redding walked into the bar that

night, I was the first to notice her. Alex had invited this red-haired girl, Jennifer, to sit in the empty seat beside me, and now he was busy trying to convince her that he was really an opera singer. "No way!" Jennifer kept saying. She looked at Nora and wrinkled her nose, hoping for an ally. "You guys are pulling my leg, right?" So Alex was trying to sing from Wagner, holding his hand over one ear to block out the sound of the jukebox. "Come off it!" Jennifer said. "That sounds so fake! Anybody can sing like that." But Alex kept on singing.

That was when I saw Theodora. She had come through the door, and she seemed to tense suddenly, like a woman who heard footsteps in an empty parking lot. I imagined she had picked up the hint of his voice, an undercurrent wavering below the smoke and the murmur of voices and the blues from the jukebox.

Then she spotted us. For a moment I wondered if I might prevent her from seeing us if I looked quickly away, or put my hand in front of my face. But I didn't. Our eyes met, and Theodora and I stared at each other blankly. Finally I raised my hand a little, in greeting I guess, and Theodora looked from me to Alex to Jennifer and at last to Nora.

As she began to walk over, I could feel my pulse beating under the pads of my fingers. I didn't want Nora to look at me. I had the sensation, as I often did back then, that people could read my mind, that every expression and gesture telegraphed my most intimate secrets. But Nora was watching Alex sing, and when Alex glanced up and saw Theodora, no one could tell what he was thinking. His face was set in that stiff smile, as if her were posed for a photograph. "Well," he said. "Theodora. Hello!" And he introduced her around. "Theodora works at the Lyric," he told us. "In the advertising department, isn't that right? I'm sorry I don't remember your last name."

"Redding," Theodora said softly. She glanced at me, and for a moment I thought I could picture the type of person she used to be, once–that she'd once felt self-conscious about her freckles and been overly vain about her long, awkward neck, that all through high school she wore an expression that suggested she was nauseated, even when she was trying to smile. Like me, she had dreamed of becoming a different person–or so I imagined when our eyes met.

"So," said Theodora at last. Alex was pouring himself more beer, and Jennifer was staring at her with frank dislike. Theodora seemed to waver there.

"Well, pull up a chair," said Nora warmly. She scooted to one side so Theodora could squeeze in beside me, and she gave me a quick smile. It sent a hollow feeling fingering through my stomach, because I knew what she was going to say when Theodora left. "Wasn't she nice, Josh? She seemed really interesting."

The first time I met Nora I was surprised that my brother had married her. I expected, somehow, a quiet girl, admiring of him–repeating the last words of his sentences and nodding the way I sometimes did when he got to talking; when he was, as he said, on a roll. I could remember the day of the family reunion, when I'd only known her for a short time. The three of us sat around the keg in lawn chairs, talking in low tones. Everything we said seemed like a secret told in confidence. We all called each other "Pie." And I remembered how she touched my wrist, and that she smelled sweet, like lotion. "Pie," she said. "Your eyes are truly green. I've never known anyone with truly green eyes before." I felt like I could tell her anything.

Or I remembered the time when we'd been out late, and we'd gone down to the lake to watch the sun rise. Alex had passed out on the beach, and Nora and

I were walking a few yards down, picking brown, mossy clam shells out of the water, brushing the sand and mud from them. The sun was coming up in the distance, a pink line that, at last, showed where the sky ended and the water began.

"You know," Nora told me as we stared at our shells. "You know, someday you will find that right person, and then you'll understand."

"Understand what?" I said.

She shrugged, and then she put her palm against my fingers. "I just feel like you need somebody," she said softly. "Aren't you ever lonely, Pie? Aren't you ever lonely?"

That's what I'd think about late at night. When everything was quiet and the air was cool, I liked to go walking. I'd do it when we got back from the bars, after Alex and Nora were asleep, walking to calm myself, to work the alcohol out of my blood. I tried not to be afraid of the city. I tried to believe that the world was a gentle place. Near the lake, the dampness and fog would hang in the air like incense. Once, I'd stepped into Sheridan Road without looking, and a car had to stop. There was no screech of brakes, I wasn't in front of them. I suppose they just wanted to make sure that I passed safely. The headlights blurred to dazzles as I looked into them, and the person in the driver's seat was just a shadow, a darker spot in the dark car. I peered through the brightness, smiling, and lifted my arm, giving the person a wave, a salute, as if we'd shared something.

Alex and Nora were both asleep when I came back in. They were sitting on the couch, heads thrown back, mouths open. The TV was on.

I just looked at them for a moment. I thought someone ought to take their picture, that there ought to be a way to freeze time before anything happened. And then I went over to them, slipped in between them on the couch, and they didn't stir.

"I didn't invite her," Alex said to me. "What do you think, I'm crazy? She just happened to come in. An accident."

What I wanted to say was that I didn't want to see him wreck his marriage, that I felt bad for Nora, that she trusted him so much. But I didn't want to seem judgmental.

"I was as surprised to see her as you were," Alex said.

We were walking along the shore of Belmont Harbor, looking out at Lake Michigan. The shoreline was walled with a jumble of cement, like pieces of broken sidewalk, and we stepped from one slab to the other. People had spray-painted the flat surfaces—mottos, names enclosed in hearts.

"Sometimes I think you and Nora need more time to yourselves," I said. "I don't want to get in the way."

"You're not."

"I just don't want to be a pest."

"Then forget it," he said. "We don't need any more time alone together." He picked up a beer bottle from between the cracks in the rocks and tossed it into the water. "Theodora really thinks the world of you, you know."

"What are you trying to do," I said. "Pass her off on me?" He stared out at the water, and we were silent for a while. Up on the sidewalk that traced the shore, a jogger went by; the air was full of bird sounds, gulls maybe.

"You're a virgin, aren't you?" Alex said at last. He turned to me expectantly.

"Of course not," I said. I didn't want him to see my eyes, though. I felt too transparent.

Actually, there were a lot of good reasons why I was almost twenty years old and had never slept with anyone. I couldn't stand the idea of being with someone I couldn't trust, for one thing, someone who

dread 165

might change her mind about me, joke about me later, or grow bored. Besides, I hadn't met anyone. But I didn't think it was any of his business. I didn't expect Alex to understand it, any more than he understood why I'd dropped out of college, or why I'd lived at home afterward. He thought I should have the same things he had: plans, confidence, a future. But I couldn't figure out how he'd been able to decide—I'll be an opera singer, marry Nora, live in Chicago in this particular apartment, and on and on. When I left home at the beginning of the summer, Alex told me, "It's the best thing you could've done," but deep down I knew it was the most terrible thing I'd done in my entire life.

"I've slept with lots of people," I said.

"Who?" said Alex. "When?"

"I don't think that's any of your business."

"Come on."

"Give me a break, Alex," I said. "I know what you think. You think I'm pathetic, don't you? Well, I'm not. I'm happy the way I am."

Alex sat down on a rock, but I just stood there, looking down at his hair. It wasn't moving in the wind, and I thought about how he joked about it—"I mousse that sucker till a blowtorch wouldn't ruffle it." He could make even his ridiculous vanity seem charming.

"Look," he said at last. "We're just worried about you. You seem so down. Half the time it's like you're not even in your body. I'll look at you, and you'll just be this blank."

"Nothing's wrong with me," I said, but Alex just shrugged. He took out his keys and ran them along the asphalt, as if carving something there. "I'm upset, that's all." I said. "I'm worried about Dad. I think I should be home."

Alex sighed. "We're all upset. I am too. I'll tell you something. Some days I walk around and I feel like I'm in a trance. I'll get worked up over the smallest thing, and then I won't even know why I'm feeling so crazy. But you've got to believe and trust that everything will be all right. What else can you do? I'm not trying to be harsh, but what good are you doing Dad when you're moping around his hospital room? Christ, Josh. The way you were acting had Mom and Dad more upset than anything else. They didn't know what to do with you." He shook his head. "You've got to take responsibility for your own life first. If you can't help yourself, what good are you going to be to other people?"

I didn't say anything. The wind was coming up, sliding back toward the trees, the streets, the high buildings with their rows of black windows.

Nora came to my table to tell me that Alex had called. He'd told her that he and some of the chorus people were going out after the rehearsal for drinks, and that they'd probably be out late. JoAnn was sitting next to me, listening. She winked at Nora. "You better keep your eye on that dog," she said.

"Don't worry," Nora said. "He's on a short leash." I watched them both laugh.

After that, I couldn't concentrate. I dialed the numbers, I spoke my rote to the tired, impatient voices, barely hearing them through the static on the line. Nora marked our sales totals on the blackboard, then turned, smiling, breezy. "Let's get a head start on that weekly goal!" she called. "Only a few thousand dollars more! Keep pushing!"

It was how happy she looked. I kept thinking of my parents, the day they spent looking over pamphlets of villas with swimming pools and game rooms, the way my father said "Sun City," relishing the sound of it. I bent to my list of phone numbers, but I couldn't quit glancing at her. I knew, suddenly, that Alex had been going out with Theodora all along. I told myself that people don't accidentally run into each other in bars when you're in a big city. I realized that he was probably still having sex with Theodora, no matter what he said about it being just that once, about them being only friends.

After we'd punched out, and I sat waiting for Nora, I couldn't stand how unaware she was. Alex seemed so evil to me at that moment. Nora stood on tiptoe to erase the blackboard. She straightened the papers on her desk, made a note in her pocket calendar. When she looked up she raised her eyebrows and smiled, surprised, I guessed, to see me staring at her.

"Do you want to go out for some drinks anyhow?" she said.

"Sure." I turned to the empty room before she flicked off the lights and locked up. I imagined them all ringing, late at night, some ghostly wrong number that would never be answered.

We were in Fibber McGee's again, and I was drinking more than usual. Later, that would be my excuse. The more beers I had, the stranger things seemed. When I got up to go to the bathroom, the shadows seemed to shift. I thought people sitting next to us were listening in on our conversation. And Nora kept turning the topic back to Alex. "I think he's more upset about your father than he lets on," she said. "I woke up one night, and he was crying in his sleep. He's gotten so temperamental."

I finished my beer, and for a moment it felt like my chair was dropping away. I wondered why she kept talking about him. "Huh," I said.

"I wish he wouldn't keep it bottled up inside," she said.

"I wouldn't worry about it," I said. "Alex can take care of himself."

"I don't know, Pie. I think he's really upset."

I don't think he's so upset about Dad," I said. "I think it's other things."

"Like what?"

I wiped my forearm through the rings of condensation my glass had left on the table. I kept my eyes closed, hoping the wetness on my skin, the air conditioning evaporating it away, might calm me. "Oh, I don't know really," I said. "I'm just babbling. Alex is Alex." I lifted the pitcher. "More beer?"

"I'm fine right now, thanks."

I filled my glass carefully, but when I lifted it, there was a small spreading pool of beer next to my glass. I put my hand on it and smoothed it across the table. Music was drifting heavily from the jukebox, and I nodded my head. "I love this song."

She smiled faintly, nodding with me in rhythm, as if we were playing a mime game. I could tell she wasn't listening to the song. She was looking into my eyes.

"Does he talk to you, Josh? Does he confide in you?"

"Not really," I said. "Not exactly." I took a drink and the room swelled forward, like the light from a camera flash. I squeezed my eyes shut, and when I opened them, Nora sighed. "Look," I said. "I'd rather not talk about it, okay?"

"What?" she said. "What don't you want to talk about?"

"It's, I don't know," I said. I could see her shrinking away from me, like in dreams, the space between us stretching out. "It was something he told me in confidence," I said.

I looked at Nora and I felt as if I could lose control at any moment. That notion came over me often enough, back then. I imagined that I'd have an uncontrollable urge to throw myself in front of an oncoming El train. At work, I sometimes thought that I wouldn't be able to stop myself from leaping up with a shriek and running out the door. But it wasn't only losing control that sent a warm shudder through me. It was also that I imagined, in a second, that I held this power over things, that everything was built on eggshells.

It flashed past me like that, and I was never sure why I didn't stop myself. It was her expectant look. I felt the same rush I'd felt that night at the family reunion, when she touched my wrist. I saw her face tighten; she drew in breath, and for a moment it seemed we shared one thought. She knew what was coming.

I hadn't imagined that she would start crying. I hadn't thought that she would stand, backing away from the table, her face contorted. She went edging away, quicker and quicker, hurrying past people who glanced up and then back to their glasses. She was out the door before I thought to go after her.

I caught up down the sidewalk a ways, calling, "Nora! Please! Nora!" I grabbed her arm. "Don't tell him," I breathed. "Don't say anything to Alex. He still loves you. Oh, I didn't mean to tell. You've got to just forget I said anything. I didn't mean it."

"Josh, how could you think—" she said, and she pulled away from me. "Do you think I can just put this out of my mind?" I snatched at her arms. I could sense the shapes of people passing us on the street, staring. "I won't let him know you told me," she said. "I don't want to ruin . . . I'll just say I found out." I pulled her closer to me, the wetness of her cheek on my arm. I wondered whether I ought to hug her. My hands wavered. "I'm sorry you had to be involved," she whispered. "Oh, he's such a liar. A fake." She started to cry again, and I bent, my lips touching her hair accidentally. "I'm sorry," I said. "I'm sorry." But when I closed my arms around her—to comfort her, I thought—she jerked away. She stared at me and I folded my arms back quickly.

"I'm sorry," I said. "I knew I shouldn't have said it."

"Josh," she said softly, and looked away, to where the orange windows of a passing El were flickering through treetops, in between buildings. "I . . . " she said, and waved her hand faintly, "I've got to go. I've got to think. I need to . . . I need to be by myself."

It was a moment before I even thought to call after her, to say her name, and by that time she was nearly running, her heels clicking faster, the ticking of a clock, a machine set in motion.

I thought that maybe she'd gone back to the apartment. But when I opened the door, the TV was on, and Alex was curled up on the sofa with a glass of wine. "Hey," he said. "Hello. Where's Nora?"

"Out," I said. I stood transfixed, and all I could think to do was pretend that I was very drunk. I wobbled as I walked over to him, stumbling.

"You're kidding," he said. "Out where?" He gave me an amused look. "Jesus," he said. "You're wasted, aren't you?"

I wavered there. "I'm wasted," I said. I couldn't imagine what else to say. My brother put his arms around my shoulders. "Okay, buddy," he whispered. "Let's sit down. That's right. That's right." I tried to pretend that I was being lifted, that I was being wheeled somewhere on a stretcher. When I opened my eyes, I was on the couch. "Christ," Alex said. "I've never seen you like this before. Nora's probably combing the city for you. How much did you drink?" He pushed my hair back from my brow. "Can you hear me," he whispered, and I felt my body shaking. A hum of electricity went down my arms, my legs.

"I'm scared," I said.

My brother put his arms around me then. And I heard, or thought I heard, him tell me that it was all going to be okay. I leaned back and the last thing I remembered was singing–something slow and gentle, like one of those country singers my father used to like so much, the ones whose voices tell you they've seen it all.

ultrasound

Ray Wilson's wife used to be a stripper. But he didn't have a problem with that. He knew that she used to be a lot of things, after she left her first husband, in those distant days before they met. And even though it seemed like the longer they were married, the more he found out—stories of lovers and communes and tarot cards, tales of odd jobs and places she'd hitchhiked through, stretching farther and farther, complex as a map—it never bothered him.

But then, shortly after they found out she was pregnant, she started acting funny. One of the first things that she did was sign up for a course in hypnotism and meditation. She said she thought it might relax her, maybe help her overcome her morning sickness. Besides, she said, she was lonely. She wanted to meet new people.

There was something about that comment that made Ray uneasy. What was wrong with all their old friends, he wondered, the ones they used to go out with on Saturday nights?

When Ray dropped her off at this place on Saturday mornings, he always saw strange-looking people in the window: willowy women with fierce eyes and layers of multicolored scarves and shawls and such; pale, shaggy-headed men not unlike the photos he'd seen of her first husband. He could sense these people peering out through the tie-dye curtains when he pulled up. The whole building looked seedy and disreputable: just a whitewashed cinder-block thing with a hand-painted sign in the window. EAST-WEST CENTER, it said. The place was all the way in the city of Boulder, in a bad section of town—adult bookstores, boarded-up storefronts, headless parking meters. The neighborhood reminded him uncomfortably of what his wife called her "weird years." As he drove home, Ray couldn't help but brood a little.

He'd never really been concerned about it before, but he married young. His wife was several years older than he, and she'd certainly seen a lot more of the world. She had eight years of experiences and adventures that he would probably never get. As he pulled into the driveway, Ray thought of this. The truth was, he thought, he really hadn't done much of interest in his life. He hadn't even slept with anyone before Ann, excepting one awkward time with an old high school girlfriend.

And now he had a baby on the way.

Sometimes, when Ray was alone in the house, he found himself going through her belongings, discovering things he knew the histories or half-histories of. Here was the little cedar jewelry case that her ex-husband had made when he was in detox. Here was a gold pen with her name etched on it, from an elderly accountant she'd slept with in Provo; a business card from Zack, the professional storyteller: "The tales he unfolds will pluck at your imagination and your heartstrings," it said. And here was the thin gold bracelet that some admirer had threaded around her G-string when she was, as she put it, a dancer.

That morning, Ray took the bracelet and threw it away. He put it in a bag and dumped some old left-over spaghetti sauce from the refrigerator on top of it. Then he took the bag out the back door and dropped it in the trash.

He'd thrown out a few of her things before—some old letters and photos—and most of the time, she didn't even miss them. Once, weeks after he'd thrown something out, she'd combed the whole house: where were those earrings, when was the last time she'd seen them, etc. She berated herself for being so absentminded. She was always losing things.

After he'd thrown these things out, he always asked himself: What's wrong with you? What a petty, childish thing to do, he'd think. During the week he'd go and buy her something new, something expensive.

But that day Ray felt especially guilty. She loved that bracelet and eventually she'd miss it. He even thought of going out and digging it out of the spaghetti sauce. But he didn't.

Instead, Ray decided to call his friend Dave. Dave and his wife Linda were the only couple in their group who had a child, so the two of them talked about that quite a bit. When Ray mentioned how odd and moody Ann had been lately, Dave told him not to worry about it. All pregnant women go through such a phase, he said.

But Ray wasn't so sure. He tended to associate her strangeness with these classes she'd been taking. Every time she came out of that place, she seemed more distant. There was something unfamiliar about the way she looked at him. And she'd stopped enjoying all the old, fun things they used to do together. The restaurants made her queasy, the movies made her sad, and she couldn't even bear to sit in a bar. When their friends came over for dinner, she wasn't as talkative or funny as she used to be. She always went to bed early. "Oh, God, I'm so exhausted," she would say after she sat there in a kind of trance for a while, not even listening. "I hope you all don't mind." No, no, they'd say, of course not. They understood completely.

But Ray didn't. He wondered. In retrospect, it seemed that even before she got pregnant she was starting to drift away from their old group. It wasn't that she didn't like them, she'd said once. But she had to admit that she was growing tired of the noisy bars they liked to go to on Saturday nights, where the smoke made her contacts sting and she had to watch young girls making the same stupid mistakes she had made, over and over. She was usually ready to go before midnight. "But you stay," she'd tell Ray. "Don't leave on my account." Later she told him that she guessed her drinking days were finished anyhow. Nowadays, it seemed as if a single beer gave her a hangover. It just didn't seem worth it, she said.

Ray didn't complain to Dave about any of this, of course. He didn't want some rumor to start going around that he and Ann were having problems, or for Linda to start to think that he was a rotten and unsympathetic husband. He knew that was how people would interpret it. So he didn't say anything.

Instead, he talked to Dave about having a little party. At first, he had worried that Ann wouldn't go for it. But she seemed to like the idea. "That sounds nice," she said, with at least a little enthusiasm. Ray slipped his arm around her waist.

"It will do us good," he told her.

So now they were down to the final arrangements, he and Dave. Originally it had just been a dinner party with the members of the old group. But then more people had been added to the list. It looked like there might be over twenty, Ray had recently told Ann, who pursed her lips. And now, actually, Dave seemed to think it might even be more than that. That morning, while Ann was at her class, Ray and Dave debated over the idea of getting a keg.

It was going to be an ultrasound party. Ann was scheduled to have an ultrasound at the clinic on Friday, and the doctor had told her that she would get a picture of the baby. So it would be a celebration. Everyone would come over to share, as Dave put it, Ann and Ray's happiness. Ray would put this picture on display, he thought, and everyone would look at it. Ann would be at the center of attention. It would be good for her. She would feel like a part of things again. Ray imagined that she would start to act like her old self.

So when he pulled up to the curb outside the East-West Center, he was feeling pretty cheerful. The talk of the party had put him in a hopeful frame of mind, though the memory of the bracelet was still there too, itching somewhere inside him, like the beginning of a cough. He honked the horn once, and Ann came out a few minutes later.

From a distance, she didn't look pregnant at all. It was only when she got up close that she seemed a little different. There was a new roundness about her figure, a delicate, almost sleepy way of walking. But it was hard, Ray thought, to pinpoint any real change. Mostly it was just a feeling he got, that there was some secret transformation going on inside her.

He still found it hard to imagine that there was a baby in there. She'd heard its heartbeat at the clinic, and sometimes Ray even lay with his ear against her bare stomach. He imagined he could hear it swimming, soft rippling sounds, and he imitated the baby for her—a butterfly stroke and a blissful, spacey grin.

This look, this embryo imitation, had been a running joke between them for a while. Ray would sometimes close his eyes and flit his fingers through imaginary water when she talked about hypnotism. At first she laughed. But recently she got this grim look when he did it, and stopped talking. Now she felt reluctant to discuss her class, though Ray tried to explain that he wasn't making fun of her.

The two of them drove for a while in silence. She slumped down in the seat and closed her eyes. Being pregnant made her tired. It was not uncommon for Ray to come home from work and find her fast asleep on the couch; often she got out of her class and napped for hours! Ray reached down and turned on the car radio, not too loud. But when he looked over, her eyes were open. She blinked slowly, as if stunned from a deep sleep.

"So," Ray said. "How was class?"

"Fine," she said. She didn't say anything more. The radio was playing a disco song Ray kind of secretly liked, the type he imagined the two of them dancing to at the bar they used to go to with their friends. He could see himself pressing Ann up close to the juke-box, the red and yellow lights blinking across their faces as they kissed. But Ann just stared at the radio. Then she reached over and turned it off.

"Well," she said after they'd driven a ways without music. "What have you been up to this morning?"

Ray thought immediately of the bracelet, and his face got warm. "Not much," he said quickly. "Not much at all. I talked to Dave for a while. I guess we're pretty much set for the party."

"Oh yeah," she said. "I forgot to tell you. I invited some people from my class to come. I hope you don't mind."

"No, no," Ray said. He hoped he sounded enthusiastic. "That will be great. I can hardly wait to meet them." He nodded when she glanced over at him. "The more the merrier!" But he felt a twinge of dismay. He could picture this parade of women coming through the door, with their flowing clothes and wild dark hair, trailing the reek of patchouli; he saw their black self-righteous eyes sneering, judging, ready to cause arguments about politics. They would walk in and a shroud would fall over his party.

"That will be terrific," he said. He gave her a big smile, though his hands tightened on the steering wheel. He stared out to the road, accelerating to cut past a slow, rusty Buick that was drifting from lane to lane in front of him. "So anyway," Ray said in a cheerful voice. "What did you do in class today?"

"Oh, not much," Ann said. She hesitated, as if whatever went on in that run-down building was a secret she couldn't trust him with. "Actually," she said, "the last few sessions have been really intense. But you'd probably think it was silly." Ray saw that she was thinking of the embryo imitation again.

"No, no," he said. "Not at all." He raised his eyebrows with a look of friendly interest.

"Anyway, I've enjoyed it," she said warily. "We've been working on the memory, and I've always been fascinated by that. There was this one older woman in our group. When she was little, her uncle was abusive to her but she blocked it out. And then, when we were all hypnotized it came back to her. It was terrible, but now, you see, so many of the problems she's had in her life make sense. And she's going to be able to get help." Ann stopped, her face pinched, and Ray nodded sympathetically. "I probably shouldn't be telling you this," she said. "You won't say anything to Dave or Paco, will you? It's really private."

"Of course not."

"It's a very tight-knit group," Ann said. "Everyone has revealed a lot about themselves."

"Uh-huh," he said. He shifted a little, imagining all the things Ann had probably told these women while under hypnosis: the ex-husband, the "dancing," all of it. He wondered if she'd said anything about him.

"We've done some fun stuff, too," she said. "The other day they took us back to when we were younger. Our instructor would say: 'Now you're twenty, now you're ten,' and in your mind, you would be. It seemed so real. And then she said she was going to take us back before we were born."

"Hmmm," Ray said. He couldn't help but think again of her weird years, back when she used to have her chart done, when she used to go to palm readers and do whatever they told her. He cleared his throat. "Are we talking about reincarnation or something?" he said.

"I knew that's what you'd think," she said. She was quiet for a moment. "But it's nothing like that at all. " She sighed, and Ray could feel the space open up between them again. "All they said was that some people believed it was a past life they saw. Malva said that she herself thought it was just another way to get in touch with a deep part of yourself. She said that we could believe whatever we liked, she didn't care."

"'Malva?'" Ray said. "Who's 'Malva'?"

"She's the instructor," Ann said sternly. "I invited her to our party."

"And her name is really 'Malva'?"

"Oh, just forget it," Ann said. She looked away from him, out to the rows of tightly huddled little houses they were passing. "You know," she said, "I really hate it when you talk to me this way."

"What way?"

She kept her face turned. "It's just this condescending way men have of talking to women. I can't stand it."

"Well, I didn't think I was talking to you in any particular way," Ray said. "I guess I'm just not a true believer, that's all." He cleared his throat again. "Look," he said, "I'm sorry." He reached over, smoothing his palm along Ann's thigh, and she stared down at his hand, expressionless, as if she couldn't imagine how it got there.

"So anyway," he said at last. "What did you see?"

"Forget it," Ann said. "It's all a big joke to you anyway."

"Oh, come on." He rubbed her leg again. "I didn't mean it. Don't be crabby."

"I didn't see anything," she said. She glanced sidelong at him, secretive, and it made his skin prickle. Was there something about him, about the two of them, in the vision she'd seen?

"Tease," Ray said. He grinned for her. But she suddenly looked so serious and tired—tired of me, he thought—that he didn't push it any further. They drove the rest of the way in silence.

They had been arguing more and more recently. They weren't real fights exactly, just little things. But it seemed like almost every day there was tension in the air, and it was no different after they got home. Ray spent the better part of the afternoon working on a leaky toilet, and he could hear Ann in the living room, laughing at something on TV. But when he came to the threshold, she wasn't laughing anymore. He didn't go in. It was as if she were a stranger, he thought, and he didn't want her to see him looking at her. Over dinner there was an uncomfortable carefulness between them. He couldn't think of anything to talk about.

Later, Paco called to see if he was coming out. Ray said no, he didn't think so. He wanted to stay home with Ann, he said, loud enough for her to hear him. She looked up. "Go ahead if you want," she said. "I'm going to bed anyway."

Their friends still got together every Saturday and Ray went from time to time, as often as seemed proper. But it was strange to go alone, with everyone else in pairs. There had originally been eight, four married couples. So Ray always felt awkward and somewhat guilty, especially when Shari or Linda or Jill would start in: "How's Ann doing?" They looked at him as he said "Fine–Great," etc. Here was a man, their eyes seemed to say, here was a man who left his pregnant wife alone and went to bars.

So he sat at home with Ann. He went out and got a couple of videos, and they watched the first one side by side on the sofa, Ann eating parsley and plain yogurt mixed together–another pregnant thing he didn't dare comment on for fear it would break the uneasy peace they'd come to. But before he could put the second video in–the romantic one with supposedly some pretty hot scenes–Ann said she couldn't keep her eyes open any longer. They kissed. He pulled Ann closer, but he could sense that he kept his mouth pressed to hers longer than she wanted. Things didn't progress.

A few months before, he thought, the evening wouldn't have ended that way. They might've made love on the living room floor, one of Ray's scratchy old Pink Floyd albums whispering from the stereo. They might've been up till three or four, talking.

Something had happened, he thought–something more than just a phase of pregnancy, and after they'd gone to bed he found himself wondering where exactly their life had taken its wrong turn. He just lay there, listening to Ann's breathing. A cold thought passed over him: would they be together in five years, he wondered. In ten? Did he really, really, believe that they'd be married forever?

It was a question Ray thought of often as the week wore on. He said nothing to Ann. "You're projecting–" That was what he imagined Ann telling him if he brought it up. "You're unhappy, you're having second thoughts, so you try to put the blame on me. That way you don't have to feel guilty." He could almost hear her. She was an expert at this kind of talk. She'd read all the books. She'd been abandoned before, and she knew all the methods of men.

Though he knew it was unrealistic, he kept thinking that maybe this party would make a difference. He and Ann used to throw huge, wonderful parties, the kind that would trail anecdotes in their wake for months. They'd been married for five years, and they still talked about some of those early parties. Like the one where Dave and Paco and Lou ended the evening by dunking their heads in a big tub of ice water, taking turns. Like the one where Shari, then only Paco's girlfriend, tap-danced and sang that old Neil Young song, "Helpless."

At the hardware store where Ray was a manager, he would stare at the blank order forms, remembering. He thought of the coffee shop where he'd met Ann, how she suddenly sat down and struck up a conversation, how shocked and charmed he'd been by the easy way she revealed personal information. He thought of the Vail hotel they'd checked into, the rich people in their ridiculous furry boots giving sour looks as he and Ann laughed at them. He recalled how he used to wake up some mornings with hands on his chest, his stomach, awaking from a dream already deeply involved.

Nowadays, she was seldom even in bed when he woke. Frequently he would rise into consciousness to the sound of Ann meditating, listening to a tape of Malva's dark low voice: "Deeper and deeper . . . that's right . . . deeper and deeper . . . good . . . " He'd find her on the living room floor, eyes closed; and this could go on, just those same repeating words, for over half an hour. By that time he had to leave.

On Friday, the day of the party, Ray and Ann both took the afternoon off work so they could go to the doctor for Ann's ultrasound. As they drove to the clinic, Ray tried again to decide just how bad things were. Ann was quiet. When he reached over to clasp her hand it felt as lifeless as a mitten.

"How was work?" he said at last.

"Exhausting."

"Oh," he said. He sighed. She worked at a day-care center, and it used to be that he knew all the names of the toddlers she cared for. He'd heard so much about her co-workers that he sometimes thought he recognized them in strangers on the street. But she didn't talk about her job anymore.

"Anything interesting happen today?" he said, and she shrugged.

"Not really," she said. "Mostly I concentrated on not vomiting."

"Sure," he said—did she think he'd forgotten that she was suffering? He tried to smile kindly.

"So!" he said, after a time. "Are you looking forward to the party tonight? Do you think a lot of the gals from your class will come?"

She stared at him for a moment, completely blank. "Oh, God," she said finally, weakly. "I forgot that damn thing was tonight."

Ray didn't like to think it was possible that his wife could become a different person. He didn't like to think that there was some hidden aspect of her personality that could consume her from the inside out, taking her over like a fever. But that was what was going through his mind as they were ushered into the tiny room that held the ultrasound equipment.

After a little while, a man came in. "I'm Ken," he said. "I'll be your technician today." He told Ann to lift up her gown, the shift they'd given her, and Ray watched as the man began to rub a gel onto her stomach, his fingers moving in slow circles just above the line of her pubic hair. Ray couldn't help but think of all Ann's other men. Had they really been as bad as she said they were? Or had she just changed toward them?

"Look at this," said Ken. He was sliding two discs over her belly, his eyes fixed on a small screen that was set in the web of machinery. "There," he said. "There, can you see it?"

Ray couldn't make out anything at first. It was all in black and white halftones, like a photocopy, and all he could see were shadows shifting, ghostly shapes circling one another. When he finally spotted something moving, he wasn't sure what it was–an arm, or the torso maybe, translucent, reminding him of some blind deep cave fish or a Portuguese man-o'-war, sliding through the murk. Ann was leaning forward. Her face was full of wonder, her mouth slightly open as if to say: "Oh!"

"You can make out the head and extremities here," said Ken, gesturing. "That darker line is the endometrium."

Ann kept nodding eagerly, and at last Ray nodded too. "Yes," he breathed. But his heart was pounding. He couldn't see anything that looked like a baby.

"Beautiful," said Ann later. "Isn't it beautiful?" They'd put the picture of the ultrasound in a little frame and placed it on the mantelpiece. Ray found it more recognizable now, though the creature, the embryo, looked hunched and skeletal, like a fossil crushed on a piece of slate.

"It's neat," Ray said. He didn't know what else to say. Ann stood staring at it, and he put his arm around her. He traced his lips through her hair, brushing against her cheek.

"I better go get ready for this party," she said.

After she'd gone upstairs, Ray began to do his last few preparations. He stirred up some dip and poured bags of chips and pretzels into bowls. He arranged everything strategically on various surfaces. He tapped the keg, pouring himself a cup of mostly foam. He felt edgy. What if no one came, he thought. What if only the women from Ann's class showed up, and he was trapped, surrounded by them.

The photo of the embryo seemed to peer down at him, presiding over the empty room. It was not the gently swimming, smiling cherub he'd imagined, and in fact there was something unsettling about its opaque little eyes, even though Ann insisted they were closed. Ray remembered some of the things Dave had said when he was depressed. "They certainly make your life different," he'd said in a grim voice. "You'll never be the same, that's for sure."

Ray had been sitting there a while when Ann called to him. "Ray?" she said. She came down to the landing in her slip and bra. "Ray," she said, "have you seen that one bracelet of mine? You know. The one I got when I used to be a dancer?"

She was still looking for it when Paco and Shari

arrived. Ray was still in the empty living room, and he greeted them expansively, wishing he could fill up the house with a festive mood.

"Where's Ann?" said Shari, and he tried to give them a big grin.

"I think she's upstairs," Ray said. He led them into the kitchen, and told them to get themselves a beer or something. "I'll be right back," he said. "Let me go find out what's up with Ann."

When he came to the doorway of the bedroom, Ann was still in her underwear. She'd moved the dresser out from the wall, and was on her hands and knees, crawling along the edge of the carpet, fingering her way through the tufts of shag.

"What on earth are you doing?" he said. "Paco and Shari are here."

She stared up at him, as if he'd just startled her out of some deep thought.

"My bracelet," she said. "I can't figure out where it could've gone to."

"Honey," Ray said. "You're not even dressed. Can't you look for it later?"

"I can't believe it's missing," she said, as if she hadn't heard. "This is my favorite piece of jewelry."

"Ann." He raised his voice a little. "Ann, people are here."

"I just saw it the day before yesterday," she said.

What a liar, Ray thought. He'd thrown the thing away almost a week before! "No you didn't," he said irritably. Then, realizing, he stopped himself.

She looked up. Their eyes met, and he felt her expression suddenly focus and sharpen. "What do you mean," she said. "How do you know?"

He could feel color coming to his face. "Why the hell are you so hot for that damn thing right now, anyway?" he snapped. "That's what I'd like to know. Why does it matter so much to you?"

She stared at him, and he could feel his blush deepening, heat prickling under his cheeks, even his own rotten blood turning against him, he thought. "You took it," she said. Her voice was hushed with amazement. "You took my bracelet, didn't you?"

"Of course not!" Ray said scornfully. "What are you, some kind of paranoid?" But he felt dizzy, afraid of what else she might see in him. "What I would like to know," he said, and straightened his shoulders. "I would like to know why you insist on clinging to some old shit you got when you were a"–he gritted his teeth–"stripper. Why is it so important? You're in a different world now."

"Where's my bracelet?"

"I haven't seen the frigging thing," he yelled, and the force of his words almost convinced him. "What are you, crazy?" He faced her, watching her mouth harden. "Are you coming downstairs, or what?"

A few people had arrived: Jill and Lou, Dave and Linda, all their old friends. A few others. When Ray got to the bottom of the stairs, a small woman with short dark hair got up from the easy chair where she was sitting with a glass of wine. She was wearing a tight, fairly short, sleeveless dress; her body was thin, yet muscular: well formed. An enormous pair of African-looking earrings swung from her ears.

"You must be Raymond," she said. She extended her hand, several wooden bracelets rattling on her wrist. "I'm Malva. Malva Rosen. Anna's meditation coach."

"Anna," Ray said. It took a moment for this to register, though this was Ann's real name. She'd never used "Anna" before, especially not the way Malva pronounced it–Ah-nah, like she'd just arrived from some exotic foreign land. Was this what she called herself now? "Welcome," Ray said. He took Malva's stiff, lotion-moist hand. "Glad you could make it." They stood there, smiling at one another.

"I've heard a lot about your course," he said. "It sounds interesting."

"Thank you," she said. It seemed to Ray that there was something slow and careful about those dark eyes. He could see how a person could be hypnotized by them. "You'll have to visit the class sometime."

"Great," he said. "Super."

They nodded at one another. Then, after a moment, she glanced around the room. Dave and Paco were over in the corner, near the mantelpiece, and they raised their beers. Ray could see they were curious about Malva. "Where's Anna?" Malva asked.

"She should be down any minute," Ray said.

And it was then, as if on cue, that "Anna" did make her entrance. Ray saw the lower part of her body appear at the top of the stairs, and the first thing he noticed was that she was wearing one of those dresses she'd had since before they were married, an oddly baggy "Indian print" with a strange, deep neckline. It was long out of style: he'd never seen her wear it before. She'd kept it, she'd claimed, only as a souvenir. She was also wearing a pair of earrings Ray immediately recognized, given to her by her former husband—silver trout with garnet eyes. She looked at Ray coldly as she moved down the steps, her hand gliding along the banister, her back straight, as if, he thought, she were entering a ballroom. Then, when she saw Malva, her expression turned pleasant. She smiled broadly.

"Malva," she said. "I'm so glad you made it!"

Shari had come over to join them and she gave Ann a big hug. "Honey," she said. "You look radiant."

"What a wonderful dress," said Malva.

She didn't look radiant, Ray thought. She looked like a kook, and he felt like telling her so. Cruel thoughts flickered in the back of his mind, even as he smiled and talked that easy party talk. He didn't know why he felt so angry.

He and Ann didn't speak to one another. People continued to arrive at the party, and they were both mingling with them. They occupied separate sections of the floor, passing from one little group to the other without ever entering the same circle. From time to time, she would catch him staring at her from across the room, and her face would stiffen. Then she would turn back to her conversation.

There must have been thirty guests at the party by that time—old acquaintances, friends of friends, all people Ray knew. He was happy to see that no one from Ann's class had showed up, besides Malva.

He stood beneath the ultrasound picture with Paco and Shari. "That's pretty cool," said Paco. Ray watched as Paco's hand slipped around Shari's waist, and they exchanged a private look.

"It's so cute," Shari said.

Ray took a sip of his beer. "Yeah," he said.

Paco continued to gaze at the picture, as if at a piece of famous abstract art. He shook his head wonderingly. "So you guys must be pretty excited?"

"Absolutely," Ray said. He took a big swallow of his beer. From across the room, he could feel Ann giving him an icy stare. "We can't wait," he said.

Ray's friend Lou had brought some marijuana, as he usually did to parties, and after a while Ray found himself gravitating out to the back porch, where they were smoking. He passed through the kitchen, where Ann and Linda were having a serious talk. He couldn't hear what they were saying, but Linda's eyes seemed to follow him accusingly as he went by. He brushed Ann's back lightly, saying, "Pardon," in a cheerful, impersonal voice. He kept on walking.

When Ray opened the screen door and stepped out on the porch, he was surprised to see Malva there. She was standing between Lou and Dave. Bridget, a tall red-haired woman who worked with Dave at his office, was sitting Indian-style in an old rocker, the chair Ray had planned to eventually move up to the baby's room. Bridget waved. Though the screens were all open, a thin layer of smoke hung just over the tops of their heads. The smell was heavy.

"Hey," said Lou. "It's Ray. The father-to-be." He grinned.

"That's me," Ray said. Malva leaned over and handed him the joint.

"Hello, Ray," she said. Her eyes seemed to hold him for a moment.

"So," said Lou, as Ray took a drag on the joint. "I was looking at that ultrasound thing. That's pretty wild that they can do that. But, geez, it took me a long time to figure out what was the head and what was the feet. You know?"

Ray held the smoke, then exhaled in a long stream. "Is that right?" he said. He didn't want to talk about it. He'd pretty much run out of things to say on the subject, and the effort of putting on an enthusiastic face was beginning to wear him down. He passed the joint to Bridget, then turned to Malva, who had loosened a little, and was leaning against the screened wall. She rubbed a hand across her bare arm, and her bracelets rattled.

"Isn't it amazing," she said, "what the human body is capable of." She smiled in a secretive way, and for a moment Ray imagined that she was thinking of something sexual.

"What's that?" he said.

"Oh, I don't know," she said. "It's just that birth is so magical and mysterious, though we seldom think of it. Did you know that we pass through all the evolutionary stages as we develop? A bundle of cells to a fishlike thing with fins and gills to a tiny person. And to think that all this goes on inside you!" She gazed at Ray. "Don't you envy Anna in a way, Raymond?"

"I never really thought about it," he said. The mention of his wife made him shift uneasily, and he thought of her out there in the living room, in her flowing dress, furious. "So," he said. "I take it you don't have kids?"

She smiled again. "No," she said. "Not in this life at least." She laughed in a low comfortable way, and Ray was reminded of the dark sound of her voice on tape, the whisper of "deeper and deeper."

"So are you honestly saying that you believe you had kids in another life," Ray said. He meant it playfully, and he winked at her teasingly to show that, taking another sip of beer.

But she didn't seem to like the comment, or the wink. "What do you mean, 'am I honestly saying'?" she said, and Ray was surprised at how quickly the smile faded from her face. "I'm not sure what you're asking."

"I don't know," said Ray. He looked around at everyone, smiling. He wasn't trying to offend. "I guess," he said, "I just was wondering. I mean, this isn't like a . . . religious thing with you, is it?"

"I'm still not sure what you're getting at," Malva said. "'Religious' is such a loaded term."

"I don't know. I mean, if you're talking about, like, reincarnation and stuff. That's sort of . . . kooky, isn't it? I don't mean kooky . . . " He glanced around at everyone again, and they were all watching him silently. "Well, I mean," he said. "Extreme, is what I mean. I mean, to me personally it's just sort of, uh, wacky. I guess maybe I'm not being open-minded enough. Goofy is what I'm trying to say. To me, it's a goofy belief. I just have a hard time understanding how anyone really . . . believes that, you know." He cleared his throat. Malva's gaze seemed to close over him, and grip.

"Millions of people do believe it, Raymond, odd as that may seem to you," she said. "Reincarnation is a very ancient belief, and I don't think it's any less valid than . . . whatever you see as . . . truth." She said these last words very slowly, and as she spoke he felt as if the grip of her eyes was tightening. She held him for a long moment, then smiled. "Isn't it amazing," Malva murmured, turning to Bridget (whom she hadn't even seemed to notice before), "Isn't it strange how men will automatically take this condescending attitude when confronted with something they don't comprehend?" Bridget blew smoke, as if in agreement, and Ray watched as Malva took the joint and put it delicately to her lips. The way she flicked her eyes over him made him wonder suddenly what Ann had told Malva about him, what confidences they had shared.

He blushed. "Hey," he said. He looked over to Dave and Lou, but he could see there would be no defense from that quarter. "Sorry," he said. "I didn't mean for you to get offended. I was just teasing."

"Right," she said. She gave Bridget a significant look. "If you're feeling hostile, why not just be up front about it?"

"I'm not feeling hostile," Ray said. Malva blinked at him, as if, he thought, she had just done an ultrasound of his brain. "Honestly," Ray said. He spread his palms to her, to all of them; his heart had begun to beat quicker as she gave him that dry, ironical look, as Dave and Lou and Bridget watched him. "Actually, I'm really interested," Ray said. "I'd really be fascinated to know what my past life was."

"Oh, really?" said Malva.

"Yes! Really!" He shook his head emphatically: He was a nice guy. Couldn't she see that?

"You should come to the class, then," she said.

"I thought it was just for women."

"It is," she said. A slow smile spread over her lips. "That's right." Something about this struck Lou as funny, because he started to giggle in that silent snuffling way that Ray was familiar with. Malva began to chuckle, too, and then Dave and Bridget joined in. Finally, Ray had to laugh also. But he wasn't sure why.

"Seriously," he said, though Lou kept snuffling. Ray felt Malva's cool fingers press the joint to his. "Seriously, I would really love to be hypnotized. Just to see what it was like. I don't really know anything about it." He was still blushing. "It's not something I've ever had contact with."

"I've got to see this," said Dave.

"Okay," said Lou. "Okay. This is a good idea."

They both looked at Malva, who was still chuckling a little, recalling whatever she had found funny. They turned to her expectantly, and after a moment she widened her eyes.

"You mean now?" she said. She cocked her head at them, as if this might be another secret joke. "Oh, no," she said. "No, no, no. This is not a parlor trick. This is serious."

"I am serious," Ray said. Because now he was: he wanted to prove something to them.

And then Lou straightened up. "Hey," he said. "Look who's here. Annabelle Lee, the mother-to-be."

Ray turned. His wife was standing in the doorway, staring in at all of them. He had been leaning fairly close to Malva, and now he slid back a bit. Ann's eyes drifted over him. The marijuana circled slowly through his blood.

"Hey, Anna," Ray said. "How's it going?"

But she ignored him. "Dave," she said. "Linda is looking for you. She says you guys need to get going. The babysitter has to be back home by one."

"Hey, Annabelle," Lou said obliviously. "Malva here is going to hypnotize Ray."

"Oh?" said Ann. She didn't even glance in Ray's direction.

"I am not," said Malva. She, too, straightened, tugging her dress down, taking the wrinkles out. She looked at us archly, wavering a little. With Ann in the room, Ray was suddenly more aware of how stoned Malva was. She raised her head in a parody of dignity. "One cannot be hypnotized while intoxicated," she said. "You'll get too relaxed and simply fall asleep." She gestured broadly, as if to demonstrate. Ann's face was a domino of disapproval.

"I'm not intoxicated," Ray said. "My mind is as clear as a bone."

"As a bell, you mean?" Ann said softly. It was the first thing she'd said to Ray in hours, and she immediately turned her head away.

"You wouldn't be able to concentrate properly," Malva continued.

"Sure I would," Ray smiled. "Of course I would." He stared at the back of Ann's head, and when she finally let her eyes rest on him, he strolled across the porch, to show how sober he was. He had something to prove, he felt. "What could it hurt?" Ray said.

Lou and Dave took up the cause, and then even Bridget. "Come on," they said, and "Why not?" and "Just do it," and "Ohhh, this would be so great."

Malva was flattered. Ray watched her expression shift from firm disapproval to hesitation as she was pressured. Ann stood there watching, almost a silhouette against the brightly lit frame of the kitchen doorway. The folds of her old dress rustled lightly in the breeze.

"Oh," said Malva. "Oh, God. I don't know. " And then: "Oh, sure. Why not. Just a little exercise." She leaned toward Ann confidentially. "I can't believe I'm doing this," she said. "This is so unprofessional."

They gathered in the living room, so Ray could lie down on the couch. Everyone had come in, and they formed a circle with Ray and Malva in the center. Ann stood at the back of the group, watching, her face expressionless. Ray met her eyes, but he couldn't tell what she was thinking. He felt his stomach tighten. Her eyes traced slowly along his face, as if he were some curiosity she had guiltily paid money to see.

Malva bent down next to him. Ray could feel her warm breath, and when she told him to picture a bright light, he squeezed his eyes closed. Surround yourself with it, Malva said. She waited, and he began to feel his blood pumping. He could imagine his veins branching beneath his skin like rivers, highways, a whole cartography. Malva asked him to count backward with her.

But as he did, his pulse began to quicken. He could sense everyone staring at him, especially Ann. It seemed that they were rising above, floating, growing blurry as Ray went down and down. Malva's voice seemed to expand and contract with his breathing. He knew he was making a mistake.

He was going to lose control, he thought. The feeling washed over him, and he began to tip end to end in slow, gentle turns. Any minute he would begin talking, he knew it. Words would come from his lips. At any minute, he would announce, in front of all of them–anything. Everything. Tell Ann how ridiculous she looked, or Malva how much she turned him on. Tell of the bracelet he'd destroyed, the other jewelry and letters. Of his marriage–that soon to be dead and lifeless thing, he'd say. He'd say that he didn't really want that child after all. And then–then, layers would begin to peel back, he'd keep talking, until he'd revealed things he didn't know himself yet. He'd talk, he'd talk, and they'd see, all of them, how ugly, how small, how empty he was at his center. He struggled, but he was sinking, and when he tried to rise up Malva's voice pulled him under again. Stop! he wanted to shout, I don't want to do this! But her voice grew distant.

There was a tunnel stretching in front of him, and he could hear her whispering. In the distance, she said, was a tiny square of light.

going out

Scott and his father have been attending Alcoholics Anonymous meetings on Thursday evenings for several weeks now, and Scott is beginning to find it hard to pay attention. Scott's father sits, hands folded in his lap, head cocked as if he's at a symphony. His father nods and writes in a small spiral notebook, and Scott watches his face surreptitiously. As always, Scott can't help noticing the eye.

Scott's father has a glass eye. His father used to be a welder, and once, when he was drunk and not wearing goggles, a spark flew up and put his eye out. This story had always frightened Scott. He remembers being about five or six and staying at his father's place, and waking up to go to the bathroom. The eye was lying there by the sink in a tiny box of white cotton. Scott imagined that it could see him. He pictured his father stretched out, sleeping, and thought of the empty socket. Whenever his father looked at him, the glass eye remained fixed. When his father was drunk, or hadn't showered, it would become encrusted with a dull gold mucus. Sometimes Scott's father embellished the story of the welding spark by telling Scott that his eye had turned to a jelly, that the doctors had dug it out with a spoon.

Even now, Scott finds himself unnerved by it–it's a token of how his father used to be, and when his father catches him staring Scott looks down quickly. His father is printing in a notebook: "I'm O.K., You're O.K.!"

The speaker has written these words on the

chalkboard and underlined them. Scott copies it down too.

As they are driving back to the father's trailer on the outskirts of town, Scott's father weeps. He often cries after these meetings, though not openly. Scott can only see the tears if a car goes by in the opposite direction, lighting his father's face in a brief flash, like a snapshot. Scott is completely still. He never asks his father, but Scott suspects that his father is crying over him, blaming himself for how Scott's life has turned out, ashamed that Scott has ended up an alcoholic even before he's turned twenty-one. That's what Scott imagines, though he knows it's self-centered. He has always had a weak spot for easy excuses, he can't help but embrace them, though he knows better. For example, Scott always felt certain that his father drank because Scott's mother had left him, despite the fact that they were divorced long after his problem became apparent. Scott also likes to think that he himself became a drunk because his mother died, though in his more honest moments he has his doubts. Not to say he wasn't upset. She died in the winter of Scott's freshman year in college, and for months and months afterward he'd wandered the campus like he was underwater. He couldn't hear people when they talked to him.

Secretly, though, Scott knows that he drank because it was wonderful. He loved it–the numb freedom that allowed him to walk across the fraternity rooftop, three stories above ground, or kiss a pretty girl at a party out of nowhere, with no fear of retribution, or catcall the big, square-jawed guys outside the next fraternity house. It was only when, on a dare, he chugged half a bottle of ouzo and ended up in a coma for three days that he began to blame it all on his mother's death.

For as long as Scott can remember, his father has lived in a two-bedroom trailer house in the country.

Scott used to spend a month there every summer until he was fourteen, by which time his father's drinking had gotten so out of hand that even overnight visits weren't possible anymore. But the memory of the place has stuck with him: the smell of sweat and leftovers, the dirty clothes and overflowing ashtrays; girlie magazines and detective paperbacks scattered on the floor, piled on the furniture.

Scott can remember his father teaching him to play poker. His father would get up in the morning and sit in his underwear at the kitchen table, and Scott would sit across from him. They'd play cards all afternoon, into the evening, and his father smoked cigarette after cigarette, drinking beer and later Jack Daniels, not wanting to eat or get dressed or even raise the shade. Whenever they played, Scott's father gave him fifty dollars. Then he proceeded to win it all back. By dusk, Scott would have lost all the money and his father would be drunk enough to begin giving him beers. Scott took them nervously, sipping at them until they grew flat and warm, grimacing at the bitter taste. He never thought his father was a monster, no matter what his mother said. For Scott, there had been something conspiratorial and grown-up about staying with him: gambling, drinking, looking at nude ladies in his father's magazines, never going to bed until he wanted. Scott didn't even hate him when he grew frightening, late at night. His father would talk about old bosses he'd had, punching the air with his fists, or describe the bodies of women he had known, grinning languorously, looming over Scott and gesturing. Scott had made believe it was a rare and passing moment of insanity, though his father got that way nearly every night.

Things have changed since then. When they walk into the trailer and his father turns on the light, Scott is again aware of how unfamiliar everything looks. The smell and the clutter have been cleared away, leaving only the acrid, flowery odor of old peoples' houses, and a certain hollowness, like the inside of a shell. He remembers the carpet and most of the furniture from childhood, the cigarette burns on the sofa, the ringed water stains left by beer cans on the coffee table. But the place has no real connection with the past, he thinks. As always, Scott's high school picture, sitting on the TV set, catches him: that bright, self-congratulatory smile makes him wince. He was the first in his family to graduate high school. He wishes it wasn't there.

"Do you want coffee?" Scott's father asks him. "Decaf?" Scott has picked up this habit, too, and he nods. There's a long silence, and at last Scott says: "Sounds good."

He takes a piece of cold toast, saved from breakfast, and begins to nibble around the edge as his father scoops instant crystals into two mugs. His father counts them out, moving his lips, one, two, three, and then puts the kettle on the stove. Scott's father seems to do everything methodically these days, as if he's gone blind and knows the room only as a diagram of its positions.

As Scott is leaning against the counter, he notices the Bible his father has lying there is opened to a different place–Matthew now instead of Luke. It makes Scott nervous. Though he's never seen his father read it, Scott knows he must, in private. He tries to imagine his father praying and it makes him shudder. Just seeing the Bible there, the first time, sent a chill through him, the idea that his father had changed so much. He dreaded the moment his father would bring it up, sitting Scott down at the kitchen table to discuss Jesus and being born again, and Scott would feel obliged to listen politely, like he did the time he accidentally invited the Jehovah's Witness girls into his fraternity's living room. But Scott's father has never said a word about religion. He doesn't seem to know what to say most of the time, and Scott often feels as if they're like strangers trapped in an elevator together, slowly shifting their weight and staring at the unopening door, the small talk drained out of them.

"So," his father sighs at last. "Pretty good meeting tonight. I like that Taylor. He's a bright guy."

"Mm-hmm. He's good."

"I don't suppose you'll want to take any psychology when you get back to college. You'll have had enough of that." His father smiles, pouring hot water into their mugs. He stirs the coffee with a fork, and his expression doesn't change, as if he's forgotten that he's still smiling.

"Probably," says Scott. This is one of the games they have going between them—at least that's how Scott thinks of it. They are pretending that Scott is going back to school in the fall. Maybe Scott's father half believes it. But all Scott himself can think of is how it will feel to be at a party, standing there with a soda while people are laughing and dancing and drunk, watching them passing out cups of beer at the bar. He imagines his friends saying guarded things: "How are you doing?" trying not to let their eyes drift down to the drinks in their hands. Scott couldn't stand it for a minute, he knows for a fact, though he can't bring himself to admit it to his father. September is still months away.

"I don't think you'll have any trouble getting your scholarship back, do you?" his father says. He keeps at this point, meticulously as at everything else.

"Probably not," Scott says. He sighs, sips coffee. They blink at one another in the sharp fluorescent light.

Even now, after all that has happened, Scott still finds himself longing for a drink. One of the first things he learned in detox was that for him, sleep and alcohol are intertwined. After the coffee and cigarettes it takes to get through a day, he'll lie down and the soft hush-hush of his heart starts to pump in his ears. It seems like only a drink can muffle the sound.

There are times, during the day, when Scott is sure there's nothing wrong with him. Everybody over-indulges when they're young, he tells himself, and maybe everyone was overreacting to the thing with the ouzo. Maybe all people wanted, really, was to give him a good scare, teach him a lesson. But then, as the day wears on, his hands will start to shake, or his head will hum, and he'll wonder whether he belongs back in the psych ward. He'll start to feel like he's become as tired and used up as his father has.

It doesn't help to be in this place, at his father's place in rural Nebraska. To see the fields and untraveled dirt roads stretching out in every direction. To hear the soft static buzz of cicadas and the cows lowing in the pasture across the road and the slow thud of a distant irrigation pump hovering in the air as he tries to close his eyes.

Scott's father is a short, dark-haired man with a heavy brow and leathery, sun-wrinkled skin. People are afraid of his looks, Scott has noticed, not just because of his eye, but also because there is a kind of inborn intensity to his expression that is apparent even in baby pictures.

He never used to have any hobbies, except drinking and reading–he liked a certain kind of lurid detective novel, the kind that featured screaming, half-dressed women on the cover. But these days, Scott has noticed, his father keeps busy. He spends a lot of time off in the shed behind the trailer, making things out of scrap metal. Maybe, Scott thinks, he finds it therapeutic. Maybe, since he is no longer a welder by trade, he does it out of nostalgia, or to keep in practice. He works with old automobile parts and barbed wire, nails and brass pipes, making things like candlestick holders, picture frames, bookends. Recently, he made Scott a belt buckle out of thin slices of copper tubing, welded together like a honeycomb. Though Scott can't imagine wearing the thing in public, certainly not at his college, he does like it. There is a kind of strange beauty to it, Scott thinks, as if it were a relic from another planet.

Four days a week, Scott's father works at a feedlot. They are looking for people, he has told Scott on several occasions, and on the morning after the meeting he brings it up again. "I really think a little hard work would do you good," he says. They are standing in his workshop when he suggests this, surrounded by bits of metal and junk, and when Scott doesn't answer it seems to him that the old engines and bedsprings close in a little. "I don't think it's good for you to sit around all day, brooding," his father says. "That's the worst thing for you right now." His father has a flat piece of metal in a vise and he's slowly pounding it into a helix. He grits his teeth.

"Or," he says, grunting, "you could try to get a job somewhere else if you want. But I've always said that it's the physical work that keeps your mind off your troubles." He looks up, his forehead sweaty. He cocks his head slightly, in order to fix on Scott with his good eye.

"Sure," Scott says. He edges his foot along the ground, scattering bolts, spark plugs, washers. He shrugs.

On Monday, Scott goes into the office to fill out an application. Cowboys and old sixties-Vietnam types with scruffy beards are milling around, and some of them turn to look at him as he passes. Scott had long hair and two weeks' growth on his face when he went into detox, but they insisted that he cut his hair and shave daily. Now he looks clean-cut, squeaky clean, he thinks, like someone who folds his hands in his lap when he sits down, someone who constantly smooths the creases of his pants.

The man behind the desk is wearing a western shirt and a string tie, and his hair is slicked across his balding head. He rubs his knuckles as he looks at the application. "We don't get many college kids out here." He frowns. "This is hard work—physical work."

"I know," Scott says. He looks at his feet, trying to shift his leg so his argyle socks aren't visible to men passing behind him. His father was the one who told him to "dress up."

"Where did you learn of this position?"

"My dad works here," Scott says quietly. He glances across the room to where his father is punching a time card. "Larry Sullivan."

"Mmm." The man's eyes narrow, and he writes a quick scrawl across the application. "We'll get back to you."

When Scott gets outside, his father is standing by the door, waiting. Scott tells him he doesn't think he'll get the job, but his father just smiles.

"Do you want to ride around with me for a while and look the place over?" he says. They are walking by a parked pickup, and Scott can see two paunchy cowboys leaned up against it, trading what looks like a joint back and forth. He can't think of an excuse to get out of staying. "I guess so," Scott says, and follows, keeping pace with his father's slow, regretful walk.

The truck Scott's father drives is an old ten-ton, the kind Scott remembers seeing when he was out at his father's place in those long-ago summers. He can recall trucks like that, loaded with wheat, bearing down on him like some roaring dinosaur as he rode his bike along the hazy dirt road.

They call it the "dead truck," his father tells him. His father's job is to drive through the rows of cattle pens and pick up the ones that have died. Wearing thick leather gloves and coveralls, he attaches a chain to their bodies and cranks them up into the back of the truck. Later, Scott's father explains, they'll be taken to be made into dog food and fertilizer.

The cattle shift and mass in their pens, staring uneasily as Scott and his father pass. After a few minutes, Scott's father spots one in the midst of the ebb and flow of brown-and-white bodies. He points it out, and Scott sits looking at it–the swollen belly, the stiff legs that point to the air at odd angles. "We lose sometimes thirty a day," his father tells him, and Scott can picture them, lying down in the heat and mud and the maggots that thrive in the fresh manure, lying down and never getting up again.

He watches through the rearview mirror after his father backs the truck up to the narrow edge of the pen. The cattle bellow, scatter away, then circle like bystanders at a respectful distance. His father bends over the dead animal and lifts its head so he can work the chain under its body. He strains, pulling the chain under the torso, then hooks it under the front legs, which sway lazily. When he activates the crank, the watching cattle bolt again, and the dead cow's body jerks once, then slowly begins to sidle along the dark, tadpole-colored ground, and finally Scott sees it lift. He stops looking. It's impossible to imagine, he thinks–days, weeks, months of this, the sickly sweet smell of the dead and the manure; the boring maze of dirt roads that trace around and around the circumference of the pens. You would almost have to be drunk or high, Scott thinks, just to make yourself go to work in the morning.

His father climbs back into the cab of the truck, and wipes his face with his forearm. Scott lets his gaze drift over his father's gloves, then, involuntarily, to his eye, which is fixed on some distant point–the hills, the faint white line an airplane is making along the sky.

"What's the matter?" His father puts his gloved hand on Scott's knee and Scott can't help but flinch. "Oh," his father says, and his expression wavers. He takes off his gloves. "Not a pretty sight, is it? But it don't take much to get used to it."

"Yeah." Scott looks away, ashamed of his own squeamishness. "No big deal," he says. He tries to sound upbeat. He doesn't want to offend his father, to seem prissy or snobbish. Besides, he's almost positive he won't get the job anyway.

"It's only to September, even if you don't like it," his father says. They nod at one another, neither sure of what to say, and Scott's father clears his throat. "Well. How about some of that coffee?"

Scott pours him a cup out of the thermos, balancing as the truck jogs forward. He is trying to concentrate on making himself believe that there will be a time when his life is back in order, when he'll be back at the university, walking through the quad with a load of books or looking out his window at night and seeing the bright dominoes of city lights on the horizon. He can remember how, once, when he was little, his father drove him to the top of a hill at night, how they stood there, watching a red airplane light move among the stars, his father trying to convince him that this tiny light held hundreds of people, all of them on their way to California or Hawaii or Japan, all of them oblivious to anyone down below. College seems at least that distant and unreal.

"Don't look so down-in-the-mouth," Scott's father says. "You should have seen me when I came back from the cure. You're tougher than I was. All you need is something to keep your hands busy."

Out the window, the white faces of Hereford cattle are ghostly in the waves of heat–pale, skull-like masks, staring as the truck rattles by. "Yeah?" Scott is playing with the neck of his shirt, crumpling it, and he smooths it out when he realizes what he's doing. He and his father nod.

A few hours later, his father parks the truck for lunch, and they pass a sandwich back and forth, trading bites. "I guess my life is pretty good these days," Scott's father says, chewing thoughtfully. "Things are calmer now. More peaceful. I fiddle around in the shop. Go fishing. I'm getting older, you know, all I want is the easy life. You're lucky. You didn't let this thing drag on and ruin your life." His eye searches Scott's face, but Scott remains blank. "Don't worry, son," he says softly. "Things will turn out fine for you, just you watch."

Scott doesn't say anything. But what he is thinking is how it would be to go back to school, the way it would feel to move his things out of the fraternity house, looking up to see his friends' stares shift quickly away; the way it would feel to stand in the doorway of an empty dorm room and see the nights ahead buzzing endlessly, like a fly around a lightbulb. He closes his eyes for a moment.

"Don't you think so?" his father says.

"What?" Scott says. And then, "Yeah." He draws in breath. "I'm sure things will work out fine."

On days that Scott's father is at work, Scott tries to think of at least one thing he can do, so when his father comes home and asks "What have you been up to today?" he can prove that he hasn't just been sitting at the kitchen table, drinking coffee and brooding. He mows the ragged patch of lawn and puts out sprinklers, or cleans in the shop, sweeping the tiny dollops of melted metal into a pile, rebaiting the mousetraps hidden behind a stack of old pipes, picking through the coffee cans full of nuts and bolts and nails and separating them into individual cans. Mostly he does these things in the afternoon, so that he won't finish too soon and have hours and hours left to kill. If he starts late enough, he's still busy when his father comes home from work. Scott looks up, as if surprised that the day has gone by so quickly, and waves at him.

Mornings are the hardest part. Scott wouldn't like for his father to see him, walking through the trailer from one end to the other, or snooping through things, as he sometimes does. His father keeps old pictures in the bottom drawer of his dresser, and Scott likes to take them out. There are photographs of his father as a young man, wide-eyed and alert in his Navy uniform, his smile taut, anticipating the flash of the camera. When he was little Scott used to dream of having a father like in those pictures–the firm, determined jaw, the noble posture. There was a picture of him on the deck of a ship, smiling an eager, innocent smile, an expression Scott had never seen.

He had a fantasy, back then, that if he could somehow trap his father in a room for a week without alcohol, that he'd be cured. He'd be transformed, suddenly, into that calm dream-father. Scott used to imagine caring for him, bringing him food as he lay there in his locked room; he even imagined sitting on the edge of his father's bed and wiping sweat from his face with a damp cloth. How grateful he would be afterward! Scott knew the way his father would hug him, knew the way his father's tears would feel on his neck.

One night, just before he turned thirteen, Scott tried to do it. He locked his father in the bedroom and barricaded the door. For a while, his father cursed him, and threatened, and hollered. Then everything was quiet, and Scott began to get frightened. And when, finally, crying, he opened the door, he discovered that his father had squeezed through the tiny bedroom window and escaped into the night.

Scott had searched for hours. He had hidden his father's car keys, and so his father had gone off on foot. Scott walked the dark dirt roads with a flashlight, calling for him, the dust-filled beam of light tunneling all the way across the fields, to infinity. When he found his father at last, he was curled up like a baby in the high weeds along the side of the road, asleep.

Sunday, after they've washed the dishes and stacked them carefully away, Scott and his father play poker. These are the times that Scott's father seems most like himself, the way he used to be–or so Scott thinks, anyway. They play for cigarettes, and Scott's father deals the cards with a smooth, magician's precision. As he does this, he tells Scott about a woman, a widow, older than him, who comes to A.A. meetings. He has spoken to her several times, seen her in the grocery store and said hello. He lingers over her physical qualities–the wide, generous mouth; the milky skin.

The father wins one pack of cigarettes, and Scott takes another from the carton. The light glares down on his cards as he fans them out. He arranges them, and his father speaks ramblingly of an idea he's had to move his trailer out near the lake. "They say there's plots in Lewellen that don't cost too much. Couple years down the road, who knows?"

"Who knows?" Scott echoes. And here is another happy memory he's reminded of–he doesn't understand why there should be so many good things when his father was such a wreck, really–but he can remember being seven or eight and going with his father to Lake McConaughy, fishing. They'd rented a boat, and he thinks of being out on the water, his father telling him that the lake had been made by a dam, and that at the deepest point, which at one time had been a valley, there had been a little town. And sometimes, his father told him, when the lake was very calm and clear, boats passing over could see the steeple of an old church down there under the water. He must have been stone drunk then, Scott knows, but it also seems that he was more whole then than he is now, that something great was happening, and Scott had sat there, believing him, staring over the edge of the boat. He could hear the sound of a radio playing somewhere along the shore.

Scott lay down his cards, frowning at the memory, and his father taps the table briskly, because he wins again, and he sweeps the cigarettes in the center to his side.

"Just like the old days," Scott says, and begins to

shuffle. "I used to get such a kick out of you giving me a fifty-dollar bill." Scott smiles, but his father doesn't. His father looks up as if accused, as if revealed. His brow furrows.

"You know," he says, "I'd give anything to have those days back to live over again. I'd give anything to make that up to you."

"I didn't mind. Things were fun for me."

Scott's father shakes his head grimly. "No they weren't."

It has been an unspoken rule between them that they don't mention the past. The only things Scott's father will say are abstractions of some sort, phrases he has obviously picked up in a clinic: "I just had to learn to turn my actions into reactions," he will say. Or: "I was looking for approval, and I lost my identity in the process." His words hang in the air like smoke after he has spoken, and it's hard for Scott to believe he has said them.

Scott doesn't feel he can forget or ignore things like his father does. He'll think of the time this girl, Traci, and two of his fraternity brothers and he sat up late playing quarters–the easy jokes; the talk of stupid things that connected their childhoods, like pop songs and brands of candy; the way Traci's hand kept bumping against his. She was rich, and beautiful, and Scott knows for a fact that if it hadn't been for the alcohol there never would have been that great moment, much later, when they slid loosely into a kiss. He remembers the parties, the night he stood on a chair in front of a crowd of dancing people and raised a cup of beer above his head, shouting a toast: "To life! To all of us! To me!" And everyone cheered. He was happy then. There aren't so many nights he regrets. He never did those types of things people spoke of at the clinic: wrecking cars, beating their wives, tearing through their life's work as if there would never be an end to it. Listening to their stories,

Scott had felt ashamed to have such fond memories, and so little desire to start over.

In the middle of the week the feedlot calls. They would like Scott to start on Friday, and they will train him to drive one of the feed trucks. He wants to say no right away, but then he thinks that maybe his father pleaded with them to offer him the job. He imagine them snorting as his father comes into the office to punch out: "Larry, your kid turned the job down. Does he think he's too good for us?" Scott doesn't know how he would explain himself. So he tells them he will be there, seven o'clock sharp. When he hangs up his whole body feels hollow.

When his father comes home from work Scott is sitting in front of the TV, drinking quinine water and eating dry saltines from the box. His father walks in and tosses his work clothes lightly into the closet. "I hear you got some good news today," he says.

They go out for a walk, Scott and his father, after supper, down the long dirt road that leads away from the trailer. Scott can tell how pleased he is from the way he walks, his springing step, as if he's trying on a new pair of shoes. His father picks up the larger pebbles he finds in his path and throws them over the sunflowers in the ditch, out into the pasture. "I got a pair of coveralls you can use," he tells Scott. "They're too big for me. And you can take the car. I won't need it. I got Fridays off, you know, and I'm just going to work in the shop."

"Great," Scott says. The air is electric with things he considers saying, then doesn't. He thinks of friends who have parted on bad terms, meeting under falling leaves, under a drizzle of rain. He could say: "I really don't think this job is right for me," or even, "Dad, will you help me, please?" But then, when Scott looks at his face, all he can see is the glass eye, which is blank as the dark bead of a bird's. Scott faces him, turning words over in his mind, and then discarding them.

His father smiles at him quizzically. "What's wrong?"

I don't know." Scott shrugs, bending down to pick up a rock. He throws it across the ditch. "Nothing."

When Scott wakes up on Friday, his father is still in bed. Scott dresses in the dark, and when he goes to the car, the sun is barely staining the rim of the sky. Once he's driving, his head starts to throb, and he can't stop himself from feeling that this day will mark an ending place. He stares ahead and can almost see his future in the distance, bearing down on him like dark weather. He lets his foot off the accelerator, watching the speedometer drift down, slower, as he heads into the gray foothills. Lots of people are worse off than he is, he tells himself. He thinks of someone his own age, with the same problems, back in the real world, going to work, content. He imagines men his age, not boys, going to war; the pioneers, with wives and kids and complete responsiblity at his age, enduring all sorts of tragedies and hardships. And yet, as he curves up to the top of the hill, and looks down to where the feedlot is, where thousands of cattle cluster like a brand against the pale fields, he stops the car. He sits there until the time when he is supposed to start work has blinked by on the digital clock on the dashboard. Then he turns the key. He drifts past the feedlot, puttering as heavy trucks roar past, his hands clutching the steering wheel like an old man, drifting toward the highway, toward town.

He drives through St. Bonaventure for hours. His car moves slowly down the street where he and his mother used to live, and he pauses for a minute in front of the old house. There is a For Sale sign in the front yard. In the corner is the tree he used to stand by when he was waiting for his father to come pick him up. His father would never come to the door, so Scott would lean there against the tree's trunk, sometimes for hours because his father was always late. He would gaze expectantly at the street, as eager as if he were going out to a party.

Beyond the tree is the place that to Scott seems most like his mother, a small fenced-in garden, where he can see a bright flash—a rag, perhaps, tied to a post. He continues on, past his old grade school, past a row of unchanged storefronts, and he almost expects to see his mother come out of one of them, holding a package, rummaging through her purse, which would be stuffed with bills and letters and lists of things she had to do, the little errands and plans that held their life together scribbled out on scraps of paper that she was always losing. She would be looking for her keys, which were always buried somewhere in that purse, and her large, light-sensitive glasses would be darkening as she stepped out into the bright sunlight. All this comes to him like a vision, and his hands feel brittle on the steering wheel. He turns the car around and around familiar blocks.

Scott is almost surprised, in the afternoon, to find himself pulling into a liquor store. He steps out of the car, wobbly on his feet, and when he walks through the door the electronic chime that announces his presence sends a slow trickle of ice through his stomach. He sets a cheap bottle of vodka on the counter. The saleswoman looks up and her long turquoise earrings swing sleepily.

"Party tonight?" she smiles. She has three gold teeth.

"Yes," Scott says, and pushes a crumpled bill toward her.

"Four ninety-three," she says firmly, merrily. "And seven cents is your change. You have a nice day now."

He is not going to drink it: That is what he tells himself as he crumples the bag and pushes it under the front seat. It was just a mistake that he bought it.

He looks at the clock and realizes he would just be getting off work about now, had he gone. And then suddenly he wonders if maybe they called his father when he didn't show up. Suddenly he can picture his father pacing, thinking Scott has been in an accident– calling the police. Or maybe rushing out of the house to search on foot, since Scott has the car, tracing the path Scott might have taken, expecting to find him encased in the bloody wreckage. And then, not finding him . . . perhaps he begins to realize what Scott done. He may even guess that Scott would end up at the liquor store. Scott can hear the vodka bottle clink as he turns onto the road. He imagines his father at home, punching the air with his fists–or worse, crushed and disappointed. Waiting. What excuse can be given, Scott wonders. All he can think of are child- ish explanations like amnesia or kidnapping.

As he drives up to his father's trailer, Scott tells himself that he's going to tell the truth. He pictures the two of them, pouring out the entire bottle. He think of his father raising his fist, then changing his mind.

When Scott opens the door, his father calls out: "Congratulations!" He's standing in the kitchen, his arms spread out expansively, but when he sees Scott his arms slip to his sides. Scott knows it must be his expression. "I figured," he says as Scott steps in. "I figured there was reason to celebrate today. You started your new job. You've been almost two months without a drink. And–" He pushes a piece of paper toward Scott, who takes it dumbly. "You got some mail from college." It's a form letter, Scott sees, con- cerning pre-registration. There are smudge marks where his father has smoothed out the folds, and Scott can see him, reading it, relishing the idea that his son's life is coming together, nodding the way he does when he finishes welding one of his creations.

Scott starts to fold the letter, and it is then that he notices the table is set for a party. He has spread it with a balloon-patterned paper tablecloth, and there is a pitcher of lemonade with real lemon slices floating in it, various kinds of cookies, cheeses and salami, all in wheels and geometric designs, arranged on paper plates. The father puts his hand on Scott's shoulder, then takes it away, as if it's a gesture he's not quite sure of, as if he has found something unsavory there. "How was work?" he says.

Scott thinks the words: "I didn't go to work." The refrigerator begins to hum in the quiet. "Dad . . . " he says. His father's jawbone moves vaguely beneath the skin, and the eye drifts blindly. "Things went okay," Scott says at last.

"Mm," he says. He's going to find out sooner or later, Scott knows. The longer it goes on, the worse it will be. But he shuffles his feet and says nothing. "Well, anyway." Scott's father looks at the table and frowns. "I don't know. I just thought it might cheer you up, some stupid little thing like this."

"It looks great. Thanks." He can see the moment for telling him passing by, growing distant. He tries to keep from looking miserable.

"It's nothing fancy," his father says. "I don't know what people do." He puts his finger on a square of cheese, then takes it guiltily away, as if he's been scolded. He puts his hand briefly on Scott's. "Be happy," he says. "Just be happy." Scott nods, and tries to smile.

Late at night Scott wakes and he is hot and shivering at the same time. He has thrown off the covers in his sleep. They are curled like a body beside him. Scott touches his own skin and it's cool and damp as clay. He hasn't felt this way since the first few nights in detox. His heart pumps in waves, and he lies there, limbs flung out, eyes open. The night sounds melt together: the rattling of tree branches against the trailer's metal sides, the scratching chirp of a cricket. A cow calls out from the field across the road.

His father begins to talk in his sleep. At first, Scott

can't quite place the sound, it weaves and curls at the edge of his hearing, barely audible. Then his father lets out a cry, and Scott sits straight up in bed. His father's words are slurred when Scott presses his face to the wall to listen. His father makes a low sound in his throat, something that is halfway between a bark and a moan of pain; there are several of them one right after another and then more indecipherable word and then a bark so full of misery that it makes the hair on the back of his neck prickle. He needs to get out of the trailer. He's got to, and he puts his hands on the glass of the window above his bed, thinking of the bottle hidden under the front seat of the car. He can picture himself, going out to a bar, a party. He drinks tall aquamarine margaritas, dances with sleek women in rhinestone stitched dresses, stays up all night, the music fast and glittery. His father murmurs again, and Scott gets out of bed. The floor seems to unwind beneath him, like in dreams, as he steps carefully down the hall, past his father's room, where he can hear him breathing heavily, through the kitchen and out the screen door. He's not sure what he'll do. He stands in the moonlit yard, which is quiet except for the sound of the sprinkler, the water hitting the cement, spraying into the grass, then back, in a sleepy rhythm. He looks at the car and steps dizzily out the gate to the gravel road where it's parked. He fingers the handle of the door, lightly, then inches it open. When he looks over his shoulder, he half-expects to see his father, framed in the lighted bedroom window, watching. But he isn't. Scott lifts the bag out, nervous even at the crinkling of the paper, as if this might wake him. Then he gazes out to where the circle of porch light ends, to where the dark line of road vanishes into shadows. He can hear the cattle call out mournfully as he begins walking, the gravel sharp beneath his bare feet. The crickets purr, whispering from the ditches. He's gone several hundred yards before he stops to think: Where am I going? He's in his boxer shorts, no shoes, miles from town. He slows, and then at last sits down in the high sunflowers that line the ditch. The shadows pull up over him like a sheet.

He would like to be closed up, that's what he thinks: surrounded by brick and mortar; the mouth, the ears, the eyes, stuffed with sawdust. He lies back and it's then, through the stems of weeds and sun-flowers, that he sees a bone-white face, bobbing in the dark, floating there, gazing with hollow eyes. His throat forms a gagging, voiceless cry, that supersti-tious sound familiar to him from horror movies, and he scrambles in the dirt for a moment in terror.

And then he realizes that it's a cow. The cattle, having noticed him, have come to the edge of the fence. Scott hears one low curiously, then snuffle. They're hungry. They think I'm bringing them food, Scott thinks. Their spectral faces nod in the darkness, staring expectantly. Kneeling in the wet grass, he clutches the paper bag in his hand, and they press closer to the fence. The cattle raise their voices again, in a deep chorus, and he can feel his hands shaking. He sinks down. Everything seems to press toward him, and he would like to believe that he's like a drowning person, that he's submerging, drifting down and down until the dim porch light and the trailer and the sunflowers above him and the moon and then finally even the pale masks of the cattle recede, grow distant and blurry, and then go out, one by one.

fitting ends

There is a story about my brother Del which appears in a book called *More True Tales of the Weird and Supernatural*. The piece on Del is about three pages long, full of exclamation points and supposedly eerie descriptions. It is based on what the writer calls "true facts."

The writer spends much of the first few paragraphs setting the scene, trying to make it sound spooky. "The tiny, isolated village of Pyramid, Nebraska" is what the author calls the place where I grew up. I had never thought of it as a village. It wasn't much of anything, really– it wasn't even on the map, and hadn't been since my father was a boy, when it was a stop on the Union Pacific railroad line. Back then, there was a shantytown for the railroad work- ers, a dance hall, a general store, a post office. By the time I was growing up, all that was left was a cluster of mostly boarded-up, run-down houses. My family–my parents and grandpar- ents and my brother and me–lived in the only occupied buildings. There was a grain elevator, which my grandfather had run until he retired and my father took over. "PYRAMID" was painted in peeling block letters on one of the silos.

The man who wrote the story got fixated on that elevator. He talks of it as "a menacing, hulking structure," and says it is like "Childe Roland's ancient dark tower, presiding over the barren fields and empty, sentient houses." He even goes so far as to mention "the soundless flutter of bats flying in and out of the single, eyelike window at the top of the elevator," and "the distant, melancholy calls of coyotes from the hills beyond," which are then drowned out by "the strange echoing moan of a freight train as it passes in the night."

There really are bats, of course; you find them in every country place. Personally, I never heard coyotes, though it is true they were around. I saw one once when I was about twelve. I was staring from my bedroom window late one night and there he was. He had come down from the hills and was crouched in our yard, licking drops of water off the propeller of the sprinkler. As for the trains, they passed through about every half-hour, day and night. If you lived there, you didn't even hear them—or maybe only half-heard them, the way, now that I live in a town, I might vaguely notice the bells of the nearby Catholic church at noon.

But anyway, this is how the writer sets things up. Then he begins to tell about some of the train engineers, how they dreaded passing through this particular stretch. He quotes one man as saying he got goosebumps every time he started to come up on Pyramid. "There was just something about that place," says this man. There were a few bad accidents at the crossing—a carload of drunken teenagers who tried to beat the train, an old guy who had a heart attack as his pickup bumped across the tracks. That sort of thing. Actually, this happens anywhere that has a railroad crossing.

Then came the sightings. An engineer would see "a figure" walking along the tracks in front of the train, just beyond the Pyramid elevator. The engineer would blow his horn, but the person, "the figure" would seem not to notice. The engineer blasted the horn several more times, more and more insistent. But the person kept walking; pretty soon the train's headlights glared onto a tall, muscular boy with shaggy dark hair and a green fatigue jacket. They tried to brake the train, but it was too late. The boy suddenly fell to his knees, and the engineer was certain he'd hit him. But of course, when the train was stopped, they could find nothing. "Not a trace," says our author. This happened to three different engineers; three different incidents in a two-year period.

You can imagine the ending, of course: that was how my brother died, a few years after these supposed sightings began. His car had run out of gas a few miles from home, and he was walking back. He was drunk. Who knows why he was walking along the tracks? Who knows why he suddenly kneeled down? Maybe he stumbled, or had to throw up. Maybe he did it on purpose. He was killed instantly.

The whole ghost stuff came out afterward. One of the engineers who'd seen the "ghost" recognized Del's picture in the paper, and came forward or something. I always believed it was made up. It was stupid, I always thought, like a million campfire stories you'd heard or some cheesy program on TV. But the author of *More True Tales of the Weird and Supernatural* found it "spine-tingling." "The strange story of the boy whose ghost appeared—two years before he died!" says a line on the back cover.

This happened when I was fourteen. My early brush with tragedy, I guess you could call it, though by the time I was twenty-one I felt I had recovered. I didn't think the incident had shaped my life in any particular way, and in fact I'd sometimes find myself telling the story, ghost and all, to girls I met at fraternity parties. I'd take a girl up to my room, show her the *True Tales* book. We'd smoke some marijuana and talk about it, my voice taking on an intensity and heaviness that surprised both of us. From time to time, we'd end up in bed. I remember this one girl, Lindsey, telling me how moved she was by the whole thing. It gave me, she said, a Heathcliff quality; I had turned brooding and mysterious; the wheat fields had turned to moors. "I'm not mysterious," I said, embarrassed, and later, after we'd parted ways, she agreed. "I thought you were different," she said, "deeper." She cornered me one evening when I was talking to another girl and wanted to know if I wasn't a little ashamed, using my dead brother to get laid. She said that she had come to realize that I, like Heathcliff, was just another jerk.

After that, I stopped telling the story for a while. There would be months when I wouldn't speak of my brother at all, and even when I was home in Pyramid, I could spend my whole vacation without once mentioning Del's name. My parents never spoke of him, at least not with me.

Of course, this only made him more present than ever. He hovered there as I spoke of college, my future, my life, my father barely listening. When we would argue, my father would stiffen sullenly, and I knew he was thinking of arguments he'd had with Del. I could shout at him, and nothing would happen. He'd stare as I tossed some obscene word casually toward him, and I'd feel it rattle and spin like a coin I'd flipped on the table in front of him. But he wouldn't say anything.

I actually wondered, back then, why they put up with this sort of thing. It was surprising, even a little unnerving, especially given my father's temper when I was growing up, the old violence-promising glares that once made my bones feel like wax, the ability he formerly had to make me flinch with a gesture or a well-chosen phrase.

Now I was their only surviving child, and I was gone—more thoroughly gone than Del was, in a way. I'd driven off to college in New York, and it was clear I wasn't ever coming back. Even my visits became shorter and shorter—summer trimmed down from three months to less than two weeks over the course of my years at college; at Christmas, I'd stay on campus after finals, wandering the emptying passageways of my residence hall, loitering in the student center, my hands clasped behind my back, staring at the ragged bulletin boards as if they were paintings in a museum. I found excuses to keep from going back. And then, when I got there, finally, I was just another ghost.

About a year before he died, Del saved my life. It was no big deal, I thought. It was summer, trucks were coming to the grain elevator, and my brother and I had gone up to the roof to fix a hole. The elevator was flat on top, and when I was little I used to imagine that being up there was like being in the turret of a lighthouse. I used to stare out over the expanse of prairie, across the fields and their flotsam of machinery, cattle, men, over the rooftops of houses, along the highways and railroad tracks that trailed off into the horizon. When I was small, this would fill me with wonder. My father would stand there with me, holding my hand, and the wind would ripple our clothes.

I was thinking of this, remembering, when I suddenly started to do a little dance. I didn't know why I did such things: my father said that ever since I started junior high school I'd been like a "-holic" of some sort, addicted to making an ass out of myself. Maybe this was true, because I started to caper around, and Del said, "I'd laugh if you fell, you idiot," stern and condescending, as if *I* was the juvenile delinquent. I ignored him. With my back turned to him, I began to sing "Ain't No Mountain High Enough" in a deep corny voice, like my father's. I'd never been afraid of heights, and I suppose I was careless. Too close to the edge, I slipped, and my brother caught my arm.

I was never able to recall exactly what happened in that instant. I remember being surprised by the sound that came from my throat, a high scream like a rabbit's that seemed to ricochet downward, a stone rattling through a long drainpipe. I looked up and my brother's mouth was wide open, as if he'd made the sound. The tendons on his neck stood out.

I told myself that if I'd been alone, nothing would have happened. I would've just teetered a little, then gained my balance again. But when my brother grabbed me, I lost my equilibrium, and over the edge I went. There were a dozen trucks lined up to have their loads weighed, and all the men down there heard that screech, looked up startled to see me dangling there with two hundred feet between me and the ground. They all watched Del yank me back up to safety.

I was on the ground before it hit me. Harvesters were getting out of their trucks and ambling toward us, and I could see my father pushing his way through the crowd. It was then that my body took heed of what had happened. The solid earth kept opening up underneath me, and Del put his arm around me as I wobbled. Then my father loomed. He got hold of me, clenching my shoulders, shaking me. "My sore neck!" I cried out. "Dad, my neck!" The harvester's faces jittered, pressing closer, I could see a man in sunglasses with his black, glittering eyes fixed on me.

"Del pushed me," I cried out as my father's gritted teeth came toward my face. Tears slipped suddenly out of my eyes. "Del pushed me, Dad! It wasn't my fault."

My father had good reason to believe this lie, even though he and some twelve or more others had been witness to my singing and careless prancing up there. The possibility still existed that Del might have given me a shove from behind. My father didn't want to believe Del was capable of such a thing. But he knew he was.

Del had only been back home for about three weeks. Prior to that, he'd spent several months in a special program for juvenile delinquents. The main reason for this was that he'd become so belligerent, so violent, that my parents didn't feel they could control him. He'd also, over the course of things, stolen a car.

For much of the time that my brother was in this program, I wore a neck brace. He'd tried to strangle me the night before he was sent away. He claimed he'd seen me smirking at him, though actually I was only thinking of something funny I'd seen on TV. Del was the farthest thing from my thoughts until he jumped on me. If my father hadn't separated us, Del probably would have choked me to death.

This was one of the things that my father must have thought of. He must have remembered the other times that Del might have killed me: the time when I was twelve and he threw a can of motor oil at my head when my back was turned; the time when I was seven and he pushed me off the tailgate of a moving pickup, where my father had let us sit when he was driving slowly down a dirt road. My father was as used to hearing these horror stories as I was to telling them.

Though he was only three and a half years older than I, Del was much larger. He was much bigger than I'll ever be, and I was just starting to realize that. Six foot three, 220-pound defensive back, my father used to tell people when he spoke of Del. My father used to believe that Del would get a football scholarship to the state university. Never mind that once he started high school he wouldn't even play on the team. Never mind that all he seemed to want to do was vandalize people's property and drink beer and cause problems at home. My father still talked about it like there was some hope.

When my brother got out of his program, he told us that things would be different from now on. He had changed, he said, and he swore that he would make up for the things that he'd done. I gave him a hug. He stood there before us, with his hands clasped behind his back, posed like the famous orator whose picture was in the library of our school. We all smiled, the visions of the horrible family fights wavering behind our friendly expressions.

So here was another one, on the night of my almost-death.

Before very long my brother had started crying. I hadn't seen him actually shed tears in a very long time; he hadn't even cried on the day he was sent away.

"He's a liar," my brother shouted. We had all been fighting and carrying on for almost an hour. I had told my version of the story five or six times, getting better at it with each repetition. I could have almost believed it myself. "You fucking liar," my brother screamed at me. "I wish I had pushed you. I'd never save your ass now." He stared at me suddenly, wild-eyed, like I was a dark shadow that was bending over his bed when he woke at night. Then he sat down at the kitchen table. He put his face in his hands, and his shoulders began to shudder.

Watching him–this giant, broad-shouldered boy, my brother, weeping–I could have almost taken it back. The whole lie, I thought, the words I spoke at first came out of nowhere, sprang to my lips as a shield against my father's red face and bared teeth, his fingernails cutting my shoulder as everyone watched. It was really my father's fault. I could have started crying myself.

But looking back on it, I have to admit that there was something else, too–a heat at the core of my stomach, spreading through my body like a stain. It made my skin throb, my face a mask of innocence and defiance. I sat there looking at him, and put my hand to my throat. After years of being on the receiving end, it wasn't in my nature to see Del as someone who could be wronged, as someone to feel pity for. This was something Del could have done, I thought. It was not so unlikely.

At first, I thought it would end with my brother leaving, barreling out of the house with the slamming of doors and the circling whine of the fan belt in my father's old beater pickup, the muffler retorting all the way down the long dirt road, into the night. Once, when he was drunk, my brother had tried to drive his truck off a cliff on the hill out behind our house. But the embankment wasn't steep enough, and the truck just went bump, bump down the side of the hill, all four wheels staying on the ground until it finally came to rest in the field below. Del had pointed a shotgun at my father that night, and my father was so stunned and upset that my mother thought he was having a heart attack. She was running around hysterical, calling police, ambulance, bawling. In the distance, Del went up the hill, down the hill, up, down. You could hear him revving the motor. It felt somehow like one of those slapstick moments in a comedy movie, where everything is falling down at once and all the actors run in and out of doorways. I sat, shivering, curled up on the couch while all this was going on, staring at the television.

But the night after I'd almost fallen, my brother did not try to take off. We all knew that if my parents had to call the police on him again, it would be the end. He would go to a foster home or even back to the juvenile hall, which he said was worse than prison. So instead, he and my father were in a shoving match; there was my mother between them, screaming, "Oh, stop it I can't stand it I can't stand it," turning her deadly, red-eyed stare abruptly upon me; there was my brother crying. But he didn't try to leave. He just sat there, with his face in his hands. "God damn all of you," he cried suddenly. "I hate all your guts. I wish I was fucking dead."

My father hit him then, hit him with the flat of his hand alongside the head, and Del tilted in his chair with the force of it. He made a small, high-pitched sound, and I watched as he folded his arms over his ears as my father descended on him, a blow, a pause, a blow, a pause. My father stood over him, breathing hard. A tear fell from Del's nose.

"Don't you ever say that," my father roared. "Don't you dare ever say that." He didn't mean the f-word—he meant wishing you were dead, the threats Del had made in the past. That was the worst thing, my father had told us once, the most terrible thing a person could do. My father's hands fell to his sides. I saw that he was crying also.

After a time, Del lifted his head. He seemed to have calmed—everything seemed to have grown quiet, a dull, wavery throb of static. I saw that he looked at me. I slumped my shoulders, staring down at my fingernails.

"You lie," Del said softly. "You can't even look me in the face." He got up and stumbled a few steps, as if my father would go after him again. But my father just stood there.

"Get out of my sight," he said. "Go on."

I heard Del's tennis shoes thump up the stairs, the slam of our bedroom door. But just as I felt my body start to untense, my father turned to me. He wiped the heel of his hand over his eyes, gazing at me without blinking. After all of Del's previous lies, his denials, his betrayals, you would think they would never believe his side of things again. But I could see a slowly creaking hinge of doubt behind my father's expression. I looked down.

"If I ever find out you're lying to me, boy," my father said.

He didn't ever find out. The day I almost fell was another one of those things we never got around to talking about again. It probably didn't seem very significant to my parents in the span of events that had happened before and came after. They dwelt on other things.

On what, I never knew. My wife found this unbelievable: "Didn't they say anything after he died?" she asked me, and I had to admit that I didn't remember. They were sad, I told her. I recalled my father crying. But they were country people. I tried to explain this to my wife, good Boston girl that she is, the sort of impossible grief that is like something gnarled and stubborn and underground. I never really believed it myself. For years, I kept expecting things to go back to normal, waiting for whatever was happening to them to finally be over.

My parents actually became quite mellow in the last years of their lives. My mother lost weight, was often ill. Eventually, shortly after her sixtieth birthday, she went deaf. Her hearing slipped away quickly, like a skin she was shedding, and all the tests proved inconclusive. That was the year that my son was born. In January, when my wife discovered that she was pregnant, my parents were in the process of buying a fancy, expensive hearing aid. By the time the baby was four months old, the world was completely soundless for my mother, hearing aid or not.

The problems of my college years had passed away by that time. I was working at a small private college in upstate New York, in alumni relations. My wife and I seldom went back to Nebraska; we couldn't afford the money or the time. But I talked to my parents regularly on the phone, once or twice a month.

We ended up going back that Christmas after Ezra was born. My mother's letters had made it almost impossible to avoid. "It breaks my heart that I can't hear my grandson's voice, now that he is making his little sounds," she had written. "But am getting by O.K. and will begin lip-reading classes in Denver after Xmas. It will be easier for me then." She would get on the phone when I called my father. "I can't hear you talking but I love you," she'd say.

"We have to work to make her feel involved in things," my father told us as we drove from the airport, where he'd picked us up. "The worst thing is that they start feeling isolated," he told us. "We got little pads so we can write her notes." He looked over at me, strangely academic-looking in the new glasses he had for driving. In the last few years he had begun to change, his voice turning slow and gentle, as if he was watching something out in the distance beyond the window, or something sad and mysterious on TV as we talked. His former short temper had vanished away, leaving only a soft reproachfulness in its place. But even that was muted. He knew that he couldn't really make me feel guilty. "You know how she is," he said to my wife and me, though of course we did not, either one of us, really know her. "You know how she is. The hardest part is, you know, we don't want her to get depressed."

She looked awful. Every time I saw her since I graduated from college, this stunned me. I came in, carrying my sleeping son, and she was sitting at the kitchen table, her spine curved a little bit more than the last time, thinner, so skinny that her muscles seemed to stand out against the bone. Back in New York, I worked with alumni ladies older than she who played tennis, who dressed in trendy clothes, who walked with a casual and still sexy ease. These women wouldn't look like my mother for another twenty years, if ever. I felt my smile pull awkwardly on my face.

"Hello!" I called, but of course she didn't look up. My father flicked on the porch light. "She hates it when you surprise her," he said softly, as if there were still some possibility of her overhearing. My wife looked over at me. Her eyes said that this was going to be another holiday that was like work for her.

My mother lifted her head. Her shrewdness was still intact, at least, and she was ready for us the moment the porch light hit her consciousness. That terrible, monkeyish dullness seemed to lift from her expression as she looked up.

"Well, howdy," she called, in the same jolly, slightly ironic way she always did when she hadn't seen me in a long time. She came over to hug us, then peered down at Ezra, who stirred a little as she pushed back his parka hood to get a better look. "Oh, what an angel," she whispered. "It's about killed me, not being able to see this boy." Then she stared down at Ezra again. How he'd grown, she told us. She thought he looked like me, she said, and I was relieved. Actually, I'd begun to think that Ezra somewhat resembled the pictures I'd seen of Del as a baby. But my mother didn't say that, at least.

I had planned to have a serious talk with them on this trip. Or maybe "planned" is the wrong word—"considered" might be closer, though even that doesn't express the vague, unpleasantly anxious urge that I could feel at the back of my neck. I didn't really know what I wanted to know. And the truth was, these quiet, fragile, distantly tender people bore little resemblance to the mother and father in my mind. It had been ten years since I'd lived at home. Ten years!—which filled the long, snowy evenings with a numbing politeness. My father sat in his easy chair, after dinner, watching the news. My wife read. My mother and I did the dishes together, silently, nodding as the plate she had rinsed passed from her hand to mine, to be dried and put away. When a train passed, the little window above the sink vibrated, humming like a piece of cellophane. But she did not notice this.

We did have a talk of sorts that trip, my father and I. It was on the third day after our arrival, a few nights before Christmas Eve. My wife and my mother were both asleep. My father and I sat out on the closed-in porch, drinking beer, watching the snow drift across the yard, watching the wind send fingers of snow slithering along low to the ground. I had drunk more than he had. I saw him glance sharply at

me for a second when I came back from the refrigerator a fourth time, and popped open the can. But the
look faded quickly. Outside, beyond the window, I
could see the blurry shape of the elevator through the
falling snow, its outlines indistinct, wavering like a
mirage.

"Do you remember that time," I said, "when I
almost fell off the elevator?"

It came out like that, abrupt, stupid. As I sat there
in my father's silence, I realized how impossible it
was, how useless to try to patch years of ellipsis into
something resembling dialogue. I looked down, and
he cleared his throat.

"Sure," he said at last, noncommittal. "Of course I
remember."

"I think about that sometimes," I said. Drunk–I felt
the alcohol edge into my voice as I spoke. "It seems,"
I said, "significant." That was the word that came to
me. "It seems significant sometimes," I said.

My father considered this for a while. He stiffened
formally, as if he were being interviewed. "Well," he
said. "I don't know. There were so many things like
that. It was all a mess by then, anyway. Nothing could
be done. It was too late for anything to be done." He
looked down to his own beer, which must have gone
warm by that time, and took a small sip. "It should
have been taken care of earlier–when you were kids.
That's where I think things must have gone wrong. I
was too hard on you both. But Del–I was harder on
him. He was the oldest. Too much pressure. Expected
too much."

He drifted off at that, embarrassed. We sat there,
and I could not even imagine what he meant–what
specifics he was referring to. What pressure? What
expectations? But I didn't push any further.

"But you turned out all right," my father said.
"You've done pretty well, haven't you?"

There were no signs in our childhood, no incidents

pointing the way to his eventual end. None that I could see, at least, and I thought about it quite a bit after his death. "It should have been taken care of earlier," my father said, but what was "it"? Del seemed to have been happy, at least up until high school.

Maybe things happened when they were alone together. From time to time, I remember Del coming back from helping my father in the shop with his eyes red from crying. Once I remember our father coming into our room on a Saturday morning and cuffing the top of Del's sleeping head with the back of his hand: he had stepped in dog dirt on the lawn. The dog was Del's responsibility. Del must have been about eight or nine at the time, and I remember him kneeling on our bedroom floor in his pajamas, crying bitterly as he cleaned off my father's boot. When I told that story later on, I was pleased by the ugly, almost fascist overtones it had. I remember recounting it to some college friends–handsome, suburban kids–lording this little bit of squalor from my childhood over them. Child abuse and family violence were enjoying a media vogue at that time, and I found I could mine this memory to good effect. In the version I told, I was the one cleaning the boots.

But the truth was, my father was never abusive in an especially spectacular way. He was more like a simple bully, easily eluded when he was in a short-tempered mood. He used to get so furious when we would avoid him. I recall how he used to grab us by the hair on the back of our necks, tilting our heads so we looked into his face. "You don't listen," he would hiss. "I want you to look at me when I talk to you." That was about the worst of it, until Del started getting into trouble. And by that time, my father's blows weren't enough. Del would laugh, he would strike back. It was then that my father finally decided to turn him over to the authorities. He had no other choice, he said.

He must have believed it. He wasn't, despite his

temper, a bad man, a bad parent. He'd seemed so kindly, sometimes, so fatherly–especially with Del. I remember watching them from my window, some autumn mornings, watching them wade through the high weeds in the stubblefield out behind our house, walking toward the hill with their shotguns pointing at the ground, their steps slow, synchronized. Once I'd gone upstairs and heard them laughing in Del's and my bedroom. I just stood there outside the doorway, watching as my father and Del put a model ship together, sharing the job, their talk easy, happy.

This was what I thought of, that night we were talking. I thought of my own son, the innocent baby I loved so much, and it chilled me to think that things could change so much–that Del's closeness to my father could turn in on itself, transformed into the kind of closeness that thrived on their fights, on the different ways Del could push my father into a rage. That finally my father would feel he had no choices left. We looked at each other, my father and I. "What are you thinking?" I said softly, but he just shook his head.

Del and I had never been close. We had never been like friends, or even like brothers. Yet after that day on the elevator I came to realize that there had been something between us. There had been something that could be taken away.

He stopped talking to me altogether for a while. In the weeks and months that followed my lie, I doubt if we even looked at each other more than two or three times, though we shared the same room.

For a while, I slept on the couch. I was afraid to go up to our bedroom. I can remember those first few nights, waiting in the living room for my father to go to bed, the television hissing with laughter. The furniture, the table, the floors seemed to shudder as I touched them, as if they were just waiting for the right moment to burst apart.

I'd go outside, sometimes, though that was really no better. It was the period of late summer when thunderstorms seemed to pass over every night. The wind came up. The shivering tops of trees bent in the flashes of heat lightning.

There was no way out of the situation I'd created. I could see that. Days and weeks stretched out in front of me, more than a month before school started. By that time, I thought, maybe it would all blow over. Maybe it would melt into the whole series of bad things that had happened, another layer of paint that would eventually be covered over by a new one, forgotten.

If he really had pushed me, that was what would have happened. It would have been like the time he tried to choke me, or the time he tried to drive the car off the hill. Once those incidents were over, there was always the possibility that this was the last time. There was always the hope that everything would be better, now.

In retrospect, it wouldn't have been so hard to recant. There would have been a big scene, of course. I would have been punished, humiliated. I would have had to endure my brother's triumph, my parents' disgust. But I realize now that it wouldn't have been so bad.

I might have finally told the truth, too, if Del had reacted the way I expected. I imagined that there would be a string of confrontations in the days that followed, that he'd continue to protest with my father. I figured he wouldn't give up.

But he did. After that night, he didn't try to deny it anymore. For a while, I even thought that maybe he had begun to believe that he pushed me. He acted like a guilty person, eating his supper in silence, walking noiselessly through the living room, his shoulders hunched like a traveler on a snowy road.

My parents seemed to take this as penitence. They still spoke sternly, but their tone began to be edged by gentleness, a kind of forgiveness. "Did you take out the trash?" they would ask. "Another potato?"–and they would wait for him to quickly nod. He was truly sorry, they thought. Everything was finally going to be okay. He was shaping up.

At these times, I noticed something in his eyes–a kind of sharpness, a subtle shift of the iris. He would lower his head, and the corners of his mouth would move slightly. To me, his face seemed to flicker with hidden, mysterious thoughts.

When I finally began to sleep in our room again, he pretended I wasn't there. I would come in, almost as quiet as he himself had become, to find him sitting at our desk or on his bed, peeling off a sock with such slow concentration that it might have been his skin. It was as if there were an unspoken agreement between us–I no longer existed. He wouldn't look at me, but I could watch him for as long as I wanted. I would pull the covers over myself and just lie there, observing, as he went about doing whatever he was doing as if oblivious. He listened to a tape on his headphones; flipped through a magazine; did sit-ups; sat staring out the window; turned out the light. And all that time his face remained neutral, impassive. Once, he even chuckled to himself at a book he was reading, a paperback anthology of The Far Side cartoons.

When I was alone in the room, I found myself looking through his things, with an interest I'd never had before. I ran my fingers over his models, the monster-wheeled trucks and B-10 bombers. I flipped through his collection of tapes. I found some literature he'd brought home from the detention center, brochures with titles like "Teens and Alcohol: What You Should Know!" and "Rap Session, Talking about Feelings." Underneath this stuff, I found the essay he'd been working on.

He had to write an essay so that they would let him back into high school. There was a letter from the guidance counselor, explaining the school's policy, and then there were several sheets of notebook paper with his handwriting on them. He'd scratched out lots of words, sometimes whole paragraphs. In the margins, he'd written little notes to himself: "(sp.)" or "?" or "No." He wrote in scratchy block letters.

His essay told of the Outward Bound program. "I had embarked on a sixty day rehabilitation program in the form of a wilderness survival course name of Outward Bound," he had written. "THESIS: The wilderness has allowed for me to reach deep inside my inner self and grasp ahold of my morals and values that would set the standard and tell the story of the rest of my life."

I would go into our room when my brother was out and take the essay out of the drawer where he'd hidden it. He was working on it, off and on, all that month; I'd flip it open to discover new additions or deletions–whole paragraphs appearing as if overnight. I never saw him doing it.

The majority of the essay was a narrative, describing their trip. They had hiked almost two hundred miles, he said. "Up by sun and down by moon," he wrote. There were obstacles they had to cross. Once, they had to climb down a hundred-foot cliff. "The repelling was very exciting but also scarey," he'd written. "This was meant to teach us trust and confidence in ourselves as well as our teammates, they said. Well as I reached the peak of my climb I saw to my despair that the smallest fellow in the group was guiding my safety rope. Now he was no more than one hundred and ten pounds and I was tipping the scales at about two twenty five needless to say I was reluctant."

But they made it. I remember reading this passage several times; it seemed very vivid in my mind. In my imagination, I was in the place of the little guy holding the safety rope. I saw my brother hopping lightly, bit by bit, down the sheer face of the cliff to the ground below, as if he could fly, as if there were no gravity anymore.

"My experience with the Outward Bound program opened my eyes to such values as friendship, trust, responsibility and sharing," Del wrote in his conclusion. "Without the understanding of these I would not exist as I do now but would probably instead be another statistic. With these values I will purely succeed. Without I would surely fail." Next to this he'd written: "Sounds like bullshit (?)"

I don't know that I recognized that distinct ache that I felt on reading this, or understood why his sudden distance, the silent, moody aura he trailed after him in those weeks should have affected me in such a way. Years later, I would recall that feeling—standing over my son's crib, a dark shape leaning over him as he stirred with dreams—waiting at the window for the headlights of my wife's car to turn into our driveway. That sad, trembly feeling was a species of love—or at least a symptom of it.

I thought of this a long time after the fact. I loved my brother, I thought. Briefly.

None of this lasted. By the time he died, a year later, he'd worked his way back to his normal self, or a slightly modified, moodier version. Just like before, money had begun to disappear from my mother's purse; my parents searched his room for drugs. He and my father had been argued that morning about the friends he was hanging around with, about his wanting to take the car every night. Del claimed that he was dating a girl, said he only wanted to see a movie in town. He'd used that one before, often lying ridiculously when he was asked the next day about the plot of the film. I remember him telling my mother that the war film *Apocalypse Now* was set in the future, which I knew was not true from an article I'd read in the paper. I remember making some comment in reference to this as he was getting ready to go out, and he looked at me in that careful, hooded way, reminiscent of the time when he was pretending I didn't exist. "Eat shit and die, Stewart," he murmured, without heat. Unfortunately, I believe that this was the last thing he ever said to me.

Afterward, his friends said that he had seemed like he was in a good mood. They had all been in his car, my father's car, driving up and down the main street in Scottsbluff. They poured a little rum into their cans of Coke, cruising from one end of town to the other, calling out the window at a carful of passing teenage girls, revving the engine at the stoplights. He wasn't that drunk, they said.

I used to imagine that there was a specific moment when he realized that he was going to die. I don't believe he knew it when he left our house, or even at the beginning of his car ride with his friends. If that were true, I have to assume that there would have been a sign, some gesture or expression, something one of us would have noticed. If it was planned, then why on that particular, insignificant day?

Yet I wondered. I used to think of him, in his friend Sully's car, listening to his buddies laughing, making dumb jokes, running red lights. It might have been sometime around then, I thought. Time seemed to slow down. He would sense a long, billowing delay in the spaces between words; the laughing faces of the girls in a passing car would seem to pull by forever, their expressions frozen.

Or I thought about his driving home. I could see the heavy, foglike darkness of those country roads, the shadows of weeds springing up when the headlights touched them, I could imagine the halt and sputter of the old pickup as the gas ran out, that moment when you can feel the power lift up out of the machine like a spirit. It's vivid enough in my mind that it's almost as if I was with him as the pickup rolled lifelessly on—slowing, then stopping at last on the shoulder where it would be found the next day, the emergency lights still blinking dimly. He and I stepped out into the thick night air, seeing the shape of the elevator in the distance, above the tall sunflowers and pigweed. And though we knew we were outdoors, it felt like we were inside something. The sky seemed to close down on us like the lid of a box.

No one in my family ever used the word suicide. When we referred to Del's death, if we referred to it, we spoke of "the accident." To the best of our knowledge, that's what it was.

There was a time, right before I left for college, when I woke from a dream to the low wail of a passing train. I could see it when I sat up in bed, through the branches of trees outside my window I could see the boxcars, shuffling through flashes of heat lightning, trailing past the elevator and into the distance, rattling, rattling.

And there was another time, my senior year in college, when I saw a kid who looked like Del coming out of a bar, a boy melting into the crowded, carnival atmosphere of this particular strip of saloons and dance clubs where all the students went on a Saturday night. I followed this person a few blocks before I lost sight of him. All those cheerful, drunken faces seemed to loom as I passed by them, blurring together like an expressionist painting. I leaned against a wall, breathing.

And there was that night when we came to Pyramid with my infant son, the night my father and I stayed up talking. I sat there in the dark, long after he'd gone to bed, finishing another beer. I remember looking up to see my mother moving through the kitchen; at first only clearly seeing the billowy whiteness of her nightgown hovering in the dark, a shape floating slowly through the kitchen toward me. I had a moment of fear before I realized it was her. She did not know I was there. She walked slowly, delicately, thinking herself alone in this room at night. I would have had to touch her to let her know that I was there, and that would have probably startled her badly. So I didn't move. I watched as she lit a cigarette and sat down at the kitchen table, her head turned toward the window, where the snow was still falling. She watched it drift down. I heard her breathe smoke, exhaling in a long, thoughtful sigh. She was remembering something, I thought.

It was at these moments that everything seemed clear to me. I felt that I could take all the loose ends of my life and fit them together perfectly, as easily as a writer could write a spooky story, where all the details add up and you know the end even before the last sentence. This would make a good ending, you think at such moments. You'll go on living, of course. But at the same time you recognize, in that brief flash of clarity and closure, you realize that everything is summed up. It's not really worth becoming what there is left for you to become.